THE PRNCESS AND THE VAMPIRE KING
by
Eileen Sheehan

This book is dedicated to my readers and reviewers. Your delight and approval of my fantasy creations helps keep my imagination alive.

CHAPTER ONE

The harsh shrill of the quarter hour whistle brought me back to reality like a crisp slap across my face. I was still in that horrid room with those horrid creatures awaiting a fate too horrid to imagine.

Horrid... was that the best I could do? This place was beyond horrid. It was so bad there was no description for how bad it was.

My mind was fuzzy.

I needed to focus.

Those creatures, what were they? They went beyond horrid to look at, horrid to be around, horrid to interact with. My brain would not function properly. I could come up with no word to equal what they were. I gave up. Horrid would have to suffice.

I smiled to myself. What did it matter what word I used to describe what was happening? Was it really that important? In the not too distant future I would become a nothing, a thing of the past. What I thought and the words I enunciated with would mean less than they already did.

"You smile human. Do you take pleasure in this?" said a deep surly voice.

My head shot up and I looked directly into the beady, yellow eyes of my scaly captor.

"Does it matter?" I slurred boldly.

"Not in the least," the lizard beast muttered as it moved away to inspect a woman to my left.

"I thought not," I mumbled as my chin fell back to my chest.

"Silence," a deep masculine voice from the back of the room roared. "I will have silence!"

I could have been defiant and said something else just to irritate them. After all, I was a dead woman soon enough. What

1

could they possibly do to me for breaking their precious code of silence that they weren't already going to do anyway? But, I didn't. My brain thought it, but my tongue stayed immobile. Also, something deep inside my feeble brain shouted for me to shut up and behave myself and I just might get out of this thing alive. Imagine that? I knew it was a fairy tale wish, but I obeyed the command and kept quiet anyway. Maybe somewhere in the recesses of my mind I was holding out for a miracle.

My long, bony arms had been trussed over my head for so long I could barely feel them. The numbness was traveling down my back and into my equally bony legs. I looked around at my fellow captives. They made sense. Each one had enough meat on their bodies to feed these lizard beasts in fine fashion. If they dined on soup then perhaps I could understand their reason for including me in the mix, but from what I'd been able to decipher they only ate meat; and they ate it fresh and uncooked. My scrawny five-foot three-inch physique barely hit the one-hundred-pound mark on a scale while soaking wet.

I didn't belong here.

But then, did any of us?

Another quarter hour whistle pierced the air. I felt the conveyor belt jolt as it slowly moved me to the left toward the dreaded room. How many were ahead of me? The great hall was long and filled with bodies. Where did they all come from? My eyes were blurred from whatever they'd injected into my neck a few whistles ago. It was a calming agent of some sort. Apparently the lizard beasts preferred their food not fight back. It was working. I reckoned that by the time I reached the end of the line I would be a drooling fool without a care in the world. Do with me what you will creep! I could give a damn!

Rough, scaly, and incredibly powerful hands started poking and pawing at my naked body. I was disgusted by the vile assault, but couldn't even manage a flinch. Yep, the injection was definitely working.

"What is this doing here? Is this a prank?" the owner of the assaulting hands demanded with disgust. "Wumonan, I just asked you a question and I expect an answer. Why is this scrawny female here?"

"I... I ... She was here when I came on duty, boss," replied a very worried lizard-like guard that I assumed was Wumonan.

"It never occurred to you to question her presence?" growled the one he called boss.

"Ahh... no boss, I did not think..." Wumonan began.

"That's right, you did not think!" Boss interjected. "Had you used that tiny worthless brain of yours, you would have realized this female is far too inferior to be presented at our table. In fact, she is an insult to even the lowest Dragos table."

My body swayed in response to his shove of disgust.

"Get her out of here," he ordered.

"Yes boss," Wumonan replied with a mixture of fear and respect in his voice.

Wumonan pulled my drugged body from the hook holding the rope that trussed my wrists together and flung me over his broad, reptilian shoulder as if I was nothing more than a sack of flour. My arms flapped against his thick, scaly back with each step that he took, but he seemed not to notice. I fought back the vomit as my face slammed into his abrasive leathery flesh. Not only was the sensation atrocious, but the stench was overwhelming. I had heard about the Dragos off and on while growing up, but always in a fairy tale. I recalled the stories stated they did not have an elimination system like humans. They eliminated waste through their skin. I now knew this to be true. My conveyor stunk in the worst way. He reeked of dirt, something that resembled sweaty urine, and blood. Having been raised near a farm in Upstate New York, I can tell you that I've been in pig pens that smelled better.

He took me to their garbage dump outside the eatery. I'm pretty sure I felt a rib or two snap when he dumped me unceremoniously onto a raunchy pile of human discard. As I lay amongst bones picked clean of flesh and smelling like blood mixed with vulgar creature saliva, my body purged whatever contents my stomach contained. When it was empty, I continued to heave. It was as if my on/off switch was broken.

By the time the wrenching subsided, I was overwhelmed by the accentuated pain in my ribs. The powerful contracting of my diaphragm as I purged and purged and purged intensified the damage from being tossed onto the pile of bones. I had no doubt at least one rib was broken, possibly two.

As much as I wanted to be free of the pile of human remains, the injection was taking hold full force. I was disoriented with virtually no motivation to move. I could feel the hollow darkness off in a distance calling; waiting to consume me. It was only a matter of time now. Although the substance they injected wasn't lethal, I got the sense I would be out long enough to be buried alive when the next load of remains was dumped on top of me. With my slight frame, my weakened condition, and a broken ribcage, it was a pretty sure bet I would be trapped beneath the rubble. Instead of meeting my death as food for the Dragos, I was going to meet my death from those who had been their food.

How droll.

I decided I'd rather not be aware of my ultimate demise. I closed my eyes and willed the darkness to overtake me.

****

I was warm; cozy, in fact. I kept my eyes closed while I tested my limbs. They were functioning. I felt my rib cage. It was bandaged. Puzzled, I slowly raised my lids to view my surroundings. I found myself in what looked like a cave that was furnished with fairly lavish tapestry of red, green, and gold woven together to create what looked like a coat of arms. The flying dove with an olive branch led me to believe the owner was of a peace loving clan. Thick, lush carpeting from the orient was spread over the hard packed dirt floor. Strategically positioned on top of it were an ornate table and two chairs, one comfy looking overstuffed chair, and the bed I occupied.

Was I dreaming?

Had I died?

I'd heard when you die you select the era and time you'd like to play out eternity in. From what I could see, I'd gone back in time, but I had no clue how far back.

I inhaled deeply. The rich aroma of a thick stew made its way into my nostrils and my stomach reacted with a vengeance. I'd purged its contents in that pile of human remains and it demanded solace. Even the visual remembrance of that horrific place did not deter it from demanding its rightful due.

I looked around the room. Was I alone? Were angels going to come in to serve me?

Spirits maybe? I gasped in trepidation. I was in heaven, wasn't I? My mind raced through my actions prior to my capture. I could think of nothing I had done that would have warranted my going to hell. Surely this was heaven. It just had to be.

The faint rustling outside the cave caught my attention. Since I was uncertain about everything right then, I decided it best to play possum. I had just enough time to close my eyelids far enough to appear asleep -while leaving them cracked open just enough to view the activity in the room from beneath my abnormally long, thick lashes- before he entered. I had all I could do not to gasp with admiration. That settled it! I was in heaven and some sort of god just entered the cave. His six-foot-tall, muscular physique moved with the power, grace, and presence of someone possessing an undeniable abundance of self-confidence. His feet practically glided when he walked. His lean, well-formed muscles rippled with each movement as he fed newly chopped wood to the embers of what had once been a roaring fire. Thick, dark hair framed his pale, aristocratic features as he fanned the fire until flames once again danced to his satisfaction. His perfectly formed mouth made me aware of my own thin, overly broad lips. I'd wager his mouth didn't consume his face when he smiled like mine did. His only apparel was a pair of black leather pants that fit like a second skin. The rest of him -including his feet- was bare. I could have admired him all day. I'd never encountered so perfect a man.

But then, he wasn't a man.

He was a god and I was in heaven.

I found heaven very different than what I'd expected it to be. There were no angels playing harps and singing as they floated by on clouds. I struggled to remember my early religious education. If memory served me correctly, heaven consisted of various levels. Perhaps I'd entered one that didn't have angels in it. After all, they worked closely with the creator God. My deeds may not have been bad enough to force me into hell, but they were also surely not perfect enough to get me seated next to the creator of all. That was it. I was in one of the lower levels of heaven. It made sense. Didn't I learn that in the lower spiritual realms they ate and drank and felt just like humans? Well, if that was the case, it was perfectly fine with me. That stew that my handsome god was stirring smelled delicious and my mouth was watering for a taste of it.

"You're awake," he said with his back still turned to me.

I cleared my throat and whispered, "Yes."

"Don't be concerned, your faculties will all return in no time," he assured me as he bent down to fill a bowl with the delicious smelling fare.

His emerald green eyes touched mine and he flashed the most dazzling smile my way.

I was probably hallucinating, but I would have sworn his teeth sparkled like the actors in a gum commercial I'd seen on television. I squeezed my eyes shut briefly and gave him a renewed appraisal. Nope, I wasn't hallucinating. His strong, well defined teeth were a brilliant white and glistening to the point they almost hurt my eyes. Had his flesh been darker, it would have made a hideous sight. As it so happened, his pale complexion blended naturally with his brilliant teeth, creating an alluring, almost irresistible effect.

"Are you a god?" I asked meekly.

His chuckle echoed through the cave as he said, "Hardly. It's a nice thought though."

"I am in heaven, right?" I urged.

"Heaven?" he said with a puzzled look. "You believe this to be heaven?"

He stood up and carried the much anticipated steaming bowl to me. I extended both hands to receive it and almost dropped it. A bit of hot broth spilled onto my leg. It was then that I realized I was still naked.

He watched me with interest as I struggled to maintain control of the precious bowl of stew while pulling a quilt that had been barely covering me over my nakedness as best I could.

"I've already seen everything you have to offer. I see no reason risking a serious burn for non-essential modesty. Please," he gestured toward the stew, "enjoy and relax. If it makes you feel better, I promise I won't look."

With that, he left the cave.

"Are... are you coming back?" I called after him with a scratchy voice that could barely be defined as audible.

I cleared my throat multiple times in hopes of lubricating my vocal chords into working condition.

"Of course," came his faint reply from the distance.

I noted how far away he'd gotten in a very short period of time. He'd moved abnormally fast.

With the stew commanding my attention, I gave my strange rescuer minimal thought as I dove into the most delicious fare I could recall ever eating. My stomach churned and hurt as I stuffed it, but I kept going. When my bowl was empty, I looked around to be sure I was alone before I slowly made my way to the boiling pot for a refill. I would probably regret it in the long run, but I didn't care. The food was delicious and I had no idea when I'd be able to eat again. It was better to stuff my gut as full as I could and hope I was able to keep it all down.

I'd completed my second bowl when he returned wearing a smirk that made me want to slap him and kiss him at the same time. His emerald green eyes twinkled with what I took to be amusement as he stared at my empty bowl, but he said nothing as he extended his hand to take it from me. As he moved to put the bowl on the nearby table, I noticed he carried a small bundle wrapped in cloth. He returned to my side and handed it to me.

I pulled the ties slowly while I puzzled over what he could be giving me. It was a soft bundle. Could I be so bold as to hope it be clothes? The thought hastened my speed of opening the wrap. An enormous smile consumed my face as I looked down at

neatly folded, one on top of the other- black leather leggings, a tan woolen tunic and a beaded belt.   I smiled my thanks and donned the tunic without hesitation. It reached my mid-thigh, which afforded me enough modesty to stand and step into the leggings. Everything fit as if it was specially made for me.

"Thanks," I mumbled, "They fit perfectly."

"I should hope so," he said, with no further explanation

"Where am I?" I asked, deciding I didn't want to know how he managed to present me with leather pants that fit like they were made for me.

"You're safe," he mumbled as he started back out of the cave.

"Safe… where?" I urged.

"Here," he tossed over his shoulder before disappearing.

I waited for what felt like hours for his return, but to no avail. I had no idea who he was, but he was my only contact at the moment and from what I could tell he was also my savior. I didn't want him to leave me. I didn't want to be left alone. I felt tired and abandoned. I longed to leave the cave and look for civilization; at this point I'd settle for anyone to keep me company. I would have at least explored outside my cozy sanctuary, had I trusted my ribs not to shift and puncture a lung.

Somewhere over time, I managed to relax enough to drift off into sleep. The warmth of the fire and a satisfied belly promoted one of the deepest rests I'd had in ages.

CHAPTER TWO

When I finally roused enough to force myself free from the sweetest slumber I can recall in my twenty-four years of life, it took a bit of struggling to remember where I was. I sat up on the bed and swung my feet over its edge. They barely touched the floor. I didn't recall being so small in it before, but then, I'd been pretty messed up with drugs and injuries.

Injuries.

I remembered my ribs and felt for the bandage beneath my tunic. It was gone. I pulled the tunic up to inspect more closely. Searching the cave interior with my eyes, I was disappointed to find no mirror. I checked myself out as best I could without it. There was no sign of any damage that I could see, nor was there any pain! How had I managed to heal so quickly? It had been quickly, hadn't it? I couldn't tell, since I'd lost all concept of time.

I made note that my rescue was the second miracle to happen since I'd been captured by those grotesque creatures; the first being my rejection in the food line. I said a small silent prayer of thanks. I was pretty sure I'd already done so, but I wanted to thank my god-like savior again with a clear head. I sensed his presence and that he'd been coming and going, but I saw no signs of him at the moment.

I hopped off the bed with more vitality than I'd felt in a long time. *What was in that wonderfully delicious stew?* I wondered as I padded over to the fire. It was still going strong with signs of recently being tended. I looked around. I was alone.

Feeling energized and curious, I decided to brave the outer limits of the cave. I needed to know where I was so I could make plans on getting home. I really hoped those beasts hadn't teleported me to some obscure location, or worse...planet! Although I knew it could be done, I had no experience with teleporting. It would be difficult for me to get back on my own. Would my altruist be willing to continue his aid and help me get back? Did he even have the ability?

. The air felt crisp and cool against my exposed flesh as I stepped out into the moonlight. I estimated it was after midnight. I listened for sounds of life around me, but all was quiet. It looked like the whole world was sleeping. All except me, that is.

I noted the fullness of the brilliant moon. This meant that I'd been in the cave healing and sleeping heavily for about two weeks. I really owed my benefactor a debt of gratitude.

The cave was on the edge of a forest. Tall pines mingled with gnarly oaks and maples. It was a perfectly normal looking forest that gave me no hint at all as to where I was or what era I was in. An owl screeched its presence and startled a small squeal out of me.

"Be careful. We don't want to give away our hiding place," said a rich, sultry voice through the night.

I jumped to look behind me to find my handsome savior with a load of firewood balanced in his arms as if it weighed no more than a sack of feathers.

"Where are we?" I asked.

"Safe for now," he replied as he turned to enter the cave, "unless you keep that howling up."

"It was a little squeal," I muttered as I followed him back inside.

"Haven't you ever heard the saying 'the forest has eyes?' " he chided.

"Is that the same as the hills have eyes?" I said sarcastically.

I was referring to the movie, of course. It was a way of testing things. If I'd gone back in time, he wouldn't have a clue what I was speaking about.

"I saw that film," he said as he dropped the wood next to the fire. "I didn't much care for it."

Okay, so I was still in my own era. That was excellent, but I still had questions such as what was a Dragos? I remembered that word from my nightmare as if it'd been branded on my brain.

"Can I know your name?" I said with more self-confidence than I really possessed. I felt it best to be polite rather than burst into a line of questions about my whereabouts and the creatures that abducted me and then left me for dead.

"Jack," he said, matter-of-factly.

"Nice to meet you Jack," I said as sweetly as I could.

"Is it?" he chuckled with a tone that could only be described as sarcastic and walked back out of the cave.

I was really growing tired of the way he just up and left as the mood struck him.

"Wait," I commanded with more intensity than I'd intended.

It left me a little shaken. I did my best to hide it from him.

He stopped in his tracks, but didn't turn around. I watched his shoulders tense and then loosen again. It was as if he was struggling with what to do while he remained with his back to me.

"Please don't go yet," I said in a gentler tone that I was only able to accomplish after some serious breathing exercises. "I... I'm very confused and lonely and... well I'm a little frightened. I was captured by..."

"By the Dragos," he interjected. "I pulled you from their refuse pile."

The tone of his voice left me uncomfortable. I'd angered him. I wasn't sure what I should say. 'I'm sorry for barking at you and thank you for all you've done' was the most obvious, yet it didn't seem appropriate for the mood, so I said, "I owe you my life," instead.

"You think so?" he almost growled.

Although I was taken aback by his aggressive tone, I refused to be deterred. I was determined to smooth things over. I needed to show him my gratitude; for my sake, if not for his. There was no doubt in my mind that I would have died had he not pulled me from that abhorrent pile of human remains.

"Yes," I said steadily.

"Be careful.... I just might take it," he half whispered before bounding out of the entrance.

Suddenly my legs refused to hold me. I collapsed in a heap.

The thick carpet acted as a barrier between me and the cold earthen ground. I could smell the earth in its fibers, yet it looked fairly new and fresh. I would have pondered on how long the cave served as Jack's plush sanctuary had I not been overwhelmed with his parting comment.

Did I hear him correctly? Did he threaten to take my life? Had he saved me from certain death at the hands of the Dragos only to kill me himself? If I hadn't heard his words with my own ears, I would never have entertained such a thought. He seemed like a perfectly normal man. True, he was a little uncommunicative, but, considering where he'd found me, I assumed he'd seen some trauma of his own. Maybe he also narrowly escaped being food for those beasts. Or... horror of horrors... he was a cannibal and scavenged the remains off the bones of the refuse!

I shook my head. Now I was being ridiculous. If he was a cannibal, he'd have surely eaten me over the course of the last few weeks; not feed me. I forced myself to giggle. It was amazing how the mind could dream up such ridiculous stuff and make it seem real in a flash.

I took a closer look around the interior of the cave that was now my sanctuary. This was clearly someone's home or -at the very least- place of refuge. If Jack hadn't set it up, I was sure he'd used this place for his own. Yet he'd barely spent any time there since I'd arrived. Did he have another dwelling nearby? That didn't seem logical, but then, nothing about what had happened so far seemed logical. Dragos weren't real. They were creatures from fairy tales told around campfires for the purpose of scaring your fellow campers. Since when did creatures in fairy tales come to life?

Several days passed with no words spoken between Jack and me. When I saw or sensed him coming, I feigned sleep in order to avoid speaking with him. I needed time to process the fear his comment instilled in me. It had to be the better part of a week gone by before I started to get restless. I'd completely lost track of time. I had no idea how long I'd actually been in that cave. When did I arrive? I estimated I'd been there a total of three weeks, but was I correct? I kept falling in and out of sleep; staying awake only long enough to fill my stomach with the ever present stew -that I never grew tired of and couldn't seem to get enough of- and then right back into slumber land I went.

"You've been here for six weeks, not three," said a feminine voice from a distance.

Startled, I jumped and quickly looked around, but saw no one.

"Over here dearie," the voice cooed.

I couldn't decide if it was a friendly coo or not.

"You're rather rude, aren't you?" I stated bluntly.

"You're an expert on rudeness?" the owner of the voice spat, clearly annoyed.

"It doesn't take an expert to recognize rude," I replied bravely.

It didn't matter that this was my first and only visitor other than Jack. Sneaking into the cave and remaining in the shadows was rude and I intended to make that clear.

"You're an ungrateful bitch, aren't you?" the voice said.

"To whom am I being ungrateful and for what? I thanked my rescuer. I see no need to be polite to someone who sneaks in here, reads my mind, and then speaks from the dark recesses of the cave instead of showing himself," I spat.

"Herself, you twit," the voice spat back.

"You sound like a man," I lied.

I'd actually meant to say 'her', but, in my nervousness, I got confused.

"You look like you just escaped Auschwitz!" the voice blurted out.

I had no response for that because I was sure it was true. I stood in stunned silence for a while and then burst out laughing. I mean, seriously...I was arguing with a bodiless voice.

"Touché," I breathed between peals of laughter, "You've got me there."

Before my startled eyes, a glowing translucent ball emerged out of the shadows and slowly grew to enormous size. The larger it got, the opaquer it became. When it reached a size large enough to accommodate a body, a tall, slender, but shapely brunette stepped out and stood not five feet away from me.

I stood mesmerized by the overlarge almond shaped eyes that were perfectly positioned on her small, creamy bronze, oval shaped face. Her pixie type nose looked at home between her smooth, arched brows and full, ruby lips. Had it not been for the pointed ears on the sides of her head, I would have labeled her perfect.

"I'm not perfect either," she chuckled good-naturedly while pulling on her ears and lifting her chiffon gown to display grotesque and hairy feet.

"It's an odd combination," I mused as I slowly admired her slender curves and perfect complexion.

"Not where I come from," she smiled, seemingly unaffected by my comment that most would consider rude.

"I'm from New York. The state, not the city. That's on earth," I replied without thinking.

Between the lizard beasts and this odd looking person, I'd come to the conclusion that I'd left earth for some other planet, but I was surprised to hear myself say it aloud.

"Me too," she chimed. "Earth, that is."

"How can that be?" I asked with genuine surprise.

"Now that's typical," she snorted as she walked to the large, comfortable looking chair by the fire. "You humans are all the same."

"I'm sorry," I said and then chastised myself silently. What in heaven's name was I apologizing for? "It's just that I've never seen anyone from earth that looked like you, so I don't understand how you can claim your look is not an odd combination."

"You can't help it, I suppose," she sighed. "It's just that I hoped you would be different. I mean, it's not like Jack to take in just any stray human." A sparkle of amusement tinted her large eyes as she continued, "It's especially not like him to let them live. You must be too skinny for him too."

"He eats people?" I gasped as my hand flew to my throat.

My fears were being confirmed.

"Ha, ha, ha, you're so funny," she chortled, but offered nothing else.

My visitor seemed to know her way around the cave quite well. She produced some herbal tea and two cups from a cupboard I hadn't even thought to investigate. We spent the next few hours sipping tea and getting to know each other. She told me her name was L'oana, a name quite common to her kind. She equated it to Jane or Ann in my language. When I asked her what her kind was, she spat, "Earthling" as if I'd insulted her. I let the topic go for a while and just enjoyed her bubbly conversation. It'd been what seemed like an eternity since I'd had the luxury of enjoying light hearted conversation over a cup of herbal tea. I wasn't in a hurry to give it up.

At some point over the course of our discussions, L'oana grew more comfortable with me. I discovered that my new female friend was well over a century old. She took great pains to explain to me that she belonged to a raced called Squachula. Although they lived upon the planet earth, they lived in an alternate dimension than that of humans.

I learned that, like the Dragos, Squachula had a life expectancy of approximately two-hundred years. This meant she was what we would consider middle aged. I compared her youthful, light hearted actions and appearance to that of a middle aged human and smiled. No wonder we were considered an inferior species.

L'oana enlightened me on the variances of Squachula around the planet. Apparently they differed in race just like humans differed. Some were of highly superior intelligence and skills while others bordered on primitive. She confided that, over the centuries, there were times when they interbred with other species, including the humans, which added to the variances in race. Her race was a product of such interbreeding.

L'oana was not only light hearted, intelligent, and beautiful. She was also highly skilled in the art of teleporting from one dimension to another. She often made trips from inner earth to outer earth; which was how she met Jack.

I learned she was a missionary of sorts. Like humans, Squachula were prey for the Dragos and, therefore, like humans, they wanted them eliminated from their planet. L'oana traveled between planets, by way of teleportation, to assist in the task of weakening the Dragos until the time came that they could be fully driven out. This was a dangerous mission that only a few were allowed to participate in. Although she made light of it, I knew she was more than she was letting on to be.

I mentioned to L'oana the fact that, for centuries, there were sightings on earth of a large, man-like, ape-like beast in various locations of earth. Some called the beast Big Foot. Some called him the Abominable Snow Man. Some called him Sasquatch. All were basically names for the same type of being. She nodded, smiled, and proceeded to tell me that they were of the Squachula breed, but significantly removed from her clan. She equated it to the Chinese of the human race verses the humans from the continent of Africa. They were human, but significantly different in size, shape, coloring, and features. One thing that was similar was their ability to move from one dimension of the earth's etheric layer to the other.

I learned that earth was made up of four vibrational dimensions that housed physical inhabitants. For the most part, the planet looked and behaved the same in each one. They even housed similar, if not identical, plant and animal life. The truest difference was the variance of species of intelligent beings in each level.

The dimensions eventually melded into one within the core of the planet where the vibrations were denser. It was in this area that the Dragos who teleported to earth from other planets dwelled. Their location allowed them to travel into any outer level with ease to capture and accumulate the life they depended upon for sustenance. They were an evil, lizard type humanoid that migrated from another part of the galaxy some millennia past when their own planet got so overpopulated that food became a scarcity. Earth and Kurr weren't the only planets they dispersed their pioneers to, but they proved to be one of the more desirable for the Dragos to inhabit.

I'd had the misfortune of being abducted while walking down a remote section of road in the wee hours of the morning. It turned out that road was one of their favorite locations for acquiring food since it was fairly isolated and easy to remain undetected. I heard discussions during the early hours of my capture that the mountains of Arizona and the Arkansas hot springs were other prime locations. L'oana gave me a detailed list of earth's hot spots for abduction. I burned it into my memory bank and vowed to heed it when and if I ever got back home.

I questioned her method of dealing with the Dragos. Did she fight them head on or was it a sneak attack? To my disappointment, she refused to discuss the topic. I'd gotten all I was going to get about the Dragos out of her for the moment.

I noticed her energy level was fading. She was no longer as bubbly and vivacious when speaking. It was clear she needed a rest. Since I was feeling a bit weary myself, I suggested we take a brief rest. When she acted offended at the concept of my thinking her weak, I emphasized that I was still in the stage of recovery and would appreciate a little down time. This appeased her wounded pride and she eagerly obliged by leaving the cave, stating she'd return in a few hours to continue our conversations.

As I stretched out onto the mattress, that I assumed Jack abandoned in order to accommodate me, I thought of my new found acquaintance. I'd never met someone who wasn't human before. It was an odd experience, but a pleasant one. I sensed she hadn't been completely honest with me. I didn't believe she was from earth and was probably a native of the planet she said I was on at the moment; Kurr. Even so, I liked L'oana. I had very few female friends back home; mainly because we lived in such a remote area and people were not in abundance. I was looking forward to L'oana and I becoming good friends.

As I lay on my back, with my arm resting over my eyes, my mind wandered to thoughts of Jack. I'd seen very little of him since he'd brought me there. He'd entered a few times to deposit firewood, stoke the fire, and stir or freshen my ever present stew with fresh herbs or meat. He said minimal words to me. In fact, I didn't recall him saying much of anything to me since he'd frightened me into thinking him a cannibal.

Of course it was still questionable what he was. After all, didn't L'oana make that odd comment about him leaving me alive? Had I survived the clutches of the Dragos only to die at the hands of Jack? If that was the case, if he truly planned on killing me, what was he waiting for? Was his dragging things out as a sick form of torture? L'oana said I'd been in the cave for six weeks or so. Why would he forfeit his home, monitor the fire, and keep my food well stocked if he planned on killing me?

I slid my hands to over my stomach and hips. Had I gained a little weight? The tunic and pants he'd presented when I'd first arrived allowed room for it. It sure felt like I had. I cupped my tiny breasts. They felt like they too had increased in size, if only a little. Was that it? Was he fattening me up for the kill? My heart reacted to the thought so powerfully, I thought it was going to escape my chest on its own and run away. The pain in my ribcage was excruciating. I was having a heart attack! I didn't need to worry about being killed and eaten by anyone. I'd be dead in a matter of minutes from a failed heart.

The raspy sound of my gasping for air that echoed off the tapestry covered stone pounded at me like a hammer against a dull, rusty nail. It brought back memories of my aunt's mini-farm and her incessant attempts to recycle the old barn wood; pulling and prying at century old nails while doing her best to keep the wood from splitting under the nail's screeching resistance.

"What's wrong?" said a deep male whisper from seemingly nowhere.

The voice sounded more in my head than in my ear. It was familiar, yet I couldn't quite place it.

I sat up in a panic and looked around for the source of the voice but saw no one.

"Come out!" I demanded.

"I'm right here," Jack said calmly from the cave entrance.

"What's wrong?"

"How did you know?" I whispered.

His ability to come and go so quickly and silently was unsettling.

"What's wrong?" he insisted.

I backed up as far as I could on the narrow mattress while I searched for an escape route. There was none. The only way out was the entrance and Jack was blocking it.

"I don't like to keep repeating myself," he growled. "I asked you a question and I expect an answer."

"Nothing!" I burst out, "I'm fine."

"Your heart is ready to explode. What frightened you?" he persisted.

I held his gaze for a few seconds that felt like an eternity, while I debated what to do. I fought the urge to fall into his serious emerald eyes. There was something about them that pulled me in, hugged me, and then debated about letting me go. Or at least that's how it felt.

I shook my head and decided to tell him the truth.

"You frighten me," I said in a voice that was barely above a whisper.

"I don't understand. Haven't I been good to you? Why would I frighten you?" he asked.

He looked genuinely puzzled.

"You made a comment about taking my life a while back and then L'oana said...," I began.

"L'oana!" he bellowed. "When was that she-wolf here?"

"Not long ago," I winced.

"I should have known," he hissed as he stomped back out of the cave.

I wasn't sure if I should still be frightened for myself or perhaps transfer that concern toward my new found friend. She seemed like such a fun and agreeable sort. I couldn't imagine why Jack would be so unhappy to discover she'd paid me a visit.

He'd called her a she-wolf. I thought it odd, but it wasn't long before it was made clear.

L'oana dashed past me with lightning speed; followed by Jack who was traveling equally as fast. I had to rub my eyes to make sure I'd seen correctly. When I was in focus again, I gasped in horror at the sight of L'oana pinned against the thick tapestry wall. She was hanging onto dear life with Jack's hand clamped around her throat. Her head was tipped to the side and his teeth were elongated, ready to sink into her tender flesh.

He was a vampire! That couldn't be, could it? I thought vampires were products of folk lore. Of course, I didn't believe in life on other planets and lizard people either, until I was kidnapped by them and brought to a planet called Kurr. I wondered what else in fairy tales was not really a tale, but fact.

I screamed for Jack to stop with every bit of air my lungs contained, filled them back up, and did it again. Eventually –and thankfully before he'd sank his teeth into her beautiful, perfect flesh- my screams penetrated his thick skull and he looked over at me. Seeing my terrified expression must have brought him back to his senses because he retracted his fangs with surprising speed and released his captive.

She raced to my side and huddled behind me as best she could while breathing heavily. I patted her arm reassuringly while I glared at him defiantly. It was clear to me he was not human. Real or not, from what I could see he was a vampire. Surprisingly, I wasn't frightened. In fact, I was relieved. At least he wasn't fattening me up to eat my flesh.

"What's your problem?" L'oana spat from behind me.

"You stay away from her!" Jack bellowed.

"Why is she so special? Why haven't you killed her?" L'oana hissed.

I didn't like the tone L'oana was using. It seemed far too hostile when referring to me and my possible demise. It actually sounded as if she resented the fact that Jack had nursed me back to health instead of draining me of my blood. This was a twist in personality that I didn't like.

"I warned you," Jack hissed.

"I don't understand," I interjected. I was shocked when I

looked at L'oana to see the fiery red that glowed in her eyes. Her lovely face was distorted to the point it was borderline unrecognizable. The animal in her was coming through loud and clear. "What are you?" I gasped.

"She's trouble," Jack said.

He reached for my arm and pulled me off the bed with such force that I propelled into his chest. My muscles tensed with apprehension about being held so closely by a blood sucking creature. When I could finally move past my fear, I noted he felt surprisingly warm and supple. Whenever I'd read or watched shows about vampires, or listened to the tales of them from the neighborhood story tellers, they were always described as being cold, hard, and corpse-like. Had I not witnessed his fangs with my own eyes, I would have never believed Jack to be anything but a human.

"You're warm," I thought aloud.

He chuckled and wrapped his arms around me protectively while saying, "You've been listening to the story tellers."

"Did they tell you he's of the devil?" L'oana shouted. "He's evil. Don't be fooled by his warmth. It's the fire of hell that burns in his body. That's what you're feeling!"

Jack's body stiffened.

"How did you find us?" he demanded.

"Ha! Do you really think you can hide from me? Do you really think you can hide from them? You fool!" she said in a tone that sounded almost animal.

"What are you?" I asked again.

"You are looking into the face of the demon's woman," Jack explained. "She neglected to camouflage her grotesqueness. Usually she appears in human form to humans." He jutted his chin in her direction, "You surprise me, L'oana. Can it be you're slipping?"

"The demon's woman?" I gasped.

My confusion was clearly apparent.

"His queen if you please," she hissed. "And he's no more a demon than you are, Jack. You're just jealous because you and I didn't work out."

"Watch what you say, L'oana," he spat.

I watched L'oana coil her body in a snakelike fashion as she transformed from the beautiful woman with odd ears and feet to a reptilian androgynous creature with an incredibly long forked tongue that darted in and out with lightning speed. I threw my hands over my mouth to stifle the scream that I couldn't help emitting and buried my face as best I could into Jack's chest. I'd spent hours talking to this creature and actually considered her a new found friend and ally.

"Be gone with you or feel my wrath!" Jack said between clenched teeth.

"Who is she to you?" L'oana hissed. "She's a scrawny thing and a poor excuse for a woman in any species. Why do you protect her so?"

Peeking through my fingers, I was mesmerized by the sight of this snake like creature moving its mouth and tongue in a manner that formed clearly understandable –if not lispy- words. In fact, I was so engrossed in the scene before me that I almost missed his response.

"She's not your concern," he bellowed with an authoritative tone.

"But, she's yours?" L'oana hissed.

"She's my ward," he said defiantly.

"Your what?" I wailed as I pushed my head back to look up at him. How preposterous was that statement? I'd never set eyes on him before in my life. How could he claim that I was his ward?

My mother and father were killed in a car crash when I was still in diapers. I was raised by my mother's sister, Jenny. Three years my senior, her son, James, acted as my protector throughout the years. How could he possibly claim me as his ward? It just didn't make sense.

Jack rested his chin on the top of my head as he hugged me close. Even in my distress, I couldn't help noticing how natural it felt. I found myself breathing in unison with the rhythm of the beating of his heart. It was an odd realization. It was like we were an extension of each other. How could that be? I barely knew him, yet I felt like I'd known him forever. It was unsettling.

I pushed myself away from him with a force I didn't know I possessed.

"Let go of me," I said with surprising bravado.

I spared a quick glance at L'oana -who had returned to human form and was now laughing hysterically at the situation- before my focus returned to Jack. He seemed undisturbed by my refusal to be held. Instead, he also looked amused. I would have been annoyed at the smirk on his beautiful mouth, had I not been held captivated by his deep, alluring eyes.

After what seemed like an eternity, I managed to regain control and pulled myself to full height before stating as firmly as I could, "You have some explaining to do."

CHAPTER THREE

"Will you listen to the demands she makes? Does she know who you are and just doesn't care?" L'oana said.

Her cackling filled the cave.

"Quiet!" Jack snapped.

I spun at L'oana.

"I know he's a vampire," I spat. "I saw with my own eyes."

"That doesn't frighten you?" she asked.

"Of course it frightens me," I replied, "I've been nothing but frightened by one thing or another since those vile, scaly creatures abducted me, but I still need... no... I deserve to know what's happening."

"She's got courage, Jack, I'll give her that. Who is she?" L'oana purred.

"I told you," he replied.

"You told her wrong," I stated firmly.

Jack turned to L'oana and ordered, "Get out."

"I'm crushed," she pouted.

"Get out or die," he said firmly.

With a few hisses for emphasis, L'oana made her departure.

I couldn't help the sadness that swept over me. In the short time I'd spent with her, I'd enjoyed her company and considered her a new found friend. I'd been lonely for companionship. Meeting her only accentuated the fact. Discovering her to be a wolf in sheep's clothing was practically devastating.

"Try not to let it bother you. I've yet to meet anyone who hasn't been fooled by that one. Even me," Jack said in an attempt at comforting.

There was no sense in denying my feelings. It was obvious he had somehow tapped into my emotions. As I forced myself to release the tension that consumed me, my legs were suddenly unable to hold me. When I reached for him to support myself, he swept me into his incredibly strong arms and carried me to the bed. He smelled of musk and spices; clove and cinnamon amongst them. The aroma caused a heady sensation that I found overwhelmingly intoxicating and pleasurable.

"Are all vampires as alluring as you?" I stuttered.

His erotic chuckle would have been enough to tell me all I needed to know, but he took it one step further. Before I knew what was happening, his lips were on mine. At first the kiss was soft, slow, and sweet. It was me that changed the course to something more torrid and frantic. I have no idea what got into me. All I knew was that I wanted to consume him. I wanted to climb inside and become a part of him.

I'd kissed only one man in a way that could be deemed passionate; my fiancé Mark.

We'd kissed often, but in no way was I prepared for a kiss of this caliber. The overwhelming ecstasy threatened to consume me. I wanted more. I had to have more.

I grabbed at the belt of my tunic and tossed it away. His firm hand slid beneath it to cup my barely formed breast. My body jolted as his thumb teased my nipple. A groan purged from deep within my throat. It sounded foreign, yet I knew it was me making it. I needed him inside me with an urgency I'd never experienced before. Under normal circumstances, I would have been incredibly self-conscious about the fact that my body was mostly skin and bones with breasts that barely distinguished me as a woman, but somehow it just didn't matter.

The only other man I displayed such confidence with was Mark. We'd fooled around, but we hadn't gone all the way. We'd decided to save the actual act of consummation for our honeymoon. It seemed so romantic to wait. Now, all thoughts of Mark, our engagement, and my virginity disappeared as I focused on one thing and one thing only. I wanted Jack to take me completely. I wanted it in a way I'd never be able to describe.

"Enough," he said as he pulled away and reached for my belt.

I sat in breathless and amazed disappointment as I watched

his strong thighs carry him to the opposite side of the cave. His tight buttocks strained against his leather pants as he bent to tend the fire.

"I don't understand..." I managed.

"Do you know who you are?" he asked.

"Of course I do," I replied. "I'm Jessica Turry."

"Who you really are... Do you know who you really are?" he persisted.

"I'm really Jessica Turry," I said firmly.

He said nothing.

After a lengthy and uncomfortable silence, I added, "I'm not a vampire."

"No," he nodded, "that is something you are not."

I shivered with a mixture of discomfort and pleasure as his eyes bore into my very core. I shook my head to clear it. Guilt replaced pleasure as Mark's image emerged in my mind. What was wrong with me? I'd behaved like a wonton woman with this stranger who obviously didn't want me. No, not just a stranger; a vampire who could kill me at any moment.

My mind searched my memory bank for all I'd seen in movies, read in books, and listened in conversation about vampires. Had he put me under his spell or something? If I recalled correctly, they were able to hypnotize their victims with their eyes. Is that what happened? No, it couldn't have been. If he'd hypnotized me to act the slut, then he wouldn't have stopped me like he had.

How embarrassing. I was mortified. I could look at him no longer. I could be near him no longer. I wanted to find a hole to crawl into or a corner to hide in or something. Damn him for putting me in a round cave with no place to hide and double damn him for standing in front of the only exit! My mind raced. What had L'oana used to disguise her whereabouts? I could see nothing that would work. Then I remembered she'd appeared from a globe of light. She hadn't hidden behind a thing. Damn! It was frustrating to be a mere human amongst mythical and magical beings.

"The time will come when you will know who you truly are.

When that time comes we will see if we should continue this... and more," he said as he started out the entrance. "I am your guardian. Get used to it," he tossed over his shoulder without looking back.

I threw myself face down on the mattress and pounded it until I'd released enough humiliated frustration to allow my body to relax and sleep. It wasn't long before the dreaming began.

I was wearing my dream wedding dress. It was cream colored; full skirted chiffon with silk capped shoulders, and the most intricate beading on the bodice one could ever imagine. James looked incredibly handsome and distinguished in a dark tuxedo and silver silk tie as he walked me proudly toward Mark, who stood waiting in the same dark tuxedo and silver tie. Mark looked sexy, calm, and poised like a model from a GQ magazine. My heart swelled with love, pride, and joy at the sight of the two men that meant the most in the world to me looking so handsome and happy.

Unaccustomed to the three inch stilettos I'd foolishly strapped onto my sneaker favoring feet, I stumbled. James was quick to catch me and set me aright. I'd waited so long for this moment I could hardly believe it was finally happening. It would have been perfect except for one thing... my parents. I'd have given anything in the world to have them be there with me on this, the most wonderful day of my life. Tears welled up as James finally deposited me next to Mark and the preacher began the ceremony. My mascara mixed with my eyes' salty fluid and I could hardly see a thing. I relied on my ears to keep me abreast of the ceremony's progress.

Mark said his vows and the preacher turned to me. It was my turn to vow to be his and his alone 'til death do us part. Just as I said "I do" my eyes cleared up enough for me to see the man standing preparing to seal our vows with a kiss. Mark was gone. Jack's hot lips consumed mine in a kiss that tingled down to my very toes.

I sat up with a start. What a nightmare! Moisture beaded my brow and trickled down the back of my neck. I was sweating, yet chilled to the bone. I spoke into the emptiness of the cave, assuring myself that I was engaged to Mark and I would find a way to get home to him so that we could marry. Hearing the words aloud brought a sense of comfort and I pulled the thick quilt up to my chin and closed my eyes. Willing myself back to sleep, I prayed for it to be a dreamless one.

It seemed like only a matter of minutes before I was sitting up in bed feeling rested and refreshed. Jack was tending the fire and stirring the pot of stew that I just couldn't seem to get enough of. After eating the same thing for so long, it was a wonder I could even look at it, let alone salivate for it like I was.

"I wasn't going to tell you I was your guardian," Jack said without turning around.

"I'm not who you think I am," I mumbled, "Whoever that might be."

Jack stood up and stretched his back in a cat-like manner. Once again I wondered where he stayed since I'd taken over his cave.

"Is your back bothering you?" I asked softly.

"It's tight, that's all," he replied, matter-of-factly.

"I have your bed, don't I?" I asked meekly.

"That you do," he said with a smile.

"Vampires sleep and get sore backs," I mused aloud.

"I need to read some of the books you've read," he chuckled.

"Do you own a shirt?" I teased.

Jack caressed his chest as he asked in a mocking tone, "You don't like?"

My heart skipped a beat as he flashed his brilliant white and perfectly straight teeth in a genuine smile. Damn, he was handsome, and then some. Too many more smiles like that and being faithful to Mark would prove completely impossible.

I suddenly remembered my behavior the night before and blushed. I cleared my throat for lack of something to say to ease my humiliation. Jack seemed not to notice my condition as he continued to stir the stew.

"It smells pretty tasty. I'd say it's ready. Are you hungry?" he cooed.

"I'm starving," I blurted as I rushed to join him near the fire.

I reached for my bowl from the roughhewn board that was

mounted into the stone wall with spikes and acted as the kitchen self. As I extended my hand toward the pot of stew, my arm brushed against his. The hairs on my flesh stood to attention, as if electrified. I'd never experienced something of this nature before. It both thrilled and confused me. I jumped back involuntarily.

"I won't hurt you," he assured me.

"You confuse me," I stammered. "Why did you save me? Why haven't you killed me?"

"Don't believe everything you read and hear about vampires. We're not killers run rampant. Killing isn't my nature," he said curtly. After a short silence he continued, "I told you why you're here."

His eyes locked mine as if to emphasize his last statement. I felt my body being pulled to him like a nail to a magnet. What was it about him that I found so difficult to resist?

"I'm engaged to be married," I stammered.

"Congratulations," he replied gently. He cupped my chin momentarily before dropping his hand and heading out of the cave. "We're leaving this place tomorrow. Rest up while you can," he tossed over his shoulder before disappearing.

I spent the remainder of the day resting and going over in my head how I came to be captured by the Dragos in the first place. It didn't make sense.

There was nothing on the news or in the gossip chain to indicate that they were raiding in my area. If there had been, then precautions would have been taken like they had twenty-two years earlier when people were disappearing without a trace.

That was also when my parents died in a car crash. I was very young at the time and couldn't remember it, but people told me a curfew was enforced for quite some time. We were only allowed out of our homes between the hours of eleven o'clock in the morning and four o'clock in the afternoon. During this time, the streets were packed with military enforcing martial law and protecting our parameters. It prevented people from traveling to my parent's funeral. In fact, more than once over the years I'd questioned if we'd even had a funeral for them because, as hard as I tried, I couldn't remember one. I relied on my memory for so much with them because there were no pictures of them to keep their image alive. Other than my vague memories, the only evidence that my parents existed was a grave site for me to adorn with flowers.

I'd been to see a movie with Mark and then gone out for a few drinks afterward. He'd driven. He'd also had, in my opinion, too many drinks to be considered sober enough to drive home. Of course he disagreed. When I refused to get in the car with him as the driver, he hopped behind the wheel and sped off; leaving me to find my own way home. Since I didn't live more than a few miles from the bar, I just started walking.

There was a stretch of road that was fairly rural and lonely; especially at one o'clock in the morning. To add to the ambiance, the moon was barely visible and a fog had settled. It was while navigating this stretch of road and contemplating on how surprisingly thick the fog was that I felt myself being grabbed, dragged, and then trussed up like some wild beast.

I was tossed into some type of craft -that silently hovered a few feet above ground- and landed on top of a mound of other unfortunates who were trussed just as I was. I remember being barely able to breathe as they continued to stack us like a pile of pancakes, with little to no regard for our wellbeing. When it seemed like the craft was too full to continue to hover above ground as it was, several lizard men hopped in and the door closed.

The stench was almost unbearable. It would have been bad enough to have to endure the stench of the dragos in those tight quarters, but there was also the odor of feces and urine from frightened humans -as well as perspiration and halitosis- to deal with. I don't know when it all became so intense that my body shut down, but it did. When I awoke, I was naked and trussed upside down on some conveyer system awaiting my turn to become their dinner. I'd always been self-conscious about my scrawny body. This was the first time I was grateful for it! I'd never long for voluptuous curves again.

When night came around I was surprised at how quickly and

deeply I fell into sleep. I'd gotten used to the little cave with its minimal comforts. Even the bed seemed to have conformed to my body, as if claiming it.

I wondered where we were going. Jack said we were leaving. Leaving where? He'd yet to tell me where we were and I had no clue. I originally thought it was somewhere in the wilderness not far from my upstate New York home -maybe Canada-, but then L'oana popped up with this story about Kurr and I was totally mixed up.

I made it a point to push my humiliation aside and question Jack –who arrived fully dressed in shirt, beaches, and shoes- about where we were and where we were going as soon as he entered the cave the following morning. He took my abrupt questioning in stride and was more than willing to oblige me with answers.

To my shock and dismay, we were not in the wilderness of New York State. Nor were we anywhere near Canada. L'oana had spoken truth. I'd been teleported to a distant planet called Kurr by lizard humanoids called Dragos, who found humans to be their favorite cuisine. I would have denied the truth of it, had I not remembered that the reason I lived was because I was "unsuitable as food for any Dragos table".

My heart sank.

I questioned him on where he planned on taking me and was relieved when he quite willingly informed me it was his intention to return me to earth. He enlightened me on the ways of time bending, something I had very little knowledge of. According to Jack, Mark wasn't even aware I'd been taken because in earth-time only a matter of minutes had transpired. I couldn't imagine how weeks on Kurr would only equal up to minutes on earth, but who was I to question it? Instead, I nodded my acceptance of the fact and allowed him to continue speaking.

"I've kept my distance from you for a reason... and it's not what you think," Jack said as he moved around the cave collecting a few things and placing them in a sack he'd slung over his shoulder. "I'm a vampire, true, but I drink the blood of animals, not humans."

"You've never drank human blood?" I asked with surprise.

"I didn't say that. I said I drink animal blood. I'm not a killer of animals either. I take only what I need to get by on, nothing more. If the animal is large enough, what I take has no more effect on him than a human donating blood to a blood bank. As for humans... there has been an occasion or two where I've been placed in a position that required I partake in their blood, but they have been far and few between. In truth, I dislike not only the taste of human blood, but the notion of it."

"Okay, now I'm confused," I interjected. "Why would a vampire be repelled by human blood? I thought you were meant to drink it."

"A lot of people think that, but it's not true. We aren't naturally meant to drink human blood. We have human DNA in us after all. It's an act that's far too close to cannibalism. It's only the perverted or the desperate who do it."

"Wow, that's a new twist on vampirism I never expected," I said.

"Isn't it?" he said as he smiled that alluring smile. "I guess the truth isn't nearly as big a sell for the movies, novels, and scary campfire stories."

"I guess not," I replied.

I watched Jack continue to select items to place in his sack and then asked, "Were you born a vampire?"

"No. Vampire babies exist, but it's rare to be born vampire. The majority are made," he replied. "It's an affliction that consumes you after are bitten by another vampire. We look at vampirism is a type of disease."

"I had no idea," I muttered.

"Very few do," Jack replied. "I was bitten when I was very young."

"So you continued to grow then. You didn't just stay the same age as you were when you became a vampire," I stated excitedly.

"Do you mean like Kirsten Dunst in *Interview with a Vampire?*" he chuckled. "I'm afraid not. I've been growing and aging right along. Though, I'll admit the aging process is incredibly slow and my strength is triple that of a human." He shrugged, "So there are some perks to vampirism."

"How old are you?" I blurted out.

"How old are you?" he chortled.

"I'm twenty-four," I replied without hesitation.

"I know," he said soberly. "You don't remember me, do you?"

I looked at him, puzzled. It felt right and natural to be in his company, but I attributed that to the fact that we'd been together for almost two months.

"We've met before?" I asked hesitantly.

"You sat on my knee when you were just a babe. I was visiting your home. It was just before your parents... died," he said sadly.

"You knew my parents?" I said hopefully. "How? How did you know them? Were you a vampire when you knew them?"

He stopped collecting items and stood looking at me. His handsome face looked so sad. I wanted to stroke it and tell him all would be well. When he walked over and sat next to me on the bed, I couldn't resist placing my palm on his strong cheek.

Again, I marveled at how warm to the touch he was.

Again, I remembered the stories of vampires being ice cold.

He pulled my hand from his cheek and held it in his own as he drew a deep breath, "What I'm about to tell you might be difficult for you to believe or even understand, but it is true. One thing I want to assure you is that you will always be told truth by me, no matter whether you want to hear it or not."

I nodded, but said nothing. Since that night I'd argued with Mark and done something as innocent as walk home, rather than put my life in the hands of a drunk, I'd discovered there were aliens that looked like lizards teleporting people to an alien planet as food, vampires that were repelled by human blood, and creatures that shape shifted from humanoid to reptilian. It all seemed surreal. What was one more bit of information to add to the fairy tale mix?

After a moment's hesitation he continued, "The people you knew as your parents were wonderful people. They were loving and kind and generous almost to a fault. I knew your mother, Sara, all of my life. We were siblings."

"But, you're a vampire!" I squealed.

"As was she," he replied.

A loud gasp escaped my lips.

I opted to bypass the comment that my mother was a vampire as I stammered, "You're my uncle? But, you .... we... we ... you know!"

He raised his hand to stop me from saying anything more.

"Wait," he said patiently. "Let me finish before you say anything else, please. Can you do that?"

I nodded and fidgeted to put a little more distance between him and me on the mattress. I was mortified at what occurred between us the night before. It was no wonder he stopped. The fact that I was still aroused by his presence filled me with shame.

"I'm not your uncle," he continued.

My head shot up and I was immediately on the alert. If he was my mother's brother, then why wasn't he my uncle? I may have been confused, but I was also overwhelmed with relief. I hadn't almost committed incest after all.

"I'm not your uncle because Sara isn't your real mother," he explained. "Remember, I told you it is rare for a vampire to have a child and, if it did happen, the child would be vampire. You are not a vampire."

He'd spoken quickly, as if anticipating the reaction that came next.

"What the hell? Are you on crack?" I demanded. "Of course she was my mother. I look just like her. Everyone says so."

"You had her coloring and you were young," he replied.

He shifted his body to face me more squarely and took my face between his hands. I had no choice but to look at him. His eyes were filled with a mixture of concern, sadness, sympathy and something else... passion?

"Please listen to me very carefully. How you grasp and accept what I'm about to tell you will make all the difference on whether we make it back to earth safely... or even at all," he said with quiet

34

firmness.

I could feel his body relax as I my expression changed from one of rebellious disbelief to that of an interested and eager listener. If what he had to say meant I could be home again, then I was all for whatever it was; even if it meant him telling me I was some alien creature.

"I was born in the year twelve-hundred and three. I was the youngest son in a family of six children. My parents weren't wealthy by any means, but we managed to enjoy life and live in comfort. I was ten years old when my parents took all of us on a hunting trip along the Canadian border.

"It was off season, but, even if it wasn't, it was such a wild and baron place I could imagine we'd be hard pressed to stumble into another hunter unless we'd searched for him. We were the only humans for miles around that fateful weekend.

"My parents fashioned a hut out of greenery, branches, and some burlap we'd brought with us. The hut looked out onto an enormous lake. My father took my two eldest brothers, Walter and Samuel, downstream for late night fishing. I have no idea what they were trying to catch. I was too young to know the difference and, quite frankly, it doesn't really matter. What does matter is that because they were a distance from our hut, they were spared the horror of what happened in their absence.

"A small group of vampires stumbled upon us while out hunting for food. They weren't the good kind of vampires. They'd been tainted by evil. We call them black vampires. They killed everyone but Sara and me.

"I loved to swim and explore underwater. I'd trained myself to hold my breath for an incredibly long duration of time so I wouldn't have to surface often. I used this skill to still my body and convince them I'd died. It's how I survived the attack."

"By holding your breath," I said in wonder.

"By holding my breath," he confirmed.

"Wow," I said with admiration, "and mom... err Sara? How did she survive?"

"She didn't actually. She died, but I'll get to that in a minute," he continued. "When my father returned, he took my two brothers and set off to hunt down our murders and kill them. I suspect by the wounds on our necks he knew they were vampires, but I couldn't be sure since our paths have never crossed since then. I assume the vampires killed them.

"I lay amongst my dead family for quite some time wondering why my father wouldn't have cared for our bodies before leaving for his vampire hunt. Of course, now that I'm older, I understand the urgency in catching up with them was too great to take the time, but back then I didn't understand. I decided to bury them myself. When I got to Sara, I could see that she was still alive; although barely. The vampire virus had already taken hold of my body and I instinctively knew what to do to preserve her. I sliced my wrist and forced her to take some of my blood and then I snapped her neck."

"You killed her?" I gasped.

"I guess you'd say that. You see, if you are so near death like Sara was, the only way to prevent it would be to die with the infection in your body and some blood still intact. My killer was sloppy and somehow managed to get cut or something and his blood got into my wound. That was not the case for Sara. She had simply been fed upon. At the rate the blood was seeping from her wounds, she was going to be dead in minutes with no chance of living, even if it was as a vampire. I made the choice to preserve her and I have never regretted it... nor does she.

"We waited a week for my father to return before going to our aunt Alice, my mother's sister, for help. Alice was a kindly soul, much like my mother, and took us in. I don't know exactly how she explained the deaths and disappearance of my family, but she somehow managed. Her home was in an isolated part of the state of Maine -similar to the way your aunt's farm is isolated, but even more so- and she was a bit of a nature child. Her knowledge of herbs and their uses for remedies and spells far surpassed that of the average person. She also had knowledge of the occult, which included vampirism. It was with Aunt Alice's assistance that we learned to deal with the vampire affliction and not let it interfere too heavily with our lives. We kept it a secret, of course, which wasn't all that easy. On more than one occasion someone was able to see the differences in us, but when they discovered who our aunt was, they attributed it to her weird and witchy ways. Being able to go to her for assistance was a true stroke of luck."

"Yes, but it still doesn't explain why you say I'm not who I think I am," I said impatiently.

He looked at me with surprise and said, "I see I've rambled... my apologies."

"No... no, it's not that at all. I mean... I want to know more about you and err... Sara. I do. Your story is fascinating. It's just... I guess I'm just a little impatient to find out...," I stammered.

"Why I say you're not my niece?" he interjected.

"Well, yes." I said.

"I'm getting to that," he said, before filling his lungs with air. "When my sister met the man you knew as your father it was love at first sight for both of them. He tried to fight his feelings for her and she him. She was a vampire after all. As hard as they tried, they could not escape the love they had for each other. When she broke down and confided her secret to him, he decided to take a chance and entrust her with his most precious secret. He was not of earth. He was from the planet Kurr; this very planet that we now hide in a cave on."

"Are you saying I'm part alien?" I wailed.

"No, I'm saying that you're entirely alien. You were born here on Kurr. More than that, you are of royal blood. The man you knew as your father was actually a captain of your true parent's guard. He was sent to earth with you in tow. You were nothing more than a babe in arms. You lived quietly for some time, but eventually your whereabouts was discovered by a band of soldiers sent to search for you. When it was clear he would be unable to protect you, he asked me to take over. Not long after I accepted the responsibility of your welfare, he was killed in a heated battle. He died, but not before he wiped out the band of soldiers and you were once again safe."

"What, I'm like some princess or something?" I practically

screeched. This was way too farfetched to even remotely be taken seriously.

"You are indeed like some princess. You are next in line for the throne of Kurr, which is why your safety is so vital."

"This is ridiculous," I said as I stood up.

I needed to get some air and clear my head. Things were getting far too weird.

He grabbed my wrist.

"I'm not finished. Sit down," he said in a tone that was far more authoritative than he'd displayed since our conversation began.

It was clear I was wearing on his nerves. Well good. His wild stories were wearing on mine, so good... good... good. Maybe he'd think twice before spinning such wild fantasies again.

"Just like time is different on earth than in Kurr, so is the growth process. Yours was stunted by earth's atmosphere. You're twenty-four, but you have the body of a fourteen-year-old." At my burst of outrage and indignation over his comment, he waved his hand and continued, "If you stay on Kurr much longer, your body will catch up with your age. We can't have that happen if we want to return you to earth as if nothing happened. It'd be rather difficult to explain; don't you think?"

"Mark would accept me no matter how I looked," I said boldly.

"What about the rest of society?" he asked.

I shrugged.

"I've been monitoring you from afar since you were a young babe," he said. "It's true, you were a task at first, but after watching you grow and become the lovely creature you are today, you ceased to be a task and became a pleasure. Caring for you brings sheer joy into my life."

"I don't understand how you cared for me. I never saw you.... Never," I said.

"The woman you call Aunt Jenny at one time was Sara's best friend. When Sara was no longer able to care for you, Jenny gladly took over the responsibility of raising you; but always with me in the background watching over. She knows who you are and what you must eventually do. She knows and understands. When we get back to earth, we'll pay her a visit and she can tell you for herself," he said calmly.

Panic welled up inside me. Could Jack's story be true? Was I really an alien princess?

I decided to change the subject.

"Tell me about what happened to you when you became a vampire," I said.

"I took on some of the genetic traits of the vampire that created me. I absorbed DNA from him," he said matter-of-factly.

I looked at him closely. He really did look human. Had I not seen his fangs for myself, I would have never guessed him to be a vampire. It was confusing; especially since he was also coming and going in broad daylight and was warm and supple. Nothing added up to the monsters of lore.

Something deep inside me told me Jack was telling the truth about everything, including me being an alien. It would take some time to absorb.

For some crazy reason, my thoughts traveled from me being an alien to me kissing Jack. Maybe it was because we were in such close proximity of each other. I remembered our kiss. It still had me reeling. How could that be when I loved and was to marry another man?

Actually, Mark never really said he loved me and I'd never said I loved him. It was just understood that we loved each other. When we decided to get married, it was during a conversation about how bonded we were as buddies and it just made sense to tie the knot. After all, if friendship is at the base of a relationship it stands a much better chance of lasting. We'd heard it on a television show. Maybe Dr. Phil, but I couldn't be sure.

Before I knew what was happening, I was wrapped in his strong arms with his lips consuming my own. How did that happen? Had I initiated it or had he? I felt like I was dreaming and would wake up any time now. It was a wild tale that was definitely more suitable for a dream than for real life. In some ways, I much preferred it.

I soon stopped worrying about who initiated what and fell into his kiss with passion that equaled his own. There was something about him that brought out a side of me that was foreign, yet exciting. When we finally found the wherewithal to separate, I sat breathlessly still and waited to wake up. After a few seconds, it was clear that this was really happening.

It was also clear that he was just as affected by our kiss as I was. The silence between us was unsettling. Neither knew what to say.

I finally popped out with, "You're wearing a shirt."

CHAPTER FOUR

Jack left me alone to think while he finished the preparations for our departure. The more I absorbed what he'd told me, the more questions accumulated in my mind. I needed to know more about where we were. L'oana told me something far different and believable about our location. I'd been a student of metaphysics for some time now, so I knew full well that there were dimensions on earth; which was why L'oana's explanation was so easy to accept. I also knew and understood that earth wasn't the only planet with humanoid life on it. Humanoid, not lizard-like! It's just that I didn't expect to be told I was one of those humanoid alien species and I'd teleported back to my planet that was apparently overrun with the lizard-like Dragos.

When he returned, I let loose with a slew of questions. He was surprisingly patient with me and answered them as best he could. He didn't deny the various dimension on earth, just L'oana's story. He explained that L'oana read in my thought pattern my belief about dimensions and created a story around them. He also said she could take on whatever shape or persona she chose, but her favorite was the woman with the odd ears and feet. It amused her. He warned me to be very cautious whenever she was around. She was a trickster and I could only find misery in her company. When I asked him how he came to be so sure of this, he turned away and changed the subject. If my instincts served me correctly, I'd have to say he was talking from experience.

Having exhausted the topic of L'oana, I switched to myself and where I came from. He told me as much as he could. Interestingly, as he shared what he knew, I managed to fill in the gaps with inherent memories. If I'd doubted his claim to my origin before, there was no denying it now.

Aunt Jenny's home was outside a small New York village near the Canadian border. With a population of less than one-thousand and no cable television, it was easy to keep me sheltered from the main world. I'd never really minded it. Aunt Jenny made life an interesting adventure whenever possible; taking us on camping trips, foraging excursions for wild herbs, mushrooms, and edible plants, and hunting with bow and arrow. To say I was a tomboy was an understatement, but I wouldn't have had it any other way. It was what Mark and I had most in common.

A neighbor of ours and the son of my Aunt's closest friend, Mark accompanied us more often than not. Looking at our relationship more closely, we were really more like brother and sister than a couple in love. Perhaps that was why Aunt Jenny had such a mild response to our engagement. She'd either expected it right along or knew in her heart of hearts it wouldn't take. Whatever the reason, my generally animated aunt was surprisingly reserved with her congratulations.

I mentioned her cool response to my engagement to Jack and he told me Jenny had been laboring over how to tell me who I was. She knew that one day I would be expected to return to my native planet and assume the role of leader. She'd done her best to train me in various survival methods while camouflaging them as hunting, camping, and foraging excursions. I'd proven an adept student and she had no doubt in her mind that I'd be able to survive, should the need arise. If she'd reacted with less than expected delight it was probably because she knew there was no room in my future for Mark and she had no idea how to break it to us.

How do you tell someone she's an alien princess who would soon have to go back home? Well, if you're Jack you just blurt it out and hope for the best. I thought with amusement.

I think Aunt Jenny would have found humor in his choice of action.

I'd seen minimal of my surroundings and was eager to find out more about them. This is where Jack fell short. He'd learned a little by my father –who I now knew wasn't my father- and did a bit of exploring while waiting for me to recover and regenerate my health, but he was fairly limited with his information.

He told me Kurr was one-hundred-fifty light years from earth. Its surface was similar to that of earth. In fact, it mirrored earth in many ways; which was why Aunt Jenny took such pains in teaching me as much as she could in the ways of survival. It was also why I didn't realize I wasn't on earth whenever I stepped outside the cave. The terrain looked familiar and the air was clean and crisp like what I was accustomed to in the wilds of Upstate New York. Although the plant life and terrain was very close to that of earth, the animal life had a more distinct variation.

He was just getting into describing a few of the unfamiliar animals that we might encounter when a tall figure filled the doorway. I craned my neck to take in the full height of the man standing with a presence that overpowered the cave. His chin jutted forward with an air that reeked of arrogance, yet there was something about him that I found familiar and likable. He was appealing to look at in his own sort of way. Oh, he certainly couldn't compare with the god-like features Jack possessed, but he could be deemed handsome in his own right. His frame was large, yet he had minimal meat on his bones. Had I been as large as him in stature, I could have possibly been described as the same. His dark eyes were centered on his square face just below brows that grew thick and burley. His mouth fit perfectly below his nose. When he smiled, it was a smile of friendship that encompassed his entire face. I liked him immediately.

"Your highness," he said with a slight bow in my direction, "Sergeant Org at your service."

I was clearly confused as I looked at Jack.

"I don't know how to get us out of here. Org will be our guide," Jack explained.

"How did you get here?" I asked with surprise.

Jack nodded his head in Org's direction.

"He's been in contact with me since I took over watching you," he explained. "When you were abducted, he brought me here to find you. I can't teleport on my own."

"It's true, your grace. I learned of your abduction and immediately fetched Jack. It was a close call," Org added eagerly.

"Yes, it was. In fact, if I'd had any meat on my bones I wouldn't be here right now," I said nervously.

It was the first time I'd spoken that fact out loud and I found it unsettling.

"Your lack of meat had nothing to do with it, your grace. We have allies in all nations that are eager to have you take the throne and bring Kurr back to a state of excellence. It was one of ours that had you tossed off the line," Org assured me.

"You're in co-hoots with lizard men?" I said, stunned.

"We work with who we have to in order to accomplish our mission. Fortunately, we had someone on the inside to get you tossed off that line," Org explained.

"Where I waited to retrieve you," Jack added.

"You never told me this," I hissed at Jack. "It would have been nice to have known the truth."

"There's a time and place for all things. It was not the time," Jack stated with a shrug. He stood and extended his hand to me, "Now it's time to leave."

I stood to join him and stopped in midstream when Org cleared his throat as loud as he could. Had I done something wrong? Was something amiss? People just didn't clear their throat in that manner for no reason.

When he was sure he had Jack's attention he whispered, "She's waiting outside."

"Damn!" Jack spat.

"I'm sorry, I couldn't convince her to stay behind. She promised not to be a bother," Org said apologetically.

"It'll be a cold day in hell when L'oana is anything but a bother," Jack hissed.

"Do people still believe hell is a burning furnace?" L'oana chuckled as she rested her chin on Org's shoulder. "I find that truly amazing. You don't think that, do you princess?"

It was clear by the way she emphasized the word princess that she was resentful of the fact.

THE PRINCESS AND THE VAMPIRE KING

"You're not welcome here," Jack hissed.

"You should have told me who she was, Jack," she said flatly. "Tell me Sergeant, what do you think of Jack as your future king? When he marries the princess that's what he'll be."

Org's eye flew open with surprise and he studied me carefully.

"Is this true, your grace? Are you planning to marry Lord Jack?" he asked.

"Is this how they think here?" I asked.

I was not only desperate to change the subject, but I was really curious about Org's ability to believe such nonsense so easily.

"Yes," Jack said flatly. He grabbed me by the elbow and pushed his way passed Org and L'oana. "No one's marrying anyone. If you're coming with us," he spat as we moved past my false friend, "you will behave. No trickery! Do I make myself clear?"

"Completely," she cooed, "but if you don't plan on marrying her, why all the coddling?"

I'd had little exposure to L'oana and her antics, but I somehow doubted she'd refrain from pulling something now and then on our journey home; however long or short it may be.

"Why is she coming?" I whispered to Jack. "She's evil. What good will having her with us be?"

"Retract your claws," he said to L'oana before turning to me, "She's a trickster, but she also wants to see Kurr returned to its rightful state. She can prove useful if we run into any Dragos or Mannadors."

"Mannadors?" I asked.

"They make the Dragos look like pet lizards," Org growled.

"The Mannadors are from a dying planet. They are the reason you were exiled from here. They killed your parents and replaced the monarchy with their own," L'oana explained. "They were not aware of your existence; which is why Captain Berger was able to get you to safety. I didn't realize he'd taken you to earth and I especially didn't realize I'd been hob knobbing with your guardian all this time."

"I don't hob knob," Jack spat.

"Whatever you want to call it, honey," she drawled.

With his hand still on my elbow, I could feel the vibration of Jack's body as it shuddered with revulsion. He'd obviously done something with L'oana that he seriously regretted and didn't want reminding of. I decided not to ask him. Some things were better left unsaid. Plus, every man deserves some privacy.

"Don't start," Org snapped to L'oana. "Everyone, follow me. I have no desire to get caught on the way to the teleportation launch."

"Is it far?" I asked.

"That depends," L'oana replied.

"On what?" I asked, ignoring her jealous glares.

"On whether we run into anyone or anything along the way," she spat before darting off ahead of us.

"I don't trust her," Jack said softly.

Sergeant Org and I said nothing.

CHAPTER FIVE

It felt fantastic to be out of the cave and using my lean muscles to walk along the hilly path that bordered the forest. Had I not known better, I would have sworn I was in the Adirondack Mountains enjoying a good excursion. The air was cool and crisp, as it should be for a mid-fall day. The sun seemed a little brighter than on earth. I questioned Sergeant Org about this and he explained that the sun emitted rays on Kurr that were slightly brighter because, unlike people on earth, the residents of Kurr refrained from using inventions that polluted the atmosphere. Earth would consider Kurr behind the times in many ways, but they were merely eco conscious beyond man's comprehension.

We walked along a well-worn path through a forest of tall pine trees mixed with oak and maple trees. We hadn't gone more than a half-mile before Jack raised his hand to signal we stop while putting his finger to his lips for silence. I'd been so busy admiring the scenery and filling my lungs with fresh, clean air that I missed his signal and slammed right into him. It felt like I'd slammed into a brick wall. Every muscle on his normally warm and supple body was cold and rigid with tension. Something was amiss. He grabbed me by the waist and pulled me close while Sergeant Org scanned the forest for signs of danger.

Having been raised to be a free spirited and independent person, I would have taken offense by Jack's possessiveness, had I not felt the vast difference in his body language. There were times to tout your bravado and self-sufficiency and times to seek the protection of others. I knew in my heart of heart this was the latter.

I watched as Sergeant Org moved stealthily from tree to tree while he sniffed the air and cocked his ear closer to the ground. It was clear he was also on the alert for trouble.

But what kind?

I'd no sooner formed that question in my mind when the answer was made abundantly clear.

Out of the blue, to the far west of Sergeant Org, sprung an enormous lion. Not only was it incredibly odd to see a lion in this type of terrain, but the lion itself was strange in appearance. It clearly had the body and head of a lion, but its coloring was all wrong. Its mane was a dark purple-grey and its body was a dark dapple grey. It was a beautiful combination, but just all wrong for a lion. Not far behind it was a lioness. She too was a dapple grey, although the tone was far lighter than the lion.

I watched in wonder as they circled Sergeant Org. Their muscles looked coiled for action, as if they'd spring at him in any second. I held my breath while I waited to see what the lions would do, or what the sergeant would do, or what Jack would do.

No one did anything.

It was as if the world stood still. If the lions hadn't boasted a loud roar once in a while to declare their presence and dominance, I'd have thought I was looking at a still photograph.

Then everything changed.

I felt Jack's body begin to do something that resembled a quiver. Sergeant Org glanced our way briefly before running toward the lion full speed. I could see a large knife in his hand, although I haven't a clue when he'd managed to pull it out from concealment. Jack tossed me on my backside and darted over to the lioness. Before my very eyes, and with lightning speed, he fed. Although she lay still where he left her, I somehow knew he hadn't killed her and she'd revive shortly.

The lion wasn't so fortunate. In the most amazing hand to beast battle, Sergeant Org pierced the lion's heart without earning so much of a scratch. I was speechless with awe.

Jack helped the sergeant drag the beast in my direction. I found myself backing away. This surprised me since I'd been trained for hunting with a bow and arrow and was considered quite skilled at it. Perhaps it was the coloring of the lion or the sheer size of it. I'm not sure. All I knew was that I shook uncontrollably at the thought of being within a few feet of it.

I backed up against a large boulder and flattened my body to create as much space between myself and the beast as I could. If Jack and Sergeant Org noticed my discomfort, they made no move to acknowledge it as they dragged the enormous beast past me and deep into the woods. L'oana reappeared with a smirk on her face as she hovered close to me. Could she actually be acting as my body guard in Jack and Sergeant Org's absence?

I was really having difficulty keeping up with what was happening. None of it made sense.

I peered over the boulder in the direction Jack and Sergeant Orb had gone. They were barely visible through the thick foliage. I strained to follow their movements. Could they be doing what it looked like they were doing? Were they burying the lion? Yes, that's exactly what they were doing. They'd dug deep into the thick debris covered forest floor with their bare hands and were now lowering a man into the ground.

A man?

I rubbed my eyes to make sure I was seeing correctly. I strained for a view of the lion, but saw only Jack and Sergeant Org balancing a very large male body as they lowered it into the grave they'd dug.

"You thought that was a real lion didn't you?" L'oana giggled.

I nodded, but said nothing.

She pointed behind me, "Look."

I looked in the direction she'd pointed expecting to see the lioness lying there, or possibly reviving. Instead I saw a naked, grayish looking female lying peacefully on the ground. My gasp brought peals of laughter from L'oana.

"This is going to be some trip," she managed between laughs.

I openly showed my annoyance with a scowl. Once again a wave of sadness swept over me as loneliness set in. I was on an alien planet with a vampire who claimed to be my guardian since childhood, a very large guard who thought me to be his princess, and a wicked shape-shifting tormentor. I longed for the comfort and familiarity of Aunt Jenny and Mark.

"Can you make any more noise?" Jack growled as he stomped back to where we were standing.

"Seriously, L'oana," Sergeant Org sputtered, "You know better than that."

Their chastising was enough to subdue my tormentor. She lowered her eyes and looked away like a child wishing to be any-where than where she was at that time. As she searched for a place to focus, she spotted the woman moving as if to get up.

Happy to take the attention from herself, L'oana directed it toward the woman.

"I thought she was dead!" growled Sergeant Org. "Grab her, quick!"

"I thought she was a beast," Jack mumbled before following Sergeant to stop the woman from escaping.

Before I could comprehend what was happening, Jack and Sergeant Org captured the woman. Her screams bounced off the trees one by one, each time getting a little louder and longer. It was a fascinating thing to hear.

My awe was short lived. With one clean snap of his powerful wrist Sergeant Org broke her neck. I was overcome with horror.

"And they were worried about me being too loud?" L'oana said, completely ignoring the fact that the woman had just been murdered.

Jack returned to me with lightning speed, while Sergeant Org continued on to the grave where he and Jack and had buried the man. Jack held me close, as if to shelter me from the view, but it was too late. The damage was done. I peered as best I could past him and watched with disgust as the Sergeant's bare hands dug the grave open and placed the dead woman next to the dead man. He covered the bodies as quickly as he could and rejoined us, wiping his hands on his tunic as he did.

"Who are you people?" I asked as I slowly pushed myself free from Jack.

"Oh, princess, don't be so dramatic," L'oana spat.

"They were the enemy," Jack explained. "We had to do it, Jessica."

"Her name is Jessica? That's not a royal name," L'oana bellowed.

"Keep your voice down, L'oana, I'm not telling you again," said Sergeant Org through clenched teeth.

"Someone with the name L'oana is criticizing Jessica?" I chuckled sarcastically. "Now that's funny."

"Jessica isn't your real name, stupid," L'oana spat. She turned to Jack, "Tell me her real name."

"Let's get moving," he said without looking at her.

"Tell me or I'll go on ahead and announce your arrival!" she threatened.

"I was never told her real name for security purposes," Jack explained resentfully.

"Then you," she looked at Sergeant Org, "You must know."

"We're moving on now and I'll hear no more nonsense about warning anyone of our whereabouts," the sergeant said firmly. "If you even think it, I'll know and I guarantee it'll be the last thing you think."

"I'm not afraid of you, Org," she spat.

"Then maybe you'll be afraid of me," Jack said quietly.

"Remember the week we shared last year?" L'oana cooed.

She may have cooed seductively with her voice, but her body clearly showed signs of unease. She was afraid of Jack.

"You spent a week with her?" I gasped, doing my best to control the unexpected and very surprising surge of jealousy that rose up in me upon hearing that bit of news. "How could you guard me while occupied with ... that?"

"He has a life, dearie," she stressed with a chuckle.

"It's no wonder I was abducted. I have a guard who'd rather run with slutty galactic freaks than do his job," I blurted before I'd realized what I'd said.

I don't know who I shocked more with that comment that reeked of jealousy, them or me. It was Sergeant Org who broke the silence by clearing his throat and suggesting we continue moving. Apparently we had a two-day trip on foot. I thought about asking why we weren't traveling in a vehicle or on horse-back, but before I could form the words on my lips we had yet another signal to be still and quiet from Jack, whose hearing was far more acute than mine or Sergeant Org's. Whether his hearing was superior to that of L'oana I couldn't say, since she was an inherent trickster and may have easily been aware of the threat and chosen not to divulge it.

CHAPTER SIX

We may have been out in the wilderness, but it seemed as if the entire world obeyed Jack's command to stand still and be quiet. From what I could tell, not one bird, not one rabbit, or rodent, or even an insect made a move or a sound. We all waited with anticipation for whatever it was he was warning us about to show itself.

Jack, on the other hand, had no intention of waiting to see what was rapidly making its way through the trees in our direction. He scooped me up into his arms like I was nothing more than a bag of laundry and leapt into the air. I sucked in my gasp of shock as we rocketed into the tree tops. I could feel his flesh wrap around my nails as I clung to him for dear life while he perched on the top branch of an enormous sycamore tree.

I buried my face into his chest and closed my eyes as tight as they'd allow. I'd always had a fear of heights. I couldn't remember ever being on anything that brought me higher than a six-foot step ladder without getting dizzy and nauseous. I peeked with one eye and regretted it instantly.

Below me were about a dozen of those horrific lizard people. This was the first I'd seen them with a clear head. They were incredibly tall. I'd have to say that if one was six foot tall he would have been considered short. I remembered them being ugly, but not this ugly. The drugs and time must have dimmed the impact of their appearance. Below me moved bodies that looked like lizards walking upright with heads shaped in a way to make one wonder if the lizards might have stumbled upon a way to mate with primates. Thick gray-green scales reflected the sunlight in the most eerie manner. My body trembled involuntarily as fear consumed me. Now, not only was I dealing with my fear of heights, but I had to contend with the paralyzing realization that the monsters I'd almost been a meal to meandered the grounds beneath me without a care in the world.

A brief question of Sergeant Org and L'oana's whereabouts flashed through my mind before I caught a whiff of the ever familiar Dragos stench as it billowed through the trees and filled the air. Even Jack's body jolted as the overwhelming foulness reached us. It was all too much for me. Slapping my hand over my mouth, I did my best to subdue the urge to vomit.

I was unsuccessful.

Jack stiffened with what I'm sure was revulsion as my body jerked and jolted while silently purging the contents of my stomach. I kept my hands steadfast over my mouth as the thick mass oozed between my fingers. The scent of bile blended with the morning's ration of stew mixed with the stench of the Dragos. I was completely grossed out and could only imagine the state Jack was in. To his credit, other than the stiffening of every muscle he possessed, he showed no reaction as we waited for the Dragos to continue on their way.

It seemed like eternity before my lizard-like abductors were finally far enough away for Jack to feel comfortable taking us back to ground. By then I was almost feverish from the ordeal. Both Jack and I were covered in vomit, although I'll admit I took the brunt of it. If his sense of smell was as acute as his hearing abilities, I could only imagine what he was going through at that moment.

Of course L'oana was the first to vocalize the disgusting sight we made and how abhorrent my actions were. She found my inability to control my bodily functions completely unacceptable and irresponsible on my part. She moaned and groaned about being unable to take a breath as the air was thick and tainted with Dragos stench and my vomit.

Jack silently slipped off his tunic and wiped the vomit off as best he could on the grass. I had no intention of baring my body to the world to clean up and, quite frankly, the mess on me was beyond wiping off on the grass.

"There's a creek not far from here," Sergeant Org volunteered sympathetically while scowling at L'oana.

"Let's go," Jack muttered before grabbing my hand and pulling me along while he followed Sergeant Org's lead.

Our detour to the creek took us off the intended path by at least two miles. I felt badly about it. I knew I was holding us up. Earlier, Sergeant Org praised me for my hiking ability and mentioned we were making good time because of it. He estimated we'd reach our destination by nightfall with a sigh of relief. Now, because of the delay, that might not happen.

I vowed silently to step up my game to make up for time. Clearly my three companions were holding back their speed of travel for my benefit. I was healthy, fit, and used to trekking through the woods. I'd show them I could keep up with the best of them.

L'oana grumbled her annoyance with the course of events so often I wanted to tape her mouth shut. Although Jack and Sergeant Org remained consistent with their orders for her to keep quiet, she paid them little mind and tortured me with her whining all the way to the creek. When we finally reached the much anticipated water source I rushed ahead of them. I could hardly stand myself and was eager to get clean. They were considerate enough to turn their backs while I removed my disgusting apparel and walked out into the creek. Since I'd been washing myself with a bowl and pitcher set up since I'd awoken in the cave, washing in the creek was not only frigidly invigorating, but a foreign action. It took me some time to develop a technique that allowed me to clean my body the way it needed to be cleaned in the shin deep water, but I eventually managed.

Feeling fresh and refreshed, I stumbled over the sharp stones that littered the creek bed to its silken grassy edge. As I pulled my tunic from the ground I frowned. The vomit had been wiped away in the same manner that Jack had removed it from his own tunic. Unfortunately, not only was there a far greater amount to remove, but it had been sitting on my tunic for a considerable length of time and some of it clung as a dried and crusted film. I shuddered as I pulled the tunic over my head. The leather leggings had come clean, so that at least was a relief.

When I was satisfied that I was properly covered, I told them they could turn around. It's debatable whose face looked more distressed when Jack and Sergeant Org saw the state of my tunic.

"You said you'd cleaned her clothes," Sergeant Org growled at L'oana.

"Why was I expected to deal with that disgusting mess?" she whined.

"You're a woman," Jack said matter-of-factly.

"What does that mean?" I demanded.

Nothing got my burs up more than a sexist person.

"We were trying to respect your feminine modesty, your highness," Sergeant Org explained. "L'oana is the closest thing to feminine we have to assist you."

"What does that mean?" L'oana screeched.

"Get over it," Sergeant Org snapped as he pulled his own tunic from his torso. "I know it's fresh from my body, but I have nothing else to offer you to wear while I properly remove the soil from your tunic. Please accept this as a temporary solution."

I was speechless as I literally accepted the shirt off his back. With gallant courtesy, Jack and the bare chested Sergeant turned their backs to me while I slipped back out of my soiled tunic and pulled his enormous one over my head. There was a familiar scent in the tunic that I couldn't place. It soothed my senses. I'd smelled it before in my life, but I couldn't say when. It gave me a sense of security.

I giggled when I realized it came down almost to my ankles, "It's a little big."

"Ha, ha!" L'oana roared, "You look like a little kid. Of course your lack of boobs doesn't help."

"L'oana!" Jack barked. "You're being warned for the last time. One more word and I'll drain every ounce of blood from your evil body."

"You love my blood, don't you Jack," she cooed as she pulled her hair to expose her neck and lowered her tunic to bare her shoulder. "It's orgasmic, is it not?"

Jack threw his hands in the air with disgust before grabbing my tunic and stomping over to the creek. Sergeant Org protested that he'd planned on cleaning my tunic but Jack just waived him back. Cupping the clear, free flowing water in his hand he splashed and rubbed at the crust of vomit until there was no sign of it. He spun it in the air so rapidly it was almost invisible to the eye. When he finished, he returned it to me. It was only barely damp and incredibly clean.

I accepted the tunic gratefully and rushed to replace the one I wore with my own. As I tied the belt I noticed that although my breasts were still small, they'd grown. They were actually defined against the tunic instead of barely noticeable. I slid my hand over one and cupped it. Yes, it was definitely larger. I thought of Jack's comment about my body catching up with my age the longer I stayed on KURR. It was clear he was speaking truth.

Jack caught me cupping my breast and slowly shook his head. He grabbed Sergeant Org's tunic from me and handed it to him, "We'd better hurry. She's starting to blossom."

Sergeant Org looked at me thoughtfully while donning his tunic, "Once it starts it's quick, you know."

"Let's go," Jack said firmly.

"Right," Sergeant Org replied as he spun on his heel to lead us out.

CHAPTER SEVEN

To all of our relief L'oana grew tired of the pace we were forced to keep –partly because I wasn't a superhuman and partly because the men were stopping often to listen and observe- and went on ahead. We walked in relative silence. I, for one, reveled in the break from her taunting, whining, and bitching. I still hadn't figured out why she was even with us, but then there was a lot about what was going on that confused me.

I used my time of silence to contemplate and absorb all that had been told to me. Both Jack and Sergeant Org were adamant that I was the heir to the throne of Kurr. I wasn't sure what that entailed, but it sounded pretty important. In fact, it had to be somewhat important since my parents were killed and I was hidden in exile because of it.

I'd been brought up to be comfortable hiking and hunting, but my body wasn't prepared for the rigorous trek we were making. The terrain was far more aggressive than anything I'd encountered. It demanded complete attention to navigate around the ruts and rocks and tree roots that covered the ground in all directions. My thighs were burning from exhaustion and I was sweating from the exertion. I looked at Jack and Sergeant Org with dismay. Neither showed the least sign of being tired.

Jack must have sensed my predicament because he tapped Sergeant Org on the shoulder and nodded his head in my direction. Sergeant Org gave a quick nod of agreement and signaled us to follow him off the path and into the thick of the woods.

At one point, the trees were so close together that, had any of us been grossly obese, we'd be hard pressed to pass through them. As it was, both Sergeant Orb and Jack's muscular torso's filled the gaps between the trees that we passed through quite thoroughly. I looked above in wonder at the way the branches were intertwined with each other. It was like they were forming their own type of net. Although what the net was intended to catch was beyond me.

I was just about to collapse from exhaustion when we reached a small clearing next to a large pool of water. I assumed it was the native's watering hole by the array of animals we found drinking their fill. A few deer spotted us and darted off into the thick of the foliage, as did some rabbits, while a small flock of ducks made it a point to announce the arrival of intruders.

Jack was a little more reserved about leaving the protection of the trees. I followed Sergeant Org to the water's edge while Jack lingered back on the edge of the forest, clearly on watch. I smiled when I discovered a large flat rock to sit on. I quickly removed my moccasins and dangled my feet in the clear blue liquid. The soothing coolness of the water traveled therapeutically up my legs, relaxing me almost instantly. This was the first I'd been alone with Sergeant Org. It felt a little odd, but it also gave me an opportunity to ask a few questions that were weighing heavily on me.

"Did you know my parents?" I asked hesitantly.

"If you mean the King and Queen, I served them and was in their company on multiple occasions, but I was not close to them. If you mean the man who swept you off to safety, Captain Berger.... I knew him well," he replied.

"It's difficult to imagine myself a princess, let alone heir to a throne. It seems surreal," I said wistfully. "In fact, this entire ordeal seems surreal."

"Believe me, it is very real," he assured me. He glanced in Jack's direction before asking, "What do you know about the Mannadors?"

"I'd never heard of them until L'oana mentioned them," I replied.

"We killed two of them on the road," he said bluntly.

"The lions," I gasped.

"Mannadors are shape shifters. When injured or dead they return to their natural humanoid state. It's because of their ability to disguise themselves that they are so dangerous. When you encounter a Dragos, there is no guessing what they are. Not so with a Mannador. Any of these creatures could be a Mannador in disguise... any of them," he said with disgust.

"How did you know that's what the lions were?" I asked gently.

"There are two ways. If you're lucky like I was, you will be downwind of them and pick up their scent. Because the Mannador takes on so many disguises, it has a unique scent. I've grown accustomed to it and can generally spot it with one whiff. Secondly, if you look closely into their eyes, you will see a hint of red and green speckles floating around. This is a pure Mannador trait that you won't find in any other creature on the planet. There are a few exceptions to the rule, of course, but for the most part you can spot ninety-nine percent of them that way," he explained.

"Jack thought the woman was a lion," I mused.

"Jack is new to the planet. He's only been here once before for a brief visit just after he took over guarding you. He understands the need to kill them, but hesitates because it's not his nature to kill," he explained.

"Which is why you did it?" I asked.

"Yes," he replied.

I looked over at Jack thoughtfully. He looked so handsome leaning against a thick sycamore tree while scanning the area. I allowed the revulsion that started to form over his participation in the killing of the man and woman Mannadors to subside as I realized just how difficult this must all be for him. He'd traveled to an alien planet and put himself at risk in order to save me. I had no right being repulsed by anything he did or was. If it wasn't for Jack and the sergeant, I'd be a part of that pile of bones Jack picked me out of. I chastised myself for my naivety and ordered myself to shape up and grow up. It was time I looked at things with a different perspective.

I caught Sergeant Org assessing me and blushed. Although I was sure he wasn't attracted to me and was merely taking note of the subtle changes my body was experiencing, it still made me self-conscious. I looked away and caught Jack's eye from a distance. Was he assessing my body's maturing progress as well? Interestingly, instead of being embarrassed, like I'd been when I caught Sergeant

Org looking, I was mildly aroused.

I quickly looked away and forced Mark's image into my head. I needed to put space between myself and that vampire. Whether he was truly my guard or not didn't matter. It was clear to me that he was trouble. He brought forth emotions, reactions, and feelings I could barely harness. If I wasn't careful, I'd be making a fool of myself again.

"Jack worries about you," Sergeant Org volunteered.

"So he says," I replied softly, while steeling a glance at him.

"I think he has stronger feelings for you than he lets on. He can't fool me. This guarding thing is more to him than just honoring a promise," the sergeant chuckled.

"What do you mean?" I asked innocently as I pulled my feet from the water and stood up.

"You need to open your eyes princess. It is as plain as the nose on your face," he huffed before walking to the water's edge and filling his water flask with the clean, clear liquid. I was still tongue tied by his statement when he added, "If we don't get you teleported back to earth soon, there'll be no explaining those curves you're developing."

"She's promising to be quite the voluptuous dish," Jack added as he walked up behind me and circled his arm around my waist.

I leaned back into him absent mindedly, while fighting the tingling that was spreading through my body. It took several moments for me to realize what we were doing and pull away. Jack chuckled softly and Sergeant Org snorted as if to say, "point proven".

"I question if she should return. It might be too late," the sergeant said to Jack.

"Of course I'm going to return!" I blurted forcefully. "I want to go home. I don't want to stay here. I want to go home."

Surprised by my sudden emotional outbreak, they stood in silence for a moment before Jack nodded.

"So you will," he assured me.

I couldn't believe what happened next. Just as brazenly as you please Jack ran his hands lightly over my breasts and hips. I was speechless.

"We're going to have to hurry," he barked to Sergeant Org and then started walking as if he'd done absolutely nothing out of the ordinary.

"Unbelievable!" I growled as I stomped behind him.

I was sure I heard a chuckle coming from Sergeant Org, but I refused to turn around to see for sure. Instead, my eyes bore into Jack's back as I followed him back to the path we'd been traveling.

It felt like we'd been traveling for days and days. The realization that we'd only left the cave a few hours earlier was hard to believe. I was exhausted, both physically and emotionally. I looked up at the sun's position. It hadn't moved much. How many hours had we been traveling anyway?

"Five," Jack said over his shoulder.

I grumbled to myself, knowing full well he could hear me, "Is there no privacy for me? Groping my body, reading my mind.... It's all so invading. I can't wait to get home. I can't wait to be in Mark's arms again."

If I analyzed my grumbling more closely, I'd have to admit that it wasn't Mark's arms I was eager to get home to. The arms that pulled at me like an undeniable magnetic force were walking ten feet ahead of me and I was doing my best to convince myself otherwise. It both embarrassed and concerned me that I was so attracted to a vampire that claimed to have been my guardian for the majority of my life. Was it hero worship and not pheromones in action? I sincerely hoped so. Hero worship would eventually fade away as I discovered more and more flaws to focus on. The pull of pheromones was far more difficult to ignore.

A soft breeze brought Jack's erotic scent my way. It caressed my senses like sinewy fingers, arousing me in ways I'd read about in books, but never thought were real. My stomach tightened and twisted like a wet rag being wrung to dry. My knees buckled beneath me and I stumbled to catch my balance.

"Are you alright princess," Sergeant Org called from a few feet behind me.

My throat was so tight all I could do was nod. Through it all, Jack never made a sign of acknowledgement of my predicament.

Although, since he'd consistently known what I'd been thinking up to that point, it was hard to believe he was unaware. I found this fact annoying.

What an arrogant ass, my mind projected with as much force as I could muster.

I smiled as I watched Jack's shoulder blades tighten.

We'd barely returned to the path when L'oana reappeared. My disappointment in her arrival was only heightened when she announced that we were approaching an encampment of Mannador soldiers. L'oana said they were searching for two members of their party that were due back earlier that day; a man and a woman.

My body was consumed with renewed fear mixed with frustration. From what I'd learned about the Mannador so far, they were a force to be reckoned with. Since they were able to shape shift, climbing the trees like we did when the Dragos were near would be useless. Since they shifted in a variety of life forms in order to cover the area thoroughly. Birds would seem a natural form.

She warned us that staying where we were would put us right in line to meet them within the next fifteen minutes. If we were forced to make a run for it, I was far too exhausted to get very far. My heart sank and my eyes filled with tears. It seemed the Mannadors would wipe out my family after all. I looked around at the beauty around me and filled my lungs with clean, refreshing air. I regretted not knowing more about this planet of my birth, but vowed to at least enjoy the beauty it was presenting me for the brief time before my death. I wondered if the spiritual dimensions that one went to after death on earth were the same dimensions for those who died on Kurr. Would I meet my parents there?

"It's not your time to die, my sweet," Jack whispered as he scooped me into his arms.

The stress of the potential encounter of the Mannadors, combined with sheer exhaustion and the nearness of Jack, was more than I could handle. My body literally collapsed against him as we moved with lightning speed through the forest in a direction that would lead us far away from the soldier's encampment.

When we finally stopped, we were in mountainous terrain

miles away from the path we'd been following. Jack set me down slowly. I fell to my knees and emptied my stomach. He rubbed my back sympathetically, while holding my long dark hair out of harm's way.

"It's natural for the humanoid body to react like that when you've traveled at vampire speed," he explained in a soft and gentle manner that was almost a coo. "I wouldn't have put you through it if I didn't think it necessary. I'm so sorry."

I wanted to tell him that even after traveling just a hair's breadth below the speed of light, my hormones were still out of control and I just didn't need him adding to my discomfort by speaking to me in such a sultry manner. I wanted to tell him that he caused emotions and feelings in me that I couldn't explain and made me uncomfortable. I wanted to tell him that I didn't trust that I wouldn't throw myself at him like I had in the cave and make yet a bigger fool of myself. I wanted to tell him that I was terrified of being caught by the Mannador and my only comfort was in knowing he was at my side. I wanted to tell him that I didn't care if he ever returned me to Mark, because I didn't know if I could go on living without him at my side. His method of guarding me from a distance was no longer acceptable. I wanted to say these things, but all I managed was "don't" before my body succumbed to more purging.

CHAPTER EIGHT

Jack held vigil at my side until I'd finally regained control of my faculties and was able to stand. He held me close while I tested my legs for stability. I rested my cheek against his chest and closed my eyes while I listened to the steady beat of his heart. It beat at twice the rate of a human heart. I estimated two-hundred beats per minute. I slipped my hand through the front of his tunic and caressed his flesh. It was warm and supple. Pulling his tunic further from his flesh, I nuzzled my face like a kitten seeking comfort.

"Where are the others?" I murmured.

My lips tickled as they grazed his flesh.

"They will take some time catching up with us. They both have about the same ability for speed, so I'm guessing they'll reach us within an hour. We can take that time for you to rest a bit. I feel your exhaustion," he said softly.

"Is that all you feel?" I couldn't stop myself from asking.

A low groan escaped him as he pulled my mouth to his. Our kiss was deep and tender. It was nothing like the frantic passionate one we'd shared in the cave, but it was equally -if not more- arousing. I wrapped my arms around his neck and clung to him as if my life depended on it. I wanted his strength, his protection, his passion.... him. I wanted him more than I'd ever wanted anything in my life. Suddenly it didn't matter if I was making a fool of myself, I had to have him and I told him so between kisses.

This time he didn't push me away, but responded between kisses as well. He asked me if I knew what would happen if he took my virginity while on Kurr. I didn't, so he enlightened me on the subject. Apparently, if he took my virginity while on Kurr it would finish the "body catch up with the age" phase and I'd become fully developed. He questioned if I was ready for and up

65

to the consequences of our actions. It would be clear to Sergeant Org and L'oana that we'd made love and also I'd have to explain my changed body when we returned to earth. He swore he wanted me so badly it hurt, but he'd refrain from taking me if I asked him to because there was nothing he wanted less than to bring me pain or distress.

My hands managed to disrobe him while he was presenting his explanation as to why we shouldn't make love. I was half-way through removing my own clothes when he gave in and finished the job for me with an urgency that surprised me.

Although I could feel his need, he was surprisingly gentle as he prepared me for the loss of my virginity. My body burned from his kisses. My breasts ached and throbbed from his attention. When he moved to my most tender private area, I thought I was going to go mad. Instead of feeling pain when he finally showed mercy and drove his manhood deep inside me, I felt orgasmic relief. It was a moment and experience I'd cherish forever.

We were suspended in time as he filled me with his power, his essence, and his love. Although we'd made love on the cool, hard ground, I felt as if I was floating on air as I watched him dress and then reach for my clothes. Extending his hand, he helped me up and then frowned. I was already swelling and filling out. The tunic was large enough to adjust to my new curves, but the pants were a lost cause. I gasped in dismay. Not fitting into my clothes was a dilemma that never crossed my mind.

I started crying.

"Damn, I didn't want your first time to be like this. What's wrong with me?" he hissed as he paced back and forth. "It should have been a time of beauty and joy with the man you love, not with me."

"But it was... and I do..." I sputtered before realizing what I was saying.

Could I really be telling him that I loved him? I knew from conversations with friends that a girl often fantasizes herself in love with the man who takes her virginity, even if she wasn't. It's just the romance of the moment taking over. I bit my tongue to prevent me from making such a childish statement as 'I love you' to him.

I'd said just enough and thought just enough to stop Jack in his tracks. His face was a billboard of emotions that shifted from one to the other and then back again. I wished fervently for the ability to know his thoughts like he knew mine.

As I wiped away the tears and did my best to compose myself, he moved to my side and wrapped his arm around my shoulder.

"I knew you'd blossom, but I didn't realize it would be this fast or to such an extent." He nuzzled my temple, "You're beautiful... Please don't cry," he said quietly, "We'll figure out how to get you a new pair of pants. In the meantime, the tunic can act as a shift. You fill it out, but there's still room in it and its long. It'll be okay."

"I don't think I can walk through the wild with bare legs," I said meekly.

He looked surprised by my comment and then shook his head, "Of course."

He looked off into the distance until he spotted what he was looking for.

"Would you like to clean up?" he asked hesitantly.

Although I didn't want to lose the sensation of him by washing it away, common sense told me it was in my best interest to do so. I nodded slowly.

"Climb on my back?" he asked more than ordered.

I did so hesitantly.

He climbed the nearest tree until we were at its very peak. After that, he basically leapt from tree to tree until we were once again at the watering spot we'd rested at only an hour or so earlier. As he set us down he asked me to see to my toiletries as quickly as possible since he'd spotted L'oana and Sergeant Org half-way up the mountain. He estimated they'd arrive at the spot where we'd just made love in ten minutes or so.

I hesitated only briefly before removing my tunic and wading into the water. To my surprise, his naked body was right next to me. He assisted me in cleaning the dirt from my back and then tended to his own body. We worked diligently and quietly and within minutes I was climbing on his back and we were once again leaping across tree tops.

Sergeant Org was holding my pants when Jack set us down on a nearby boulder. He wore a distinct frown on his face, but said nothing. L'oana, on the other hand, was vocally clear with her opinion.

"What the hell did you do, you fool? No... don't answer that. One look at little Miss Princess and I can clearly see what you did. Are you out of your mind? Have you no sense at all?" she hissed as she stomped back and forth. "I have half a mind to abandon you right here and let you fend for yourselves. You obviously don't give a fig about anyone or anything."

Wow. I knew they'd be a little uncomfortable when faced with the knowledge of our making love, but I didn't expect a reaction like this. She actually made me feel ashamed. I shuddered and fought the emotion. What Jack and I did was beautiful and I wasn't going to let anyone take that away from me.

"What business is it of yours what I do?" I snapped defensively.

"Jessica... stop," Jack said firmly.

"I'll do no such thing. I won't have this... this... thing carrying on over something that has absolutely nothing to do with her!" I roared.

"Newsflash, you're not on earth anymore. You're on Kurr; the planet where your parents were killed so that monsters could steal their throne. The planet that you were whisked away from in order to save your life. Have you looked at yourself lately? You're the image of your mother and now, with that body, you fit the image of a twenty-four-year-old princess. The only thing we had going for us if they happened to catch us was that scrawny boobless body. Now it's gone," L'oana spat angrily.

"How do you know I look like my mother? How would anyone know I wasn't just a woman?" I asked defiantly.

"They had their labs do some sort of progressive graphics by taking your baby pictures and your parent's pictures. Whatever they did and however they did it, I have no clue. All I know is that you're the image of the photo they have posted of you. Or should I say the photo they have of the offspring that they discovered somehow got away, but had no idea where you went to. Thank your lucky stars that earth is a remote planet and the galaxy is so large. They're looking for you on other planets. They just haven't made it to earth yet," Sergeant Org explained.

"You could have sexed your heart out with the earthling lover of yours with no consequences," L'oana said to me as she scowled at Jack. "Damn it Jack, what were you thinking?"

"I wasn't," he mumbled as he turned his back on us and walked away.

I couldn't believe my ears. Had he really just said that? If he'd punched me in the stomach, I think it would have hurt less. I was devastated. The realization that Jack regretted what we'd done suddenly turned what had been a beautiful act of love making into something ugly and dirty. My heart felt like it'd been shattered into a million pieces. I felt an emotion for him that was new. I felt hate.

My eyes bore into Jack's back. I truly hoped he was getting the message that I hated him. I wanted him to know it... to feel it. How could I have been so stupid? How could I have let my hormones take over like they did?

Sergeant Org was the first to take control of the situation and bring us around to coming up with a solution to the matter at hand. Jack refrained from joining in and allowed the sergeant, L'oana, and me to create a plan. The more Jack failed to participate with us as we discussed what to do about my new body and the change in circumstance, the heavier my heart.

Jack finally broke into the conversation to announce that he was certain the hawk that flew overhead wasn't a hawk at all, but a Mannador. L'oana agreed. This changed things completely. They reluctantly agreed that we had no choice but to travel through the subterranean.

I wasn't sure why they'd be so reluctant to go below ground. After all, we traveled in subways and tunnels on earth all the time. I assumed they had the same set up.

I was wrong.

CHAPTER NINE

I was forced to climb onto Jack's back again so that we could all travel at a decent pace. Jack was actually going much slower than we'd traveled before in order to allow for our companions, but it was at a speed much faster than it would have been had I gone on foot. We traveled on ground instead of the tree tops until we reached the opening of a small cave that truly didn't look like much. This unimpressive little opening in the hillside turned out to be a portal to the world beneath our feet.

I learned from Sergeant Org that this was L'oana's world. It was a world full of illusions, tricksters, and evil doers. This explained their reluctance to entering it. He warned me to be cautious about speaking to anyone other than the three of them and told me of the many species of life that lived in the world below the surface world, including some of my own who'd managed to escape the chaos when the Mannador arrived. Some of the subterranean residents were able to travel back and forth between worlds like L'oana did, while others were strictly for that world.

It was at this time that L'oana divulged the reason she insisted on being a part of the party to return me to earth. The Mannador were her arch enemy too. Apparently L'oana's people were the only other species both above and below ground that were able to shape shift. The Mannador considered this fact, along with their inherent ability to trick and confuse, a major threat. They were working on either enslaving each and every one of her kind or eliminating them altogether. The only thing that saved them from either so far was the fact that the Mannador were terrified of going underground.

L'oana worked for a coalition sworn to return balance to the planet. She'd vowed to do what she could to remove the Mannador from power and save her people's shrinking population. She may not care for me, but she knew enough to recognize a solution to their troubles when it was right in front of her.

Sergeant Org was with this same coalition. He operated above ground and L'oana acted as an intermediary between the two worlds; keeping them each informed on the other's progress. The sergeant had only ventured into the subterranean world a few times for coalition convocations. A guide met him at the portal and took him directly to the location and returned him above ground almost immediately afterwards. He knew very little of the terrain and dangers that we'd face. We were completely reliant on L'oana.

No one was less happy about this than she. L'oana was a loner and a free spirit. She made it clear that she found the burden of keeping everyone safe miserably oppressive. She took great pains to dictate to us the do's and don'ts of her world. She especially singled me out; making sure I understood that she resented the job of being my babysitter and I was to use my head and pay attention.

The world below ground looked remarkably similar to the one above ground, with a few variances. First of all, there was no sky, no sun, no moon, and no stars. The plant life received their nutrients and growth encouragement from within the soil. It contained florescent properties. These properties caused many of the plants to glow. Water that contained this mineral also glowed. This gave the sub-world a subtle light source. It had a continual twilight or pre-dawn illumination.

Trees stretched as far as the eye could see. I wanted so badly to ask Jack to take me to their tops so I could see if they were touching the earth above or if there was still more to be seen, but I refused to ask anything of him. If I never had to speak to him again, it would be too soon.

L'oana led us to a path that looked remarkably similar to the one we'd been traveling on above ground, explaining that much of the subterranean world mirrored the world above. The truth of this statement couldn't have been clearer when I was reminded that my legs were bare while trying to follow her through the thick brush. I stifled a cry of pain and did my best to pull the brush out of my way with my hands, since they were far tougher.

Jack whispered something to Sergeant Org, who nodded and moved up next to L'oana. After a brief conversation, she scowled at me and nodded. Other than that minor interaction between my companions, we all moved silent and steadfast while L'oana led us to a small village.

The village was amazing to look at. It was like we'd stepped back in time. It was easy to distinguish the more affluent section of the village. Its roads were made of cobblestone and lined with small whitewashed stone houses with slated roofs, while the less prosperous section had dirt and gravel roads lined with brick huts and thatched roofs. The residents were going about their daily routine with no interest whatsoever in our arrival. Their attire added to the nostalgic ambience. The women wore tunics similar to the one I had on and long skirts or leather leggings like the ones I'd outgrown. The men were dressed in tunics and leather pants. Jack and Drake fit right in. Since the subterranean world mimicked the surface, I wondered if there was a village like this above ground. Was that where Jack got my clothes?

We stopped at a brick hut with a sign over its door that read, "A Song of the Shirt". I followed them through the small door into a dimly lit room lined with tunics, skirts, and leather pants.

L'oana guided me, none-too-gently, by the elbow, grabbed a pair of leggings, and shoved me behind a screen in the corner of the room.

"Put these on," she barked and then left me to do my business.

I was both annoyed at her behavior and relieved by her choice of leggings. The leather was soft and supple. It molded to me like a second skin, yet moved with ease when I moved. To add to my delight, there was still room for expansion, should my body decide to fill out a little more. I wondered what type of animal forfeited its life for this wonderfully made apparel.

When I stepped out from behind the screen, I earned a nod of approval from L'oana. I couldn't resist peeking in Jack's direction. Did he approve as well? My annoyance heightened when I realized he was deep in conversation with Sergeant Org and the shop keeper. He wasn't even looking.

So, he's had his way with me and now he's tossing me aside. He may be a vampire, but he's a typical male pig, I thought.

I must have been sending my thoughts across the room loud and clear because Jack immediate looked at me and scowled. I didn't care. For the first time I was happy he could tell my thoughts. I wanted him to know how much I hated him. He deserved it.

L'oana briefly joined the men in conversation before they shook hands with the shop keeper and headed out the door. Not one of them turned to look in my direction. I might as well have been invisible to them. I grunted my displeasure and stomped out behind them while wishing with all my heart to be back home in familiar surroundings with people who I knew genuinely loved and cared for me.

In the steady and vague illumination of the underworld, I couldn't tell if it was day or night above ground. My body was acting as if I'd put in a full day's journey, so I assumed I had. I longed to stop. I needed rest. I needed a good night's sleep. From the way my companions were forging forward, I doubted I'd get either. Jack picked up on my exhaustion. He slowed the other two down and walked back to talk to me.

"Can you go a little further?" he asked gently.

"I don't need you to worry about me. Stay away from me," I hissed.

"I know you're upset. You don't understand," he started.

"I understand perfectly," I spat before he could say more.

"If only you did," he sighed as he turned back to speak with Sergeant Org, who in turn spoke to L'oana.

"The shopkeeper told of an inn a few miles up ahead. We can bunk there for the night. Can you make it?" the sergeant asked the group, although I knew the question was for me.

L'oana chortled and Jack stifled a grin, but neither said anything to him about the obvious statement. Instead they nodded and kept moving.

I sighed with resignation and willed my legs to keep moving.

The question of what constituted a few miles occupied my head. My legs were like rubber and threatened to stop cooperating. I stumbled twice before Jack swept me up into his arms, completely oblivious to my outburst of indignation and scarlet face.

"You two lovers keep it down now, will you?" L'oana snapped sarcastically as she picked up the pace.

I had to admit that we were able to cover far more ground with me in Jack's arms. It probably felt good to them to be able to pick up speed. It must have been tortuously frustrating for them to travel at a pace slow enough for me to match. At least, I'm sure it was for L'oana. It was at that point that it dawned on me just how much they were going out of their way to accommodate me; even L'oana. I felt a little foolish about my childish outburst.

It was hard to stay angry with Jack while nestled in his arms. My body was reacting shamelessly to his touch and scent. I had to keep reminding myself that he'd used me to appease his lust and there was nothing more than carnal pleasure for me with him. From the way he was behaving, I questioned how much pleasure I'd actually given him. Sure, he made all the right sounds and said all the right things. I may have been a virgin, but I wasn't raised in a convent. Mark and I fooled around a lot and I also was an avid movie goer and reader. It was impossible not to know some things about love making, even if I hadn't actually ever completed the act.

Did men fake it like women? I doubted that possible. It was more the fact that he'd had his sexual release and was ready to move on to the next victim.

I looked over his shoulder at L'oana and wondered once again what had transpired between the two. From her words and behavior, I was tempted to believe they'd been lovers, but it was difficult to tell. Jack certainly disliked her. I allowed my mind to ponder on his reasons for these feelings. It helped to settle and relax my body.

CHAPTER TEN

We reached the inn none too soon for me. Jack put me down just outside its door and I fell back behind Sergeant Org. I wanted to put as much space between us as possible. I could be mistaken, but I think I saw a look of hurt in his beautiful green eyes before they clouded over into an emotionless void.

Sergeant Org offered me his arm and escorted me into the large public room. There were wooden tables placed strategically around the floor with a small counter in front of beer kegs against the back wall for the barmaid.

"Why it's a tavern," I murmured with surprise.

"That it is, your grace," the sergeant explained. "These little inns all have rooms like this that double as a dining room and tavern. We'll grab a bite to eat and a pint of ale and then off to bed with you."

"That sounds good," I replied with gratitude.

The mention of food made me realize I hadn't eaten since my morning's fare of Jack's ever present stew; which I'd vomited along the way. I wondered if I'd be fed something similar at the inn or if I'd finally experience a bit of variety.

"I only know how to make stew," Jack whispered apologetically as he sat in the chair next to me. "Anything else would have made you vomit more than you already have done."

"Your stew was fine," I replied, choosing to ignore his comment about the many times I'd emptied my stomach. I knew he could read my mind yet, remarkably, I was still startled when he explained the constant presence of stew for my fare. I needed to remember to watch my thoughts when he was nearby. "It was delicious, in fact. I was surprised that I never tired of it."

His green eyes twinkled as he smiled gratefully. My heart swelled and skipped a beat. I scowled to myself. What was I doing? Why was I so worried about hurting his feelings when he'd crushed mine? I needed to toughen up and remember who he was. He was a user who'd taken advantage of my innocence. It didn't matter that he'd held back while I forced the issue. What mattered was that I cared for him and he cared not one fig in return. I was an obligation to be fulfilled and nothing more. I needed to remember that.

"When this is over, we need to talk," Jack said softly.

"Sergeant Org," I said quickly, relieved to capture his attention immediately. "Do you know how long it will take to get to the teleport station now that we're taking this alternate route?"

"I estimate we'll be there by nightfall tomorrow," he replied gently.

"There's a problem," L'oana was breathless as she rushed to the table. "That shopkeeper recognized our little princess."

"We took care of it," Jack said with confidence.

"We paid him a goodly sum to keep quiet," the sergeant added.

"I warned you about this place. You can't trust anyone. He's blabbed to anyone who'll listen," L'oana said disgustedly.

"Oh no," I bemoaned.

"Oh yes," she hissed. "It cost me a pretty penny to convince the innkeeper to let us stay here. I promised him we'd stay only a few hours; just long enough for precious here to get some much needed beauty sleep."

I ignored her insulting jab and asked, "Can we at least have some food before he kicks us out?"

"It's not safe in the public room. I've ordered your food be taken to your room," she replied.

"What about everyone else?" I asked.

"We don't need to rest," she said with sarcasm, "and we aren't fugitive royalty. We can eat here."

I started to gasp in protest, but immediately thought better of it. We were in L'oana's world and she knew best. I stood up, feeling like a child being sent to her room, and followed L'oana up the rickety wooden stairs. She led me to a narrow wooden door at the far end of the hall and inserted a key into the large metal lock.

With a loud snap the lock released and the door swung open.

The room looked like one of the modest rooms I'd toured while visiting a working colonial museum in my younger days. There was a narrow cot-like bed with a thin feather mattress rolled up on it. L'oana kicked the mattress roll with her hairy toe and it flipped open, spreading out over the roped bed. Other than the cot-like bed, there was a wooden stand beneath a small dirty window with a bar of soap, a course looking towel, a wash-bowl and a pitcher filled with tepid water.

L'oana caught me eyeing the pitcher of water and said, "Don't try to drink that. There's no telling how long it's been sitting there. I'm sure it's tainted. I'll have fresh wash water sent up and a jug of watered down wine to drink."

"Thank you," was all I managed to say before she slammed the door and turned the key in the lock.

I ran to the door and pulled at it. I was locked in! Panic filled me. I'd never been good about being locked into small, confining places. I estimated the room as being eight feet by ten feet. It definitely constituted a confining place. It was much smaller than the cave I'd spent all those weeks in. Not to mention I was free to leave the cave whenever I desired. I'd just had no desire.

I recalled L'oana's warnings about the natives of the subter-ranean being tricksters. Jacks warnings about L'oana's trickster ways echoed in my mind. Was this one of those tricks? Had she partnered up with the natives to steal me away from Jack and Sergeant Org? Had it been her plan all along? Were we even in danger of running into Mannador soldiers?

The light tapping at the door and the clicking of the lock as it was once again released by the oversized key warded off the hyperventilating that was a heartbeat away from happening. If she'd only leave the door unlocked... I'd be much better if I knew I could leave if I wanted to.

My thoughts were interrupted when a slender young girl appeared with a tray of food. Following her were two young men, one with a small table and the other balancing two chairs. They'd barely set the table up for me before I'd slid into one of the chairs.

I did my best to discreetly wipe the drool from the corner of my mouth as a bowl of cold stewed chicken, potatoes and carrots was put in front of me.

The girl informed me apologetically that L'oana didn't want them to take the time to heat my food before scurrying out of the room. I shrugged my shoulders and dug into the deliciously seasoned fare. Even cold it was wonderful.

I'd emptied my stomach thoroughly after traveling at vampire speed with Jack. It now beat the food against its walls, threatening to reject it as punishment for leaving it empty for so long. I slowed my eating pace and willed my body to embrace the nourishment I was giving it. I promised myself this food would remain in my stomach, no matter what.

I thought about the fact that Jack had kissed me with such slow, sensual passion only moments after I'd vomited my guts out and shuddered. Either he had no sense of taste or he was some type of weirdo who enjoyed the taste of bile.

"I'm neither," Jack said with sincerity as he entered the room. It was then that I realized the help hadn't locked me in. "It's just that being able to kiss the lips that drove me crazy for years was worth the aftertaste of bile."

"I... I don't understand," I stuttered with confusion.

"Don't you know?" he said as he walked up behind me and rested his hands on my shoulders. "I have loved you for so long. To finally be able to hold you, kiss you... have you completely. It was like a dream that would disappear at any moment. I had no intention of letting a little vomit stand between me and such bliss."

I was taken by such surprise that I swallowed a half chewed carrot and nearly choked on it. What was he saying? Was he telling me he loved me? How could that be?

"Do you really think I'd take the virginity you've held so dear if I didn't love you? Do you really think, after all the effort I'd put into keeping you safe and well that I'd do such a thing?" He sighed, "What must you think of me?"

I felt his lips against my temple. The heat of his breath shot down my neck, sending shivers the length of my spine.

"How can you be a vampire and be so hot?" I whispered.

"I'm a vampire, true, but I'm also a man. I told you... vampirism is a disease. I'm not the walking dead. I'm more what man would consider a mutation of life; a species if you like," he explained in the sultriest voice I could ever imagine could come from a set of vocal cords.

"I guess I need to forget the myths, books, and movies," I managed to get out of my contracted throat.

"Let me help you," he whispered as he pulled me to my feet.

Our bodies melded as one as he guided us to the cot-like bed that was barely big enough for me, let alone the both of us. Somewhere in the recesses of my mind I heard it creak and groan under our weight, but I paid it no mind. Jack loved me. He hadn't actually said he loved me, but I was sure that's what he'd been trying to tell me.

When we finally stopped kissing long enough to disrobe, I decided to gamble and seek a confirmation for what I believed to be true.

"I love you, Jack," I said hesitantly.

My breath stuck in my lungs and my heart hurt while I watched his face wrestle with a myriad of emotions. Could I have assumed something that wasn't true? Was I right when I accused him of using my body for carnal pleasures? Tears threatened to surface at the mere thought of it.

Then it happened. My gamble paid off.

"There are no words to tell you how much you mean to me. Saying I love you falls short, but that's all I can think to say right now," he whispered softly as he lowered his body onto mine once more. "I have loved you for so long and I will love you always."

Our love making was a dance of surrender and abandonment. I gave myself to him fully and he to me. All thoughts of Mark were tossed to the wind. If you'd asked me who he was or what he looked like at that moment I wouldn't have known who you were talking about. Jack was the only one in my world right then.

CHAPTER ELEVEN

Confusion took over as Jack's body went limp and heavy, pinning me beneath him.

"I've never met a vampire that had such a tough time keeping it in his pants like this one does," L'oana complained to her companions. "Someone please tell me what it is about this creature that makes him do such foolish things."

I gasped in horror as I heard a strange male voice remark about what he'd like to do with my voluptuous body. Not only was it odd to hear anyone refer to my body as voluptuous, but it was shocking to hear someone claim desires to do to it the things he was claiming he wanted to do. I didn't know if I should be horrified or mortified.

I knew immediately which one of the two burly men pulling my unconscious lover off me made such an offensive statement of desire by the wicked lust displayed on his face. Interestingly, his companion was clearly embarrassed by my nakedness. The contrast helped to balance the situation.

"Get dressed," L'oana snapped as she tossed my clothes at me. "It's late. We have to go."

"What about him?" the larger of the two men asked.

"Tie him to the bed with the silver chain in that bag," she replied as she started for the door.

"Can't I kill him?" the larger one asked.

"Ha... you're crazy to even try," she spat over her shoulder as she left the room. "Just do as I say and be quick about it."

I could have killed L'oana for leaving me alone in that room with the very man who'd described to her in detail the vile things he wanted to do with my body. My only hope was that his companion had enough influence to prevent him from acting upon his desires. I stepped into my leggings as quickly as I could but was unable to get my tunic on before he'd grabbed one of my breasts with such mighty force it sent me to my knees.

"Stop Bodigan!" the other man ordered. "Stop or I'll tell Rastus!"

"Rastus... Isn't that the innkeeper?" I gasped. "L'oana's working for the innkeeper?"

"Ha," my burly tormentor laughed, "Rastus works for L'oana."

"Touch her again and you'll answer to me," L'oana snapped from the doorway. "Why is it I can't trust you to do your job without mucking it up?" she barked at Bodigan as she walked over to inspect my breast. "You could have caused some serious damage. Then what would we do?"

"She's just so hot!" Bodigan volunteered. "I just couldn't help myself."

"Help Dorwig tie up the vampire and then meet me downstairs," she ordered as she tugged my tunic over my head and shoved my arms into it like I was a five-year-old needing help dressing before pulling me out of the room behind her.

"Why don't we just kill him?" Bodigan asked gruffly.

"Have you ever tried killing a vampire?" she asked as she stopped at the door to inspect their work.

"Once," he replied.

"Were you successful?" she asked with amusement.

"Nope," he said hesitantly.

"Do you know who he is?" Dorwig asked Bodigan.

"A vampire," Bodigan said in a tone that was meant to demean Dorwig.

"He's a vampire king from earth, you twit," Dorwig volunteered. "Unless you want every vampire roaming that stinking planet coming here for vengeance, I'd just tie him up like L'oana said and get out of here. We knocked him hard enough that he should be out long enough for us to get above ground and to our king before he awakes."

"What king?" I asked.

"Not your father," L'oana spat, "He's long gone. We'll be taking you to King Orvis, the Mannadorian king. You know the one...

he killed your parents and seized the throne of Kurr."

"You're working with that king? What about your people? What would he want with me?" I said before I realized how stupid I sounded.

"I could have made the perfect mate for Jack, but he wouldn't give me a chance. He wouldn't even touch me... yet he touches you. I guess he requires stupid and ugly to get aroused," she hissed vehemently.

I stumbled down the hall while L'oana propelled me forward with shoves to the middle of my back. I barely made it down the precarious stairs without falling head over heels; something I'm sure she secretly wished I'd do. As we passed through the dining room, I saw Sergeant Org face down on the table. L'oana assured me he'd been fed something to knock him out long enough for her to get me above ground. I looked around the room. Other than the unconscious sergeant, it was empty.

Rastus was waiting for us at the front door.

"Why isn't she bound?" he demanded.

"Do it now," L'oana ordered.

He grabbed my wrists and tied them together so tight it felt like the rope was going to sever my hands from my wrists. I started to protest, but before I could say a word a scratchy and incredibly smelly cloth bag was shoved over my head. If I thought I'd die of suffocation from being locked in that small room, you can only imagine the emotions that surged through me as I struggled for air.

"She sounds like she's suffocating," L'oana said with concern.

"I'll make a slice near her mouth," Rastus said calmly. "Hold still, girl, so I don't mess up that pretty face of yours with my knife."

I didn't need to be told twice. I stood as stiff as a board and held my breath until he'd finished slicing a wide opening near my mouth. Raunchy fabric folded into my lips as I sucked in air, but I didn't care. I could breathe again and that's all that mattered.

Heavy footsteps came up behind me. I heard Bodigan and Dorwig assure Rastus and L'oana that Jack was bound so tight he'd never get free. They figured that, even if he did wake before Sergeant Org did, he'd have to wait for Org to revive and free him. They both were so smug with themselves that I wanted to kick them where it counted. I would have too if I'd had any idea of the direction to aim my foot. Unfortunately, they'd moved me around just enough to get me disoriented.

A rope was tied to the one on my wrists and I was pulled along like a dog on a leash.

I could feel that we were walking at an upward slope. We were heading for the upper world and the fate that Jack and Aunt Jenny had worked so hard to avoid.

I needed to find a way to stall them until Sergeant Org roused and set Jack free. Why couldn't he be like the vampires in the movies? They'd never be knocked unconscious and bound like that. If he was like the vampires in the movies, L'oana and her cronies would be dead by now.

"I have to pee," I shouted as loud as I could. "I can't walk anymore until I relieve myself."

L'oana groaned, but took mercy on me and directed us to a nearby body of water. She ordered the men to move away and look elsewhere before pulling the sack off my head. The world spun just a little as my eyes adjusted and my body grounded itself.

"Do me a favor and wash while you're at it. I'd rather not smell Jack for the entire journey," she spat.

I could feel her pain and jealousy as she slapped me with her words. I actually felt a little sorry for her. She obviously cared for Jack a lot more than he wanted her to. Unrequited love is a bitch. Watching Jack and I together had to hurt.

She was right. I wasn't given an opportunity to clean up before I was bound and pulled away like an animal. I could smell the remnants of Jack's love making as I pulled my leggings down. I removed my clothes completely, did my business, and headed for the water. I could have been embarrassed about the confirmation of L'oana's complaint, but I was happy instead. Taking the time to clean up was just adding to my opportunity to stall them.

With any luck, Sergeant Org and Jack would catch up with us before we made it to the king and my eventual death.

"Hurry up," L'oana shouted.

"How does he plan to kill me?" I asked.

I was both curious and wanting to distract her from the time I was taking.

"Who's killing you?" she puzzled.

"You're taking me to the king so he can kill me, like he did my parents. How does he plan on doing it?" I asked in a voice that sounded much calmer than I felt.

"Who told you that?" she chuckled.

"I'm a little tired of being spoken to like a child, L'oana," I growled as I splashed cold water on my body.

L'oana cocked her head and watched me bathe in silence.

"No one's going to kill you, princess," she finally said in the same irritating condescending tone. "In fact, you're soon to be the blushing bride."

"He's going to marry me?" I gasped in disbelief.

"He's expecting a flat chested virgin. I'm not sure how he's going to feel about Jack getting to you first," she said smugly. "Maybe he'll change his mind."

"I hope so," I sighed.

"Then he'll kill you," she smirked.

"How would he know I hadn't developed already? You said the only reason I didn't develop was because I was on earth," I said accusingly.

"Oh honey, how naïve you are. Did you really think you were kept hidden all those years?" she laughed. "He's known where you were for years."

"How come he didn't come to kill me then?" I asked.

"There was no need. He killed your fake father and sent his vampire wife to the prison planet. Jack somehow got her back though. He's a very resourceful vampire, I'll give him that. Fortunately, with the captain gone, she wanted nothing to do with you, so the king no longer considers her a threat. It was the king's intention to bring you back to Kurr and raise you until you were old enough to marry. Little did anyone know that Jack would step in to guard you. That put a monkey wrench in his majesty's plans just a bit," she said wistfully.

"What's so special about Jack?" I asked. "Why would he put a monkey wrench in the imposter king's plan?"

"Careful what you say there, princess. King Orvis won't take kindly to being called an imposter," she cooed. "Jack is a king in his own right. Did you know that?"

I shook my head.

"Well he is," she said with an admiring tone. "He's king of the vampires of earth. He has a legion of vampires at his disposal, should he wish to call them forth."

"Aren't you risking that by taking me to marry the king?" I asked. "He is my guardian after all."

"Killing you would give him cause for war. Marrying you would simply free him of his responsibilities. Once you are married and assume your duties as queen on Kurr, there is nothing he can do about it."

As if suddenly realizing the time we'd wasted talking, she ordered me to get out of the water and get dressed. I whined that I hadn't been able to get Jack's love making fully washed away due to lack of soap and a cloth. She visibly winced from my intentional cruelty and stormed into the water. I watched in wonder as she grabbed a handful of tall grass and approached me with determined strides until she was standing only inches away. Grabbing my shoulder with a vice grip, she scrubbed my private area with the abrasive grass until I cried out for mercy.

"There…. You're clean. Now get your ass out of this water and into those clothes," she ordered between clenched teeth.

Tears of mortification and pain rolled down my cheeks and my nose ran like a sieve as I made my way to shore. I made no move to tend to either. I felt more violated by her actions than I had when her goon grabbed my breast. Was there no end to this nightmare?

Oh Jack, where are you? Don't let them reach King Orvis. I beg you, my mind cried.

I couldn't resist getting in one more jab in return for the pain and humiliation she'd forced on me.

"You can scrub away his seed, but you can't remove his love. I have Jack's love and I'll have it forever!" I hissed.

"Well, he can love you from a distance, my queen," she said smugly.

"When I am queen, I'll be sure to see that you're well taken care of," I spat.

"Oh my.... Should I feel threatened?" she said with a feigned wince. "Maybe I shouldn't address you as queen. Maybe I should forgo the formality and just call you sister. That's what you'll be when you marry my brother the king." Her laughter filled the air. "That's right, sweetie. I'm a shape shifting Mannador who just so happens to not mind going underground. It's come in handy on so many occasions."

CHAPTER TWELVE

We were above ground and still no sign of Jack or Sergeant Org. I wondered if the sergeant was in on the ruse all along and simply pretending to be knocked out for my benefit. I was beginning to be suspicious of everyone around me. How sad that it had come to that.

We were barely on the trail when we met up with a small troop of Mannadorian soldiers. The King was notified of my capture and had traveled to meet me. It seemed my time as a free woman would be shorter than expected.

Although my legs were relieved when they placed me on a beautiful black gelding for the remainder of the journey, my heart was heavy. Every step that my steed took put my vampire guardian and lover further and further behind us. I questioned if it might be better to die. I didn't know how I'd be able to live without Jack at my side.

I closed my eyes and the memories flooded into my head. Making love with Jack must have broken down the barrier that had prevented me from remembering.

I saw myself sitting on Jack's knee while the people I thought were my mother and father laughed at something I'd said. What was it I said? I could hear me speaking, but I couldn't make it out. I was young... possibly two or three.

I gave up trying to remember what I'd said to him and the visions in my head moved forward. I was still quite young, so it had to have been not long after the time I sat on Jack's knee. An evil man was standing over my father's lifeless body. He was holding a bloody knife. My mother was gnashing and snarling. She was trapped in netting and being bound and immobilized. It took six men to overtake her. She was incredibly strong. Someone was holding me close with a hand over my mouth. I struggled to be free and the hand clamped stronger. My face was so small that the hand not only covered my mouth but it blocked my nasal passage. I was suffocating. I was able to see the men carry my mother's bound body away just before the world went black.

My next vision was of someone breathing life into my mouth. It was Jack. He was giving me mouth to mouth resuscitation. When I was finally able to suck in air, I wailed my pain and indignation as loud as I could. Aunt Jenny picked me up and showered me with kisses while Jack chastised her for her carelessness. The people I knew as my parents had been warned of the Mannadors coming and had hidden me with Aunt Jenny. She neglected to take heed of their warning and actually took me to visit them after I'd cried over our separation. Horrified about the danger she'd put me in, they urged her to take me to safety, but it was too late. The Mannadorian soldiers were upon us. Aunt Jenny was overtaken by one of the soldiers. He knocked her out and smothered me. Fortunately, Jack arrived in time to give me mouth to mouth before my body failed me. Jenny regained consciousness just as Jack finished breathing life back into my little body. She begged for another chance and Jack gave it to her, with a strong warning that he would always be watching.

I remembered another time not long after that when Jack once again blew the breath of life into my body. This time I distinctly tasted dirt, but I had no idea how or why it would be in my mouth.

I recalled seeing him standing at a distance on numerous occasions while growing up, but I never paid him any mind. He'd been watching me, like he said, for the majority of my life. It was no wonder I felt so secure with him in the cave and why he felt so familiar. Now I understood.

My mind went back to me sitting on his knee and I strained to hear what I'd said. For some reason it seemed important to know. I closed my eyes tight and strained to block out the outside world, but I couldn't come up with my words. All I could hear was their laughter. Whatever I said even had Jack laughing joyously.

My horse stumbled and brought me back to reality.

"Hey there," the leader shouted from behind me, "someone

check on the princess. Her horse just stumbled."

I straightened my back and looked straight ahead while two soldiers closed in to see what was about. One grabbed my horse's reigns and, once again, I was being pulled behind them. The difference being that I was riding with dignity instead of stumbling like a drunken dog.

"We're almost there princess. Soon you'll be enjoying the royal comforts you deserve," said the soldier to my left with respect that surprised me.

"As it should be," called back the soldier leading my horse.

"As it should be," I whispered to myself, "but with Jack, not him."

I rode the rest of the way with a heavy heart. I ceased looking back for signs of Jack. There were none. Now that we were so close to the king's encampment, more and more soldiers were arriving to lead us to King Orvis.

My body jolted with a start when the trumpets sounded our arrival. Soldiers formed a path for us to pass through, with swords joined at the tip to form and arch. At the end of the procession arch stood the tall imposing figure of the king.

My heart felt like it was going to beat out of my body as we drew closer to my fate. I could see his facial features now. He looked surprisingly normal. From that distance he actually looked handsome. It wasn't his facial features that I needed to see. Good looks could be deceiving, especially on a shape shifter. I needed to see his eyes. The eyes were the window to the soul; providing this king even had a soul.

My opportunity came when my horse stopped just feet in front of him and I was lifted to the ground. I stood boldly before him, refusing to kneel, and stared him straight in the eye. He bore the look of surprise and admiration for my behavior. He also had difficulty disguising his disappointment at the sight of my full, voluptuous figure.

"Are you a pedophile?" I ask boldly.

I could barely hear the king ask what I meant by that over the shocked gasps from the crowd that surrounded us over my boldness and lack of respect.

"You seem disappointed not to be presented with a child-like body," I said as I smoothed my hand over my breasts and hips. "I know you were expecting one. So, I ask you again if you are a pedophile."

"You go too far girl," the king roared.

His eyes flashed with green and red speckles, just as Sergeant Org said they would.

"I went too far you mean," I chuckled brazenly, "and with a vampire king, no less." I walked closer to King Orvis until I was standing only inches away and he could hear me whisper, "You see, a king has already made me his queen."

"Get her out of my sight!" he bellowed as he stomped away.

I smiled as I was led away to a nearby tent that was prepared for me. I'd angered the king. Hopefully I'd angered him enough to make him not want me for his bride.

"That was a dumb thing to do," L'oana spat as she walked up beside me. "You really are stupid, aren't you?"

"I'd rather die than become his queen. Hopefully, I've made that happen," I replied spitefully.

"Hopefully you haven't declared war!" she said as she turned on her heels to leave me. "Get some rest, sister dear. The wedding is tomorrow."

I stood in the center of my tent, too numb to move. The wedding was going to happen the following day and she expected me to get some sleep? When I was finally able to get my body to function again, I rushed to the entrance and looked out. There were four soldiers standing guard and many more roaming around. Escape was impossible. Even if Jack could find me, he'd never get past that many soldiers.

It was hopeless.

A young woman came in carrying a pile of fabric. She curtsied timidly before hanging several beautifully crafted dresses on pegs that were driven into the poles that supported the tent.

"We must make some alterations for you, your highness," she said as she pulled out her sewing kit.

I walked over to the one that I assumed was to be my wedding dress. I had to admit it was beautifully made and tastefully decorated. Metallic gold threads were woven through white linen. The bodice was the perfect size for me before I'd started developing from my time spent on Kurr and my love making with Jack. There was no way I'd be able to squeeze my newly enlarged breasts and rounded hips into that lovely creation. Two more women entered the tent. Their arms were also laden with fabric. It matched the fabric the dresses hanging on the pegs were made of.

Without fanfare, or even a little warning, they stripped me of my clothes and started draping fabric over me while they measured and cut. When I wasn't being poked and prodded and draped in fabric, I was allowed to wear one of the softest robes I'd ever had the pleasure of resting against my skin. It caressed my body when I moved in a way that could only be described as sensual.

I thought of how Jack's fingers and lips roaming my body created a similar feeling before I collapsed to the floor. I could stand no more.

CHAPTER THIRTEEN

I could hear the faint whisper of the young maid as she lightly tapped my cheek in an attempt to awaken me. I don't know how long it was since I'd passed out, but it wasn't nearly long enough. My body was exhausted. The last thing I wanted to do was to be roust out of the marvelous semi-coma I was in.

"Princess, please... you must awaken. Time is short," came the whisper through the dark.

Time is short? Short for what? Oh yes, I remembered. I was to be married.

"I don't want to get married. Let me sleep," I mumbled.

"No, you can't sleep. I've come to set you free, but only if you arise now and flee. The encampment will be coming to life soon," she said in a hushed and urgent tone.

I needed no more prompting than that to spring to life. I sat up in the darkness and looked around. It was so black; I couldn't see my hand in front of my face. Had I been imagining that someone had come to save me? Was I dreaming? Frustration consumed me while I fought to subdue my claustrophobia. My body trembled and my breathing grew labored. It wasn't that I was afraid of the dark. It was that I had no idea where the exit was. I felt trapped. Panic was rapidly setting in.

As if on cue, a small candle flickered in the corner of the tent near my dresses.

"Over here, princess," she urged. "I don't dare come out further with the light. Someone might see it and come to inspect why you are wandering around the tent in the middle of the night."

I picked my way across the tent floor, stifling a groan or two when I stubbed my toe or stepped on a stone that was trying to invade the tent through the canvas floor. Eventually, I was huddled next to the girl holding the light. To my surprise, I looked straight into the large brown eyes of my seamstress.

"Is this a trick?" I asked a little louder than I'd intended.

"Shhh, they might hear you," she whispered. "I'm risking a lot to get you from here."

"Why do you?" I asked suspiciously.

"I am a true subject, your highness. I am a Kurr slave with no loyalty to the Mannador King and his people. They are evil," she hissed. "I can't bear to see you being forced to wed King Orvis. He is cruel. You would suffer."

"What's your name?" I asked.

"Sheshua," she replied softly.

"How do you plan on getting me out of here, Sheshua?" I asked. I was still not convinced she was a friend and not a foe. "Aren't there are guards outside?"

"They have gone to sleep with the assistance of a little powder in their flasks. They will sleep for a few more hours," she explained.

I thought of Sergeant Org face down on the table and shook my head. It seemed drugging one's victim was a common practice on Kurr.

She shoved my leggings and tunic into my arms and urged me to put them on post haste. I'd just finished securing my belt when the flap to the entrance moved ever so slightly and another maid slid in. My eyes had adjusted to the barely illuminated darkness enough for me to be able to make out her shape, but nothing more.

"Someone else has entered," I whispered urgently.

"She has come to help," Sheshua explained. "You will need her in order to get out of the camp safely."

"Where am I to go?" I asked with concern.

As much as I wanted to be free of the king's clutches, I had no clue where I was or where to go should I reach freedom.

"Follow the river north. It will lead you to the teleportation station," she replied.

"You know about that?" I asked in surprise.

"You hear much when you are an invisible slave of the king," she replied softly.

"How do I reach the river? Is it far?" I asked.

Just then, the late comer walked up to the light to allow me to see her face. She was also one of the women who had worked so diligently to create a gown that would fit the king's future bride's new body.

Sheshua told me the young woman was called Mangoot. She then took my hands firmly in hers and asked me to please listen to all she had to say with an open mind. She insisted that my future and my freedom depended on it. There was a long moment of silence while I debated what to do. I was so tired of being tricked and captured, but what was my alternative? These women could be on the up and up. I decided it was worth the gamble.

What she told me next took me completely by surprise.

Mangoot wasn't a servant. She was of Mannador royalty and was very much in love with the king. The queen died a while back, leaving the king looking for a new bride. Mangoot was expecting to be the one chosen. When I showed up on the scene she was completely thrown. She wanted me gone and was willing to do what was necessary to make that happen... short of murder.

I looked into Mangoot's eyes and could see her pain. They were telling the truth. I took a deep breath and asked what they had planned for my escape.

Mangoot had special shape shifting abilities. Where most of the Mannador could shift into the shape of an animal native to the land they lived on, Mangoot was able to literally think of a creature and become it. It was a secret she'd shared with few.

She asked me about my survival abilities. I told her I was quite adept with a bow and arrow. She spoke in a language I couldn't understand and Sheshua disappeared. We stood in awkward silence while waiting for her return. Fortunately, it was a short wait. When she reappeared, her arms were laden with an impressive looking bow and a quiver full of arrows, a large hunting knife, and very soft and comfortable looking moccasins that far surpassed the quality of the ones I'd worn upon my arrival. Tucked in the bottom pocket of my arrow case was an extremely thin blanket. It folded so small I questioned how much warmth it would provide, but they assured me it would be more than adequate. Mangoot also shared with me that, besides providing warmth, it would provide me with protection in the way of invisibility.

Time was passing far too quickly. We needed to leave before the encampment started its day. We could already hear a little activity stirring. The women fitted me with my survival ensemble and then urged me to cloak myself completely with the blanket. I was amazed when I held my blanketed arm out in the candle light and saw nothing. Mangoot said she would meet us at the edge of the encampment and left the tent. Sheshua urged me to follow her as she hurried out after Mangoot.

I walked hesitantly out of the tent and looked around. It was still dark, but signs of dawn were peeking over the horizon, providing a dim light for visibility. The morning air was a cool and refreshing slap in my face. I filled my lungs and immediately felt alert and ready for action. Sheshua walked with quick determination through the organized rows of army tents toward the edge of the encampment. She greeted the occasional worker or soldier with confident authority as she walked forward with a purposeful manner. No one questioned why she was out and about at such an early hour. They simply greeted her respectfully and went about their business.

I began to wonder who this Sheshua really was. The respect and consideration she was receiving was not something I would have expected a seamstress slave to receive. It annoyed me that I hadn't had the presence of mind to question who she was prior to her enslavement.

When we finally reached the edge of the encampment, she stopped as if to adjust the lacings in her high lace shoes. I stopped next to her. My breathing filled my ears and I wondered if it was as loud as it sounded to me.

"This is where we part," she said without looking up from her lacings. "Mangoot is waiting for you over that ridge. You must not dally. The guards will be making their rounds very soon. Go now and may luck be with you."

I looked wistfully at the seamstress. I wanted to give her a hug and thank her for helping me in this way. I wanted to tell her that it was no small matter to me that she cared enough to risk her life for my escape. I wanted to ask her who she used to be.

Of course I did none of these things, as we couldn't risk anyone hearing my voice or seeing exposed parts of my body, should I attempt to hug her. Instead, I hurried off in the direction she'd pointed and hoped to meet up with Mangoot soon.

When I reached the ridge and didn't see her, I began to question if it was yet another set up. Panic welled within me. It was true that I had a bow and arrow and a knife, but I also had absolutely no idea where I was or where I should be going.

I wanted Jack. I felt naked and vulnerable without him. I wondered if he'd managed to get free yet. A sudden gloom swept over me. Was he even alive? L'oana was such a liar. Had she actually had Jack and Sergeant Org killed and told me otherwise to get me to cooperate? She had to have known that if I was aware Jack was dead I would have sought death myself. Even with the thought of him alive, I'd tempted fate with the king.

"Oh Jack, where are you?" I whispered.

"Who is Jack?" came a voice from behind me.

I recognized the voice as belonging to Mangoot and spun around to face her.

"Jack," I explained, "has not only been my guard and savior for most of my life, but he's the one I love. L'oana tricked him and Sergeant Org while supposedly leading us to safety underground. We'd stopped at an inn to rest when she made her move. The last I saw either of them, Jack was unconscious and trussed up like a bundle of hay and Sergeant Org was face down on the dinner table.

"Sergeant Org?" Mangoot spoke in an excited hushed tone, "You've met him?"

"He was taking Jack and me back to the teleportation station so I could return to earth," I explained.

"This Jack, he is a vampire?" she added.

"Yes," I replied.

"You call him Jack?" she continued.

"What else would I call him?" I asked curiously.

She smiled softly and, after a brief moment of silence, said, "You could call him by his rightful title. He is Lord Jack Devon, King of the earth vampires. He is very handsome and very powerful."

"This isn't the first time I've heard him referred to as the king of the vampires," I said thoughtfully, "but it is the first time I've heard his full name. He never told me and I never thought to ask."

It struck me that I was making a habit of not asking people more about themselves. It was a bad habit that needed to be corrected. Not only was it important to know exactly who I was dealing with in this strange and formidable world, but a name was one's personal identity. To ignore such a thing was rude and unforgivable. It was like declaring they meant nothing to the world. I vowed to change my ways.

"How can you say you love someone when you don't even know his true identity?" Mangoot asked gently.

She had a point that I had no answer to.

"Do you know Sergeant Org well?" she continued.

"Jack introduced him to me only recently. He was the one to discover the Dragos had abducted me and warned Jack. He brought Jack here to fetch me home," I said.

"The Dragos abducted you and you live to tell of it? My, you are blessed," Mangoot said with admiration. "Are you aware you travel in high company, my dear? Sergeant Org is no mere sergeant in the military. It is a nick name he took on when King Orvis seized the throne in order to take attention away from him. His real name is Prince Mandrake Organna. Prior to the king and queen's death, he was expected to inherit the rulership through marriage to you. I am very surprised to discover he is tolerating a love affair between you and Lord Devon. You have been promised to him since birth."

At her last comment I missed a step and almost fell on my

face. She giggled at my clumsiness and said we'd taken enough time chatting. If we didn't get on our way immediately we would miss our chance.

At Mangoot's request I walked an easy twelve feet away and waited for her to shift into a creature that would see me safely to the river. To my surprise, and apprehension, she transitioned into a very large, very scaly, very reddish-green dragon. She snorted and pointed to her back with her snout as she lowered her body for me to climb on her back. Although she was a dragon and not a lizard, the sight of her scales filled me with memories and apprehension. I swallowed hard and commanded my legs to obey.

Once I moved past the scale thing, I found her body surprisingly warm and supple as I did my best to find a secure place on her back. I would have never guessed it just from looking at her. I would have thought her scales to be leathery and rough like the Dragos. I caught myself wondering if real dragons were like this, or if it was because she was a shifter and chuckled. Dragons weren't even real.

I almost fell off when she stood up and launched herself into the air, but I somehow managed to regain my balance. Her scales were large enough for me to grab onto and use as a stabilizing aid. Even so, I hoped the flight would be a short one as we flew above the tree tops.

To my relief, we arrived at the river's edge in a very short period of time. I'd feared falling off her back during the entire flight and was eager to have the solid ground beneath my feet. The balance I'd managed to maintain during the flight failed me during her landing and I tumbled to the ground with a thud.

"You're not very graceful, are you?" she chuckled as she returned to her humanoid self. "Follow the river north until you reach the teleportation station. Don't leave the river if you know what's good for you. They'll be looking for you soon, so hurry. If you run into a Mannadorian troop, go deep into the water. They're afraid of water. You can swim, can't you?"

I nodded.

"Good," she continued. "I must leave you now. Good luck."

I watched with wonder while tiny lights flew around her as she turned into a beautiful bird. I've never been good at identifying species, but, by her coloring, I assumed she was of a tropical sort.

As she flew away, I heard her call out, "If I run into Lord Devon or Sergeant Org I'll tell them where you are. Remember to take good care of that blanket. It could save your life."

I waived my thanks and set to task rolling up my blanket and carefully stuffing it back in the bottom of my arrow case. I hoped I wouldn't need it again, but, if I did, I wanted quick and easy access to it.

Upon hearing the horns announce my escape from the encampment, I frowned. I'd hoped we were farther away than we obviously were. A renewed sense of urgency pushed me onward. I had no intention of getting caught by the Mannador.

Traveling through the air eliminated the possibility of them picking up on my scent and knowing the direction I'd gone. My only hope was that L'oana wouldn't realize I knew the way to the teleportation launch and would assume I was wandering aimlessly instead of following the river to my destination. I also hoped no harm came to Mangoot or Sheshua. At the risk of over worrying and distracting myself from my mission, I assured myself that they were intelligent women who had thought things through and had a plan for covering up their participation in my escape.

Grateful for the beautifully made new moccasins, I headed up the river's edge at an easy jog.

CHAPTER FOURTEEN

I had no idea how far up the river I had to go to reach the teleportation launch. I also had no idea what to do when I got there. These thoughts, as well as thoughts of Jack and Sergeant Org, filled my head while I kept a steady jog. I was surprised at how well my legs were holding up. Either all of the intense walking had strengthened them, or it was part of the maturing process my body was experiencing. Whatever the reason, it was good fortune for me.

I pictured Sergeant Org in my mind. Had my parents really pledged my hand in marriage to him? It seemed so abstract. He certainly was handsome in his own way. He didn't fall into Jack's category of handsome, but never-the-less he was good looking enough. Had my life gone differently and I not met Jack, I could have possibly accepted being married to him. He was not just handsome, but he'd proven himself to be a kindly person. Someone of this nature was such a rarity on earth, and I was guessing on Kurr as well.

Like Mangoot, I wondered what effect my relationship with Jack had on the sergeant. I remembered his look of displeasure when he saw the undeniable signs that Jack and I made love. What went on in his mind? Had he planned on sticking to his promise to marry me and was simply waiting for the right opportunity to tell me? Was Jack aware of this promise between my parents and his friend? I hoped not. I would hate to think Jack capable of being so cruel.

Of course, promise or no promise, I had no intention of marrying anyone but Jack...providing he asked me. I wondered what it would be like to marry a vampire. He said he aged slowly. Would that mean that I'd be an old hag and he'd still be his handsome self? I shuddered at the thought.

After a few hours of steady jogging, my body finally demand-ed a break. I spotted an old, gnarled apple tree and sat down with my back against its trunk. The landscape was beautiful and serene. Mangoot made it a point of depositing me on the side of the river that bordered the forest, just in case I needed to disap-pear amongst the trees. As I looked upon the other side of the river, I couldn't help wishing I was there. It was as if the river divided two worlds. Behind me was a dark and sinister looking menagerie of gnarly trees while across from me was a beautiful field coated with an array of wildflowers and berry bushes. They looked like they might have been cultivated, although I saw no signs of life other than the birds and butterflies that fluttered from bush to bush.

My stomach rumbled at the thought of eating a juicy berry. Did I dare try crossing the river? I was tempted, but then thought better of it. I did, however partake in the light snack of cheese, bread, and water that the women had been thoughtful enough to supply. It was a sparing amount, but it was enough to take the edge off my hunger without bogging me down when I started jog-ging again.

Feeling rested and satisfied, I stood up to resume my journey. It was then that I saw him. Off in the distance, a man was walk-ing very cautiously along the riverbank I'd just jogged along. He hadn't spotted me yet because he was focusing on the ground, as if he was tracking something.... or someone. I'd gained a little weight when my body blossomed, but I would still be considered a lightweight. I looked down to see what type of tracks my moc-casins left. Although they barely left a dent in the grass, if you knew what to look for, it was enough.

I cursed my misfortune and backed into the trees. Mangoot's warning about not leaving the river echoed in my head. I looked from behind the trees at the man. Was he Mannadorian? Would I be able to get into the river without him seeing me? Was he even after me?

The man was very near by the time I had wits enough to remember the blanket. I pulled it out as quickly as I could and shrouded myself with it while hoping my rustling and fumbling wasn't loud enough to be heard.

He was only yards away from me when he stopped and cocked his head. Was he sniffing the air? Yes, he was sniffing the air! Did I stink? Had he caught my scent? The hours of jogging had coated my body with perspiration. Was it that distinctive?

I held my breath.

"Who's there?" he shouted at nothing in particular. "Come out. I won't hurt you."

I had no intention of divulging my presence, so I just kept quiet.

"Come on. I know someone is there. Show yourself," he continued.

I stood as still as I could while I waited for him to give up and move on. I prayed it would be soon because my body needed to relieve itself and I wasn't sure how much longer I could hold it in.

I was just about to take a chance and show myself when Jack's transparent image suddenly floated before me. He looked worried. His words sounded in my head, *'It's a trick. Stay put.'* I stifled a gasp with both my hands and stared in wide eyed wonder at his handsome face floating before me. I longed to reach out and touch him, but of course he wasn't there.

"I know you're there and I'm not leaving until you show yourself," the stranger barked.

His tone was getting progressively more frustrated.

Whether it was my imagination playing tricks on me or Jack really had projected himself to me didn't matter. I decided to heed the warning and stay put. Hopefully the stranger would give up before my bladder did.

Minutes seemed like hours as I stood, statue-like, waiting for him to leave. Panic threatened to surface when he walked in my direction. My muscles prepared for flight as I assessed my pursuer. He was lean and muscular and looked to be quite strong. He reminded me of the hunters Aunt Jenny and I often encountered during deer season. His mannerism was alert and ready to strike. If he wasn't Mannadorian, he was probably working for them. What was it the sergeant had told me to look for to distinguish if someone or something was a Mannador? I was so stricken by fear of discovery I struggled to remember as he drew closer to where I stood.

When he was just about upon me, I caught wind of his musky odor. It was the same odor the soldiers carried. Then I remembered to look into his eyes, like I had the king's. Sure enough, he had little green and red speckles floating around in them. He was Mannadorian alright and he was about to walk right into me.

"I can smell you princess," he cooed as he extended his arms and started searching the air. "I know you're here somewhere. Who gave you the cloak of invisibility?"

He was only inches away from me. I needed to do something, but was unsure what the right move was. Should I take my chances and stay put in hopes he'd miss me, or should I try to make it to the river?

Once again Jack's face appeared in front of me, *'When I say go, run to the river like your life depends upon it. Go as far into it as you can and stay there. I'm coming.'*

I coiled my muscles for action. Adrenaline was building up so strongly I felt I'd explode if I didn't move soon. The Mannadorian tracker walked past me and then stopped and cocked his head. As he turned to walk in my direction Jack shouted '*Go!*' so loud in my mind I was sure the tracker heard it. I responded like a race horse at the starting gate and sprang into action.

Grateful that I was a good swimmer, I plowed into the river until I was waist deep and then dove under the water. The current was stronger than I expected. I was unable to save my blanket from its clutches. Sadly, I watched it bob with the current until it disappeared. The Mannadorian tracker paced the riverbank. He was furious, but, true to what I was told, he wouldn't enter the water.

Battling to keep myself steady and upright in the current was hard enough, but dealing with the freezing temperature was even more so. The only good thing that came out of the situation was my bladder went into shock and was no longer bothering me for relief.

"You can't stay in there forever, princess," the tracker called out. "I happen to know the water's temperature is not much above freezing. You picked the wrong river for a stunt like this!" I watched as he sat down and made himself comfortable on the river bank. "I'll just wait here until you come to your senses!"

He was right. My limbs were already tiring and I could barely feel my arms and legs. My body was getting numb from the cold. Soon I'd be experiencing hyperthermia. My mind raced at what to do.

"Where are you Jack?" I cried out. "You said you were coming!"

His translucent face appeared before me, *'Look above.'*

I looked up into the sky to see something flash across the sky like a comet before landing just feet from where the surprised Mannadorian tracker sat on the river bank. Before he could react, Sergeant Org leapt off Jack's back and snapped his neck. It all happened so fast, I found it hard to believe I wasn't making it up.

I watched as Jack barreled into the icy river, reaching me in record time. I surrendered eagerly to his strong embrace. He cradled my frozen body close to his as he hurried to the river bank.

Sergeant Org looked pale and worried as Jack set me down on the grassy bank.

"Are you alright, princess?" he asked feebly.

"Yes, thank you. I'm just a little c-cold," I replied.

Without a moment's hesitation the sergeant removed his tunic for the second time for me to wear. As he tossed it in my direction, he dashed off to the edge of the forest to purge the contents of his stomach. Apparently he didn't fare any better than I did when traveling at vampire speed.

Jack helped me remove my clothes and slip the dry oversized tunic on. Assuring me he'd have them dry in no time, he took my clothes and held them away from his body before spinning at such a rapid speed I could barely distinguish him. True to his word, when he'd finished spinning, my clothes were almost completely dry.

Sergeant Org bade me wear his tunic just a little longer to assure my body temperature returned to normal. I didn't argue. The question as to why it was always the sergeant and not Jack to offer me his tunic crossed my mind, but I decided to save it for another time. I found out much later, when all was well and peaceful, that it was an honor for a subject to offer his princess and future queen assistance whenever possible and Jack didn't want to interfere with Kurr ways.

Sergeant Org's scent was strong around me. It felt familiar and comfortable. Once again I remembered what Mangoot had said about our being betrothed. I wanted to ask him, but I didn't know how to broach the subject; especially in front of Jack. If I did have a conversation with the sergeant, I wanted us to be alone so that we could each say what was on our mind without fear of hurting or offending those listening in.

Jack held me until my body stopped shaking and I was warm enough to return the sergeants tunic to him. Fortunately, it was a beautiful, sunny day, so the prince in disguise didn't suffer during his time without his tunic. When we were all back in our respective clothing, Jack suggested we get moving. He was sure there were more trackers out there searching for me.

As I was hopping on his back to allow for faster travel I asked, "Why couldn't you tell L'oana is Mannadorian?"

"She is?" said the sergeant with surprise.

"I knew I didn't trust her," Jack growled.

"You said you could tell by their scent and their eyes," I complained.

"She was clever ... claiming to be Squachula like that," Sergeant Org said thoughtfully.

"The Squachula have traits similar to the Mannador," Jack explained. "It would be difficult to tell them apart just because they had a scent and flecks in their eyes. She knew this."

"Did you know she's also the king's sister?" I asked as I finished adjusting myself on Jack's back and wrapping my arms around his shoulders.

"Damn!" Sergeant Org bellowed as we started up river.

CHAPTER FIFTEEN

To Sergeant Org's dismay we were about a day's travel from the teleportation launch. This meant we'd have to find a place to spend the night. Although Jack could continue on, Sergeant Org and I required rest.

He remembered a cave he'd hidden in on several occasions and guided us to it. It was not big, but it was dry and very difficult to spot until you were right upon it. Since Jack didn't require the same type of rest that we did, he volunteered to stand watch outside while we slept a few hours.

Once alone in the cave, an awkward silence fell between the sergeant and me. I longed to ask him what was on his mind, but I felt insecure about doing it. I got the impression he was holding back asking me something as well.

"Can I ask you something, princess," he finally said.

"What's that?" I asked.

"Can I ask how you managed to get free?" he said.

"Mangoot didn't find you?" I said with surprise.

"Mangoot? Is that a person or an animal?" he replied.

"She's the Mannador that helped me escape. She shifted into a dragon and flew me to the river," I explained.

"You don't say?" he chortled. "Well, I'll be."

"She's of royal blood and wanted me out of the way because she's got plans of becoming queen," I explained.

"Ah... I see," he said thoughtfully.

After a moment of silence, I added, "She told me something."

"Oh yes? Do you want to share it?" he asked curiously.

I nodded slowly.

His face looked soft and vulnerable in the firelight as he waited quietly for me to continue. It dawned on me that this was the first I'd seen him relaxed. His confidence in Jack was enormous.

"She said I was promised to you in marriage by my parents," I said softly.

He couldn't have reacted more violently if I'd slapped him in the face with a brick.

"How did she know?" he bellowed in a loud whisper.

"So, it's true? We're engaged or betrothed or however you want to say it?" I asked in a hushed tone.

He looked away, his face a mask of sadness.

"Jack doesn't know," he said softly.

As relieved as I was to hear this, my heart broke in half for the sergeant.

"How horrible it must have been for you to see me with Jack and know what we...err...what we...," I began.

"He can't ever know," he emphasized.

"I don't understand," I stammered.

"How much do you know about Jack?" he asked.

"Well, I recently discovered... from Mangoot of course... that he is the king of the vampires of earth and that I should be addressing him as Lord Devon."

"Did he ask you to address him as such?" he asked.

"He never even told me who he was," I replied.

"Then continue to call him Jack until he says differently," he said.

I chuckled nervously, "Do you think he'll want me to call him Lord Devon?"

"He will if you tell him we're engaged," he said flatly.

"Are we?" I pushed.

He nodded.

"That was an agreement between you and parents I don't even remember. You can't expect me to honor it," I said anxiously. When he didn't respond I added, "I love Jack and he loves me."

"I know," he said. After a brief moment of staring into nothingness, he added, "We should probably get some rest. We have a long day ahead of us tomorrow."

"Why can't Jack know?" I asked.

"If you love him, you'll keep quiet," he replied.

"I don't understand," I persisted.

"Please do me a favor and get to know him before you tell him anything like this. Once you get to know his nature, you'll understand why I don't want him to know," Sergeant Org replied.

"Will he hurt me?" I asked hesitantly.

His head whipped around with a shocked look.

"Are you serious?" he asked incredulously.

"That would be the only reason I could think to keep a secret like this from him," I replied.

"That just goes to show how little you know him," he half whispered, half hissed.

"It's just that..." I began.

"Listen," he said with growing impatience. "It's like you said. It was an agreement between me and your parents. You had nothing to do with it and you don't want to honor it, so let's just call it void and forget about it. It makes no sense upsetting things by telling Jack."

I was not comfortable with keeping a secret of that caliber from Jack, but it seemed I'd already upset Sergeant Org considerably, so I decided to let it drop. There was time to confide such things with my vampire lover later; once we were free from this planet and on home turf again. I may have been the true heir to the throne of Kurr, but it was a foreign land to me. Earth was my home and earth was where I wanted to go. I snuggled into the fetal position near the fire and closed my eyes. He was right. We needed to rest. We could talk again later.

I'd just about fallen asleep when I felt Sergeant Org's strong hand on my shoulder. I sat up with a start and he held his finger to his lips to indicate I be quiet. I nodded my head and looked at him quizzically.

"I can't sleep until we finish our discussion," he whispered.

"Okay," I whispered back.

He sat down beside me so close our shoulders were touching. I made no move to put space between us. I somehow felt he needed the body contact and I also knew that the closer together we were the quieter we could speak. Jack was probably nearer the entry of the cave than Sergeant Org would have liked and his vampire hearing was acute. It was this fact that made me realize what he had to say must have been pretty important for him to risk being heard.

My body fought sleep while I waited for him to speak. Why couldn't he have come forth with whatever it was he had to say when I was wide awake and ready to talk? I vowed that when I finally made it home I was going to sleep for a week.

"My name isn't really Org," he started.

"I know. You're Prince Mandrake Organna," I said smugly.

He sucked in his breath as if he'd been punched in the stomach.

"Is there any secret that Mannador doesn't know?" he asked with dismay.

"It's a secret?" I gasped.

"Absolutely," he growled.

"I didn't know," I apologized.

"Did you really think your parents would promise you in marriage to a sergeant in the militia?" he asked incredulously.

"I... I don't know," I said.

His question made me feel just a little foolish.

"Well, they wouldn't. You are royalty, and royalty can only marry royalty," he said flatly.

"If you're a prince, then why am I in line for the throne? Shouldn't it go to you?" I asked.

"On Kurr it is the woman who inherits all titles and land," he explained. "It probably seems strange, since it's the opposite on earth, but it's the way it is here."

"If you're a prince and I'm a princess, then we are brother and sister! They were going to marry brother to sister?" I gasped, "That's disgusting."

"We are not related by blood," he said quietly. "My mother died and my father remarried. He died and then your mother married your father."

"That's complicated," I mused as I rolled his words over in my mind.

"Complicated, but the truth," he went on to explain. "Because we had no blood ties, but had strong title ties, they felt we'd be an ideal match."

"So, technically you're my step brother?" I asked hesitantly.

I was still trying to make sense of what he'd told me.

"I suppose you might say that. Your mother was my step mother, but she sent me away when she married your father, so I don't know what you'd really call us..." he hesitated, "except engaged."

"Wow. That's a lot to absorb," I said softly.

"It is," he agreed.

"Think of it," I chuckled lightly, "a prince and a princess huddled together hiding in a cave while being guarded by a king. That's something, isn't it?"

There was a brief moment of silence before he continued.

"I take my promises very seriously," he said somberly. "We were to be married when you reached the age of nineteen."

"That was five years ago," I interjected.

"I would have come for you, but the conditions here were not favorable for your return," he said with sincerity. "They still aren't."

"If all was well here on Kurr, you and I would be married by now?" I said with disbelief.

He nodded.

"But, Jack...." I started.

"Ah, Jack.... Yes," he interrupted me. "He's my best friend. Did you know that?"

I shook my head.

"We met when the captain married his vampire sister. Captain Berger introduced me as his second in command for the liaison between earth and Kurr and it's been that way ever since."

"Jack doesn't know you're a prince?" I asked.

"No, and I wouldn't advise telling him," he continued. "Jack's a pretty standup guy. He's stuck on doing the right thing. He only drinks the blood of animals and never to the point where they expire. He's compassionate toward humans to a fault. In fact, it was his compassion that earned him the kingship. He disagreed with the way their former king was handling the interaction between vampires and humans so strongly that he got some vampires to support him and led an uprising."

"He overthrew their king?" I said with wonder. "Isn't that like what King Orvis did with my parents?"

"It's nothing like it," Sergeant Org hissed with disgust. "Orvis seized the throne and killed your parents for power. Jack expressed his disapproval of the king's condoning of the slaughter of innocent humans by his vampire kingdom and he rose up against him to stop the madness. He didn't kill the king. In fact, the king still reigns a small region as the Black King. They call Jack the White King because of his goodness."

"I see...." I mused.

"I hope you do," he said breathlessly. "Jack comes from an era where honor and honesty prevail. If he had any idea that you and I were engaged, he would break it off between you two." He clapped his hands together for emphasis. "Kaput...that would be the end of it, no matter what he felt for you."

"I don't believe you. He loves me. He told me he loves me and would love me forever," I said defiantly. "Those aren't the words of a man who'd turn his back so willingly."

Just then Jack sauntered into the cave.

"Who's turning their back on who?" he asked.

Fool that I am, I ignored the sergeant's warnings and told all to Jack.

CHAPTER SIXTEEN

I couldn't believe it. After hearing the story of Sergeant Org's true identity and how we'd been promised in marriage when I was just a babe in arms, Jack stormed out of the cave and refused to talk to either of us. After one of the most excruciating hours I've ever endured, he finally returned. What I expected to hear and what I heard were two different things.

"Sit down, both of you," he commanded. We did as he bid. He looked directly into Prince Mandrake's eyes –I could no longer think of him as Sergeant Org-, "Why didn't you tell me your true identity? You know I would have kept it a secret."

"I know," the prince replied. "It's just that I'd promised Captain Berger never to tell a soul and I honor my promises. Besides, it was safer for you to not know."

"I suppose," Jack murmured. "We have a dilemma now." He turned to me, "I have watched you grow and loved you from afar since you were just a babe in arms. Being able to hold you and consider you mine was like a dream come true. I will always cherish it, but it can be no more."

I started to protest and he held his hand up to stop me.

"I am a King. You are a princess and he is a prince you were promised to by your parents at the time of your birth. You are destined to be King and Queen in your own right. I do not take brides-to-be away from fiancés. It is not done," he said firmly.

"So, now I suppose I must call you Lord Devon," I spat with rage. "Or should I call you Your Majesty?"

He looked stunned for the briefest of moments before his face grew like expressionless stone.

"My name is Jack. You may continue to call me Jack," he said softly.

"Well you can call me Her Majesty!" I screeched as I stomped out of the cave into the cool night air.

The cold air slapped some sense into me almost immediately. Prince Mandrake's words rolled around in my head, *'He comes from a different era.'* I turned on my heels to reenter the cave. Storming out would accomplish nothing. I needed to somehow make him see that we were in an age when arranged marriages weren't the in thing.

To my dismay, I entered the cave just in time to hear Jack insist that the prince and I be married right away. He apologized profusely for any pain he might have caused my fiancé by making love to me and taking my virginity. Then he went so far as to declare our marriage a wise political move that just might be the ticket to overthrow King Orvis.

Was I dreaming? If so, it was a nightmare and I needed to wake up. I slapped my face for good measure, but nothing changed. I was still standing behind my one true love while he apologized for loving me and gave me body and soul to another.

"I can't believe what I'm hearing," I said in words that were barely audible.

Jack turned to look at me. His emerald green eyes consumed me. It was as if he was drinking in his fill of me in hopes it would last him his lifetime… or at least mine. I could see the pain in his eyes and I could feel the pain in his heart. I didn't understand.

"Why?" I whimpered.

"It will be light soon. We should get moving. The sooner we get you two out of here, the better. Once we're back on earth, we'll discuss our strategy," he said as he moved past me like I wasn't even there.

I stood in the middle of the cave and wept like I'd never wept before. My fiancé came to hold me, but said nothing. What was there to say? He'd warned me against telling Jack and I hadn't heeded that warning. Now, Jack had spoken. I'd only known him for a short while, but I somehow knew that when Jack said something was law there was no arguing the fact, whether you were his subject or not.

When I finally calmed down enough to breath normally, I

looked up at my prince's handsome, compassionate face through tear filled eyes.

"Is there something I can call you besides Sergeant Org or Prince Mandrake?" I asked between hiccups.

He brushed the wet from my cheek with his thumb and planted a light, brotherly kiss on my forehead.

"My real name is Mandrake Buhemm Organna. You can call me Org or Drake, whichever suits you better," he said in a soft, soothing tone.

"What did my parents call you?" I asked.

"Drake," he replied.

"Drake," I repeated as I nestled my head against his chest.

"You don't have to marry me," he whispered. "This isn't the dark ages. It was a promise, that's all. No law will be broken if you decline. I.... I will still be there for you no matter what."

"Do you care for me?" I said hesitantly.

He wrapped his arms around me and held me tight against his torso. There was no erotic sensation in the act. It felt nothing like what went on inside me whenever Jack held me close. Even so, I felt comfortable and secure. I felt loved and safe in his arms and right then I needed that.

"I've known you since you were in your mother's womb. A day hasn't passed that I haven't at least checked in on your welfare. I couldn't imagine not having you to protect and care for. The only reason Jack was given the responsibility of guarding you full time with me as a backup was because I promised your parents on their death bed that I'd do whatever I could to regain the kingdom for you. I've been working with the coalition all these years trying to devise a way to seize back what is rightfully yours. Had it been otherwise, you would have felt my loving embrace daily," he said as his lips grazed my ear. "I've loved you all of your life."

Surprised by his admission, I turned my head to look at him and ran smack into his lips. Our kiss was slow and timid at first. I think we both felt guilty about Jack being so near. At least I did. Then I grew angry. Jack had literally thrown me away to this man, so why was I worrying about him being just yards away and possibly walking in on us? I allowed myself to embrace the kiss.

It was a nice kiss. It was a friendly kiss. It was a sensual kiss. It was a passionate kiss. But, it was a kiss I would forget within minutes, for it didn't compare with Jack's kisses. It left me flat. As the kiss grew more intense, so did Drake's body's reaction. I pulled away. I may have been okay with kissing him, but I had absolutely no intention of bedding him. His eyes were misty with emotion when I looked at him next. It was clear he had true feelings for me. I wished I could have said the same.

As I turned from Drake, I stopped short. There, leaning in the cave's entrance as if he didn't have a care in the world, was Lord Jack Devon, Vampire King. I wanted to slap him silly! The only thing that gave me any satisfaction at all was the hardened look in his eyes. It told me all I needed to know. He may have thrown me to the wind, but he still had feelings for me and he didn't like watching me kiss Drake. I wondered how he thought he'd deal with Drake marrying and bedding me. Damn his pride and honor anyway.

What a mess. I was a princess who had a fiancé back on earth, a fiancé on Kurr, and a vampire lover who wanted me, but wouldn't break a stupid marriage promise between two dead people and his best friend -who, in actuality, was my step brother and a prince. I made up my mind right then and there that I wasn't going to be manipulated by any of them.

I stopped at the doorway of the cave and looked Jack squarely and defiantly in the eye. I could have been imagining it, but I think I caught him flinch just a smidgeon. After staring long enough to get my point across, I turned to Drake.

"I will have to think about things," I said proudly. "Marriage is not something to take lightly. My parents made a promise to you, Drake, that I had no knowledge of. I made a promise to a life-long friend back on earth that must be broken if we wed. You and his majesty seem very stuck on the importance of honoring your promises. That being the case, well... you can see my dilemma, can't you?"

I left them open mouthed and at a loss for words as I walked proudly from the cave. I would be a victim no more!

Jack was the first to regain his sense. If I'd had my bow and arrows, I would have driven an arrow through that cold vampire heart of his from where I stood just outside the cave when the only thing I heard him say was, "So, your name is Drake?"

CHAPTER SEVENTEEN

We managed the remainder of the trip with no encounters with the enemy and no mishaps. We also shared no words. Each of us was lost in our own thoughts. Drake made a grunt or two when guiding us in this direction or that, but otherwise we moved in silence.

My eyes bore a hole in Jack's back as I seethed over his loathsome behavior, while wondering what he was thinking. I hoped he was thinking about the mistake he'd made and was searching for a way to make it right, but I guessed he was planning my wedding to Drake.

We reached the teleportation launch in the early evening. Once again I was exhausted. Jack hadn't offered to carry me at all, so the pace was far slower and the trip much longer than I could have been had he decided not to be an ass.

I groaned and stumbled onto the launch pad, earning looks of concern from Jack and pity from Drake, but nothing more. Drake positioned us for the transference and then hit the switch.

When the Dragos brought me to Kurr, I was one amongst a pile of people inside a craft and I was unconscious. I had no idea what to expect as one of three people huddled together on the launch pad. We held each other tight as the world vibrated around us. I looked to Jack for comfort and instantly regretted it. His eyes were locked on Drake's hand as it rested around my waist. Even in teleportation, he couldn't mask his true heart. He was infuriating.

When we stopped vibrating, we were still in the same spot. I moaned my dismay over the transference not working and earned a hug, a chuckle, and a peck on the cheek from Drake.

"We're on earth sweetie," he said gently. "It does look identical though. I'll give you that."

I chose to ignore the fact that he called me 'sweetie' as I stepped carefully off the launch pad. I looked around for Jack, but he'd disappeared. My heart fell out of my chest and rolled onto the ground, but I tried not to let Drake see. Instead, I allowed him to lead me by the hand off the launch pad and into the woods. We walked a short distance until a familiar looking cabin appeared. I looked around. Even in the darkness, I could tell that I was on home ground. I'd hiked and hunted these woods many times over the years and I'd slept in that cabin with my Aunt Jenny and James as well.

I was home.

"This is where I leave you princess," Drake whispered as he released my hand.

"What?" I panicked.

"Your Aunt Jenny is in there. She has your fiancé with her. Mark isn't it?" he added.

I nodded.

"Why?" I asked.

It was all too bewildering.

"We were gone longer than Jack or I expected. You've been missing on earth for one week. With Jack gone too, she went into a panic and has come here to search for the teleportation pad," Drake said softly.

"She knows?" I stammered.

"She knows about it, but she's never seen it. In fact, she's never seen me either; which is why we part company here. Explaining your... err... new shape will be difficult enough, without explaining me as well," he said sympathetically.

"If L'oana hadn't pulled her stunt then maybe..." I started.

"You would have been gone a day or two less, but your absence would have still been notice," he explained. "L'oana held us up by a few days, which is only minutes on earth."

"How old am I on Kurr?" I suddenly wanted to know.

"Kurrs live to be hundreds of earth years, so I wouldn't worry about it," he chuckled.

"How old is Jack?" I asked and then gasped as I realized what spewed out of my mouth without my realizing I'd be saying it.

Since he'd already told me the year he was turned vampire, the question was not only hurtful to Drake, but thoughtlessly senseless.

A look of sadness and pain swept briefly over his face before he regained composure and smiled.

"He's hundreds of years old. Somewhere around eight hundred, I think," he said.

"Eight hundred," I gasped, pretending that I didn't already know and also marveling at the thought of being that old. "How long will he live?" I continued asking with sincere curiosity.

"Thousands of years, if rumor is correct," he replied.

"You never asked him?" I was amazed.

"I never asked him," he said quietly.

"Are you curious about anything?" I mused.

"I'm curious about how you're going to explain that fine figure you're sporting," he chuckled.

I slapped him playfully on the chest and he pulled me close. Before I knew it, he had me in a lover's embrace. It was nice, it was sensual, it was a passionate kiss, and once again it left me flat. I cursed Jack silently for showing me how truly erotic kissing could be, while doing my best to respond to Drake in a way that wouldn't hurt his feelings.

As he pulled his lips from mine, he whispered, "I'm also curious who you'll end up choosing."

I wanted him to elaborate on that remark. What did he mean by who I'd end up choosing? Did he mean as a choice for husbands between him and Mark? Did he mean as a choice of the heart between him, Mark, and Jack? Just what did he mean?

I wasn't given the chance to ask him. Behind me came Aunt Jenny's loud squeal when she spotted me standing on the path. I looked for Drake, but he was gone. I longed for the ability to disappear like that. I had no clue how I was going to explain my new set of boobs and my well rounded back side to my aunt.

I searched the night for signs of Jack. I could feel him near, but he too was nowhere in sight. Squaring my shoulders, I took a deep breath and started toward the cabin. Cursed Jack anyway! It was his doing that caused my physical morphing to this extreme. Had he left me untouched I would have come home only slightly different. She may not have even noticed a little more curve, but what I was presenting to her was impossible to hide. He should be standing at my side helping me deal with this. I couldn't help wonder if that would have been the case, had he not learned about my parent's promise to Drake. Would he have stood by my side and declared his love for me to my aunt?

I'd never know.

I was so filled with frustrated rage over the state of everything that I thought I'd explode. I needed a release. I wanted to slap Jack until my hands fell off. That would be an excellent release. Instead I settled for turning to face the dark and empty looking woods and slowly presenting every inch of it the middle finger of both hands as I made a full circle. I knew he was out there. I knew he got the message.

I entered my aunt's arms with a satisfied smile.

CHAPTER EIGHTEEN

To say Aunt Jenny was shocked by my new look was an understatement. Since she'd been privy to my true story longer than I was, I decided to tell her the truth. We walked arm in arm around the clearing of the cabin while I described the horrors of what the Dragos were up to. We spent a few minutes focusing on missing people reported on the news and speculating whether or not they had been unfortunate victims of the Dragos before moving on to the next part of my little adventure.

Telling her about Jack rescuing me was both heart breaking and heart soothing. She smiled proudly as she praised him for the attention and care he'd always provided for me through the years. She confided how she didn't know how she'd have managed to keep me safe and hidden if it wasn't for him. To my surprise, she confided that there had been several attempts on my life since she'd taken parental responsibility and it was Jack who'd thwarted them.

When she whispered that she'd had a crush on Jack since she'd met him, my heart sank. The one person in the entire world I would never want to hurt was Aunt Jenny. Yet, if I continued with my story, I would do just that. Instead, I focused on Drake's role in it all and then introduced L'oana to the mix. I wanted to stall discussing my relationship with Jack as long as possible.

Aunt Jenny had limited knowledge of the Mannador, but she was at least aware of who they were and what they were capable of. She told me that she'd been hiding me from them and was aware they were searching the galaxy for me. As long as I was alive, I was a risk to King Orvis's claim to the throne; even if he did seize it instead of inherit it. I told her of my capture by King Orvis and his plans of marrying me to seal his claim to the throne. She said it made complete sense. His marrying me would solidify his claim to the throne and remove all doubt from anyone on planet Kurr. It was the logical thing for him to do, even if it wasn't the right thing for me.

It was then that I told her of my parent's promise of marriage between me and Drake. She said she was also aware of this fact, which was why she was not overly excited about my engagement to Mark. She told me she debated about telling me, but, since she'd never met Drake and had no idea how to reach him, she kept quiet.

She asked me what I intended to do about the fact that two men wanted to marry me. I couldn't give her an answer.

Of course, I knew that I could no longer marry Mark. I'd changed drastically both physically and emotionally. I was certain we'd no longer be what I'd considered a perfect fit. As for Drake, I still just didn't know. If Jack hadn't been in the picture, I would have readily accepted him into my life. He was handsome, strong, gentle, loving, caring, nice....and a prince. What more would a woman want? Sadly, even though he'd pulled back from me, in my mind Jack was still very much in the picture. Memories of his love making plagued me. I was actually comparing Drake's kisses to Jack's for crying out loud. How could I do the right thing for Kurr and honor my parent's agreement when every touch I received from Drake made me think of Jack? Of course, it didn't help that the two were best of friends.

I needed time to get used to all that had happened. I needed time to think.

When I finished my story, my aunt pushed for the answer to the question that had been on the tip of her tongue since we'd embraced. What happened to my figure? I took a deep breath and braced myself for what was to come. I couldn't lie to her. I just couldn't; no matter how much I wanted to. It was bad enough that I was going to admit to being foolish enough to fall for Jack's vampire wiles, but now that I knew she had a crush on him that was never fulfilled, I was going to hurt her as well. I closed my eyes and got it over with.

When I'd finished my story, she remained silent for so long

that I began to worry about how much I'd hurt her. Had my news cut her that deeply?

"He has always loved you, Jess," she said softly. "I'm not surprised that he succumbed to that love." She sighed deeply while standing up, "What surprises me is that he'd walk away from you so easily. That isn't the Jack Devon I know."

"You know his full name?" I asked.

I was annoyed that he'd share it with her and not me.

"Of course I know his full name. I also know his date and place of birth and home residence location. He's a vampire king you know," she replied.

"So I've heard," I said flatly.

"I see. Now that you've learned you're a princess of an entire planet you're unimpressed by a king of a mere species on earth," she snapped.

"A Mannador told me he was a king. Jack didn't think it necessary to tell me much of anything. I even had to learn his full name from someone else. I'm just irritated," I explained. "Plus, I'm exhausted."

"You've had a rough time of things, my sweetheart. Let's get you home and into a hot bath and bed," she cooed.

"That sounds like heaven," I smiled.

As we started walking to her SUV, I remembered Mark.

"What about Mark?" I asked.

"I'll take you home and come back for him. It'll give me time to make up some cock 'n bull story about where you've been and why you're suddenly sporting an impressive set of boobs!" she said laughingly.

"They are pretty great, aren't they?" I chuckled.

She reached over and tweaked my nipple in a light playful manner.

"You betcha!" she agreed. Then she said thoughtfully, "I always suspected you'd blossom into a beauty when you came into your own. I'm only glad I was around to witness it. I was afraid you'd be back on Kurr when it happened."

"I was," I said flatly.

"You know what I mean, you little minx," she chuckled.

"Yeah," I said as I climbed into the passenger's side of her SUV and settled in for the ride home.

As we drove down the long wooded dirt drive to the main road, I couldn't help scoping the woods for signs of either Jack or Drake. I sensed Jack was near, but what about Drake? Had he returned to Kurr?

I'd no more than thought the question than I got my answer. There, walking as casually as you please about fifty yards from the road to my right was Drake.

"Stop!" I shouted. "Stop, please."

Aunt Jenny slammed on the brakes and I hopped out. I called out to Drake. He must have been deep in thought because it took my calling to him several times before he looked up and recognize me. When he did, he smiled broadly and waved.

"Wait here," I said to my aunt before dashing off to speak with him.

If Jack was out there watching, I was sure his curiosity was eating at him. It made me glad. Of course that wasn't the reason I had her stop the car. I was genuinely concerned about where Drake was staying if he didn't plan on going back to Kurr right away. I needed to be sure he was okay before I settled in.

"You stayed?" I asked breathlessly when I reached him.

"Do you think I'd leave at the peak of the suspense?" he chuckled.

"What suspense?" I asked and then immediately remembered his remark about wondering who I'd pick. "Oh... that."

"Is that your aunt?" he asked curiously.

"She's just as curious about you," I teased. "Are you up to meeting her?"

He shrugged his shoulders, displaying an insecure side that I didn't know existed. After a little coaxing, he allowed me to lead him by the hand back to the vehicle. As I pulled him around to her side of the car I could clearly see the look of appreciation she had for his tall, rugged good looks. I studied him closely while he smiled and made polite conversation with her. He was truly a handsome man. His loving, gentleness served to heighten the visual. It was a shame I felt more sisterly toward him than anything else. I realized it was similar to what I felt for Mark. Once again, I cursed Jack Devon for showing me what true passion and love felt like.

I came around from my musing just in time to hear my dear aunt inviting Drake to be our houseguest. Although I wanted to be sure Drake was okay while on earth, that wasn't what I'd had in mind, but there was nothing I could do about it. He looked at me with childish delight and accepted. It was then that I realized what a difficult life he'd really led. Being invited into a home that was filled with loving warmth was probably a rarity for him.

CHAPTER NINETEEN

I didn't sleep for a week, but I did sleep around the clock. It was evening of the following day when I finally crawled out of bed and headed for the kitchen. I pulled my robe as best I could over my newly acquired figure, hoping it closed in places that it needed to close since the night shirt I found to go to bed in barely covered my crotch and what once were my underpants now resembled G-strings.

As I drew closer to the kitchen, I could hear the laughter of a man and a woman. It was a nice sound. I entered the kitchen with a smile on my face only to find Drake sitting alone at the table and my aunt and Jack huddled together near the counter in obvious conversation about something they both found amusing.

When they saw me they separated, but it was too late. The damage had been done. My smile was lost.

"There she is," Aunt Jenny cooed as she moved toward me with arms extended.

I accepted her hug and kiss while pulling at the flap of my robe self-consciously, hoping to close the gap just a little more. It didn't help that both Drake and Jack were openly admiring my bare legs and barely covered torso.

"You might want to take her shopping in the morning," Jack chuckled before turning his back on me and occupying himself with the drink he had in front of him.

"You drink coffee?" I barked.

"I drink a lot of things," Jack replied, still not looking my way.

"I thought you only drank blood!" I hissed.

"Oh, honey, that's just in the movies," Aunt Jenny said jovially. Either she missed the tension between Jack and me or she chose to ignore it. "I can't tell you the number of coffees and brandies Jack and I have had together over the years. It's just the first we've let you see it."

"Why is Drake sitting all alone at the table while you two are huddled together like... I don't know... something?" I bellowed.

I knew I was being ridiculous, but I couldn't stop myself.

"You're still pretty tired, huh?" my aunt said as she shoved a mug of coffee in my hand. "This'll help."

"I just finished a juicy steak, complements of the chef here," Drake smiled at my aunt and rubbed his belly gratefully. "It was more than Jack was able to witness, I'm afraid. He's over there drinking a cup of coffee for self-preservation." Drake let out a low laugh, "I almost had the pleasure of watching him vomit for a change."

"I would have liked that," I said as I took a seat next to Drake.

"I'll bet," Jack mumbled from the opposite side of the room.

He glanced at me only briefly, but it was long enough for me to recognize the heat of passion in his eyes before he took control and turned all stony faced on me.

"So, are you still watching me from afar, Uncle Jack?" I spat as sarcastically as I could.

He nodded, but said nothing.

"I hope you saw that very special wave I gave you last night," I said sweetly.

"It made my evening," he said with humor.

I'd expected him to be annoyed, not amused. This vampire was exasperating!

"How did you sleep?" Drake asked me softly as he put his hand over mine.

Once again I glanced at Jack just long enough to see him battle with jealousy before regaining control.

"Like a baby," I replied in a tone that I'll admit was a little overly sweet. "Knowing you were just down the hall was all I needed to feel safe enough to just let go and sleep the sleep of the dead."

I was sure I saw Jack's shoulders tense more than they should from just lifting a coffee mug to his lips. I could tell my comment took my aunt by surprise as well because she choked on her coffee. Call me a bad, but I was enjoying myself. It felt good to dig into that stony exterior that Jack decided to display whenever I was around. He may have been laughing merrily with my aunt just before I came onto the scene, but now he was a scowling fool.

It was a juvenile move on my part, but it made me happy.

Drake was eating the attention up. I felt a connection to him. Maybe it was because of our supposed betrothal or maybe it was because he'd been so sincere in his efforts to protect me and return me to my home. Whatever the reason, I wanted him to have something that I inherently knew he'd never known. If he did, it hadn't been since he was a very young boy. I wanted him to be happy. If talking to him in this way and letting him hold my hand made him happy, then what was the harm in it? Besides, it really was comforting to know he was just down the hall, so I wasn't telling a lie.

I could feel the cool night air on my breasts as Mark came through the back door. Drake made no effort to hide his pleasure in watching me do my best to cover them up, but when he saw the obvious discomfort I was in he changed his demeanor to one of genuine concern.

"Is everything alright?" he asked softly.

I pulled my hand from beneath his and used it to hold my robe closed at my throat.

"That's Mark, my fiancé." I whispered.

Drake's face turned scarlet for the briefest moment before he regained composure and turned to greet Mark. I didn't know him well enough to tell if his face went red from embarrassment or from jealousy. Funny how I'd known Jack only a little longer than Drake, yet I could easily tell his emotions. Catching myself comparing Drake to Jack once again, I scowled and shook my head.

"What's no?" Mark asked as he slid in the chair next to me.

"What are you talking about?" I asked nervously.

"You were shaking your head. Why?" Mark said as he turned his attention on Drake. "Who are you?" he asked in a manner that

I found terribly rude. Before I could chastise him on his lack of manners he looked at Jack and added, "And you..." He turned to Aunt Jenny, "Who are these guys?"

"I'm surprised at your lack of manners young man," she said, beating me to the punch.

It was just as well. Her tone was far more condescending than mine could ever be. It probably came with age and living.

"I didn't mean to be rude," he said as he turned to look at me. "It just that Jess disappeared for a week and when she returns two strangers come with her."

"Who said they were strangers?" my aunt snapped.

"Well... I..." he stammered and then suddenly his eyes flew open, "You've got breasts!"

I was mortified.

"You didn't tell him?" I whine to my aunt.

"I didn't know how," she replied.

"Tell me what?" Mark demanded. "What's going on here?"

"I... went away and had plastic surgery," I said with haste.

After which I immediately bit my tongue. I was never good at lying and Mark saw right through me. His eyes narrowed to tiny slits as he stood up and walked to the door. He stared vehemently at Drake before turning his look of hate on Jack.

"When you're ready to stop spewing bullshit, give me a call," he spouted before turning on his heels and leaving without so much as a good-bye.

The room was abnormally silent and still while we processed what just occurred. It was Aunt Jenny who finally broke the silence.

"Well, that went... well," she said.

I expected at least a chuckle from Drake or Jack, but they both remained silent. Definite looks were exchanged. I tried to catch the attention of at least one with my eyes, but neither would look my way. It was clear to see they shared the same opinion of my fiancé and lifelong friend, and it didn't look like it was a good one.

I finally gave up on the subtlety.

"Why don't you like him?" I blurted, none too softly.

Aunt Jenny gasped at my outburst before looking at Jack. It was as if she was searching his stony face for an answer.

"He's the son of my best friend and neighbor," she said in a manner that led me to believe she was insulted for Mark and his mother.

"How long have you known them?" Jack demanded.

"Since we moved here," she explained.

"Why wasn't I informed?" Jack continued.

"That I befriended the family next door?" she said, exasperated.

"I'm to know everyone she associates with. You know that!" he shouted.

I was shocked to see them arguing. I was even more shocked that it was over Mark.

"Well, if you were guarding her like you were supposed to be doing, then it would have come to your attention at some time over the last twenty-two years, wouldn't you think?" my aunt hissed. "But then, she was also kidnapped and almost eaten."

"That's harsh," Drake said softly.

"So is his attacking me over Jessica's friendship with the boy next door," she replied.

Emotions were certainly flying.

"I need to know all you can tell me about them," Drake continued.

"You need to...." Aunt Jenny stopped to level her breathing. "Excuse me a moment," she said before storming outside.

CHAPTER TWENTY

"Is someone going to tell me what's going on?" I asked cautiously.

Jack looked at me as if realizing I was still in the room for the first time. He walked over, took the seat next to me, and then took my hand. Drake took the other one. There are no words that would even remotely touch on the impact my body had when those two held my hands. The closest thing to it would be to say it was like a bolt of erotic lightning surged through me.

I visibly shuddered. Jack released my hand. Drake did not.

"I want you to tell me all about this boy, Mark," Jack said firmly.

"Why don't you like him?" I asked again.

"How did you meet him?" Drake interjected.

"He's always been around for as far back as I can remember. We grew up together," I replied. "I don't understand. I told you I was engaged..."

"His mother... what's she like?" Jack continued.

"I don't know, really. I rarely see her," I said thoughtfully. "Mark is mostly over here. She calls Aunt Jenny on the phone a lot, but hardly comes over."

"Is Mark her natural son?" Drake asked boldly.

My eyes flew open at his astuteness.

"He's adopted, like me," I said with surprise. I looked Jack in the eye and then continued, "In fact, there are so many similarities in our circumstances it's uncanny. His mother is also not married and they moved here only a six months after we did. They live just down the road. Our lands border each other. If you've been watching me, I'm surprised you didn't notice him." After another lengthy silence I tried again, "Why don't you like him?"

"I knew you had the boy next door coming around. I just didn't.... He never tried to have sex with you?" Jack blurted out.

"You of all people know better," I spat.

"Why is that?" Jack continued. "Aren't you engaged?"

"Well, Mr. It's-None-Of-Your-Business...unlike someone else I know, Mark wanted to keep it special and wait until our wedding night," I replied in a huff.

Pow! That nailed him right in the heart. I smiled to myself as I watched him struggle to hide his reaction to my slam from Drake and me. Drake didn't take such pains to hide his surprise at my cutting comment. He lifted an eyebrow and shook his head.

"It's hard to believe the man never laid a hand on you, princess," Drake said softly. "Even in your pre-development stage, you were a rare beauty."

I almost cried at his gentle complement until I looked at Jack and the anger rose again. So, for Jack's benefit, more than anything else, I told the truth; hoping I'd hit my mark just one more time.

"I never said he didn't touch me," I confessed. "I just said he didn't take my virginity."

Bam! Oh yes... that remark hit its mark just fine. In fact, it brought the jealous dragon to life in Drake as well. Feeling I needed to say something to tone down the fiery sparks of hatred and jealousy in the air, I continued, "Do you know how rare it is these days to find a man who isn't hot to take your maidenhead and then drop you at the first opportunity?" Oops... I didn't mean that to slam Jack, but it sure came out that way. I didn't wait for his reaction. "What I'm trying to say is that Mark is a rare find in today's world. Times today aren't like they were when you were young, Jack. You come from a different era. In today's world, taking a girl's virginity is as common as buying a pair of designer jeans. In fact, it's considered unpopular to graduate high school a virgin. If I'd been with any other guy, I probably wouldn't have. It was because of Mark that I retained some semblance of innocence."

"How did he touch you?" Drake asked between clenched teeth.

Oh boy, this was going badly.

"What?" I asked with as much innocence as I could muster.

"You heard me," he practically bellowed.

Boy, he sounded cold.

"Well…. We did some exploring," I stammered. "We're engaged after all."

"You were engaged," Jack spat. "No more!"

"You can't tell me…." I began.

"No more!" he roared.

"Mark and I are consenting adults," I said defiantly. "If we want to marry, we'll marry. You have no say, Jack."

In truth, I'd made up my mind to break off the engagement with Mark at my earliest opportunity, but I wasn't about to tell that pain in the ass vampire my decision. Let him stew on it for a while.

"That's true, you don't" Drake broke in.

Jack's eyes flew open.

"You'd let her go ahead with this?" he asked.

Drake closed his eyes and hung his head.

"She is my princess… my queen… and my one true love," he said. "I only want her to be happy and safe."

"You believe she'd be safe with him?" Jack said with disbelief.

"She'd be taboo to King Orvis," Drake replied.

"She'd be taboo to you too," Jack spat.

Drake shrugged his shoulders and shook his head slowly. His sadness over Jack's comment permeated the air. Before I realized what I was doing I pulled my hand free and cupped his cheeks. Tears prompted by his sadness welled inside me.

"Tell me why?" I said softly.

"It's a very long story," Drake whispered.

"I have all night," I said firmly, while I searched his eyes.

"I'll leave you two lovebirds to your story time," Jack sputtered.

Before either of us could protest, he was gone.

"He loves you so much, he can't stand it," Drake said quietly before laughing weakly. "The problem is that I love you too."

"Would you give me up as easily as he did for the sake of honor?" I asked.

"I hope I never have to find out," Drake replied.

I looked at him curiously and then stood up.

"I need more coffee, how about you?" I asked.

"Have you got anything stronger?" he asked.

"We have some brandy," I said with surprise.

It just never dawned on me to offer my hero from Kurr alcohol.

"That's perfect," he replied.

I went to the liquor cabinet and pulled out a bottle of Don Pedro. As I reached for two snifters, I spotted my aunt and Jack outside through the window. They weren't arguing, but they looked like they were in a pretty intense conversation. I shrugged off my jealousy and moved back to the table. After pouring us each two fingers of brandy, I sat back and swirled mine absent mindedly while I waited for him to speak.

To my surprise, he tossed the brandy back in one gulp and motioned for more to be poured. I said nothing and did as he asked. This time he treated my top shelf brandy with the respect it deserved.

"I told you about how you and I came to be somewhat related... by law at least... and then engaged," he started.

I nodded.

"What I didn't tell you was that my mother had an affair while married to my father," he began. "She gave birth to a boy. It was immediately apparent to my father that the child wasn't his. He inherited too much from his true father." Drake hesitated for a moment before continuing. It was clear he didn't want to say what came next. "My father went into a jealous rage and killed my mother."

"Oh Drake! I'm so sorry," I gasped.

He waived his hand as if to brush it off and then continued, "Soon afterward, my father married your mother. Because of my mother's infidelities, he imposed his distrust on your mother. She couldn't even go from one end of the palace to the other without an escort. It was like she was living in a prison and she resented it." He looked me in the eye, "Do you remember me telling you that it is the woman who has the rule on Kurr?"

"I do," I replied.

"When my father married your mother, all of my mother's power was transferred to her. One day, she could take no more of my father's jealousy and possessiveness and she arranged for him to have an accident."

"Are you saying my mother was a murderer?" I gasped.

"I'm saying that she used her power to free herself. If that means she was a murderer, then so be it. I don't look at it that way," he shrugged.

"But, he was your father," I said.

"He was my father, but he never cared for me. I wasn't a girl to inherit the throne and he couldn't look at me without remembering my mother. I was shut away from him. I didn't really know him," he said softly.

Now I understood the pain and loneliness I felt from him and my desire to give him just a piece of happiness, if I could.

"Your mother kept me around for a while, but when she married your father I was sent to live in a country estate with plenty of housekeepers and a governess... No mama and no papa."

"You poor, poor man," I said as I wiped a tear from my cheek.

He reached over and completed the job for me with his strong thumb.

"I'm not telling you this to gain sympathy," he said, "but I thank you for it. I'm telling you this because you need to know."

"What? What do I need to know?" I asked.

"The bastard my mother gave birth to... my half-brother. Well, my father tried to kill him, but a wet nurse took pity on him and scooped him away before my father could accomplish the task. She hid him underground on Kurr until she was able to find someone to take him far away." He stopped and looked at me with pain in his eyes.

"I'm trying to understand," I said.

"The father of my half-brother is King Orvis. My mother had an affair with a Mannador," he almost whispered.

"Oh!" I gasped.

"My half-brother is also a prince from a very strong lineage. He is of both Mannador royalty and Kurr royalty. The Mannador males inherit and it's my understanding King Orvis is trying to change the laws of Kurr in the same way. If that is the case, it makes him quite a catch in the galaxy."

"I should say," I agreed.

After a moment of silence, I looked at Drake and panic filled me. Oh no... it couldn't be!

"Has your half-brother ever met you?" I asked.

"Once," he replied.

"Do you know where they've hidden him?" I continued.

"I knew the planet, but not the location, until recently," he responded.

I took a deep breath and closed my eyes. I needed to ask, but I wasn't sure I wanted the answer.

"Does he know who he is?" I asked in a voice just above a whisper.

"I'm not sure, but I don't think so," he said softly.

I poured more brandy and downed it in one gulp.

"Mark?" I asked.

Drake nodded slowly.

The room went black.

CHAPTER TWENTY-ONE

When I awoke I was lying on my bed in my room, the sun was shining, and there was a pile of new clothes on the chair next to me. Aunt Jenny was bustling around the room tidying up what didn't need to be tidied since I'm an obsessive compulsive neat freak. It was clear she was just looking for something to keep her occupied while she nervously waited for me to rejoin the world.

"Good morning," I yawned.

"Good afternoon," she replied with a smile.

"What time is it?" I asked.

"Somewhere around three o'clock, I think," she said as she fidgeted with the tie backs of my draperies.

"You went shopping?" I asked.

"Without you... I know, but I only picked up a few things. You can get the rest yourself when you're ready. I just didn't think you wanted to go shopping when you had nothing to wear shopping," she chuckled.

"That makes sense," I said with a yawn.

"Everyone is downstairs waiting for you," she said nervously.

"Everyone?" I said with confusion.

"Get dressed. They're waiting," she tossed over her shoulder as she left the room.

I stared at the pile of clothes that clearly looked like they'd been purchased at the local western store while remembering my conversation with Drake. It all seemed so surreal. Talk about a tangled web! If only Jack would just take me away from it all. Did he know Mark was Drake's half-brother or did he simply recognize Mannador in him once he'd gotten a closer look at him?

"Well, if he didn't know, I'm sure he does now," I mumbled, "Wonderful. Just wonderful."

I pulled on a straw skirt that fell just above my ankles, a pair of decorative cowboy boots and a beaded tee shirt before running a brush through my bed head and tying my long hair in a pony- tail, after which I scooted to the bathroom just outside my bed- room door to wash my face and brush my teeth. I was about to go downstairs when I remembered the moccasins Mangoot gave me. I searched the room and eventually located them beneath my bed. Pulling off my new boots was no easy task, but I finally man- aged and tossed them away with a grunt. It felt wonderful to slip on the soft supple moccasins and wiggle my toes. That was more like it. Now, if only I hadn't left my bow and arrows on Kurr. If I was going into battle it would have been nice to dress the part.

The moccasins allowed me to slip downstairs unnoticed. I stalked across the dining room while eavesdropping on the con- versation between several people going on in the kitchen. From the sound of things, they were not in agreement on a very impor- tant topic.

Me.

Aunt Jenny was clearly unhappy with the chain of events and was airing her opinion to the others. She felt strongly that she should have been kept better in the loop since it was her respon- sibility to raise and watch over me. Of course Jack was always in the background, but the fact of the matter was he did not contrib- ute to the day to day hands on responsibilities that might have been handled differently, had she been properly informed and updated.

"Oh, shut it, Jenny," Mark barked.

My eyes flew open as wide as they could go and I covered my mouth to stifle a gasp. I couldn't believe my ears. Had Mark really spoken to my aunt in that manner?

"I want everyone to listen to me for a minute," Mark contin- ued. "That means you too, vampire." The sarcasm in his voice when he addressed Jack was undeniable. "Did you really think I wouldn't know who I was? Did you actually think I didn't know who you both were when I came here yesterday? It's no wonder the Dragos got their hands on her. You two are nothing more than bumbling fools." It sounded as if they were trying to respond, but he gave them no opportunity, "I am Prince Markmannon Orvis, son of the great King Orvis and the true queen of Kurr. My claim to the throne is far stronger than yours, Mandrake. Since the princess agreed to marry me prior to learning of your claim to her, and considering my royal lineage, I'd say your agreement with her mother and father is null and void."

I flew into the kitchen.

"How long?" I spat, "How long have you been lying to me?"

Mark wore a look of surprise as he tried his best to regain his composure.

"Good day, Princess," Drake said softly. "I trust you are better?"

"I was until I heard the bullshit coming out of this son-of-a-bitch!" I roared. I glowered at Mark. He moved toward me and I backed away. I had no intention of letting him touch me ever again. "Did you know your dear old dad abducted me and tried to marry me against my will?" I hissed.

"No, I didn't... but don't worry. Once we are married and return to Kurr he will be forced to abdicate the throne. He'll have no choice," Mark replied.

"There's always a choice, my man," Drake said. "It's my understanding your father's grown accustomed to the throne. Considering the fact that he's never laid eyes on you, you might want to rethink his level of loyalty."

Mark looked uncomfortable, but said nothing.

"There's also the fact that Jessica has been made aware of this agreement you claim is null and void and has met the man her parents promised her to," Drake added, "Did you think about the fact that she just might prefer me to you?"

"You don't really think I'd marry you, do you?" I spat in Mark's direction. "I hate to burst your bubble, Mark, but I'd made up my mind to call off the engagement before I knew this about you. I was going to tell you at the first opportunity. Now that I see who you really are, I'm sure I made the right decision."

"Oh, thank the saints," Aunt Jenny blurted.

"You don't mean that Jessophlyn," Mark said breathlessly.

The name he used for me sent a buzzing through my body

and felt incredibly familiar. I didn't like it.

"What did you call me?" I asked.

"He used your birth name," Jack said flatly. "It appears he's done his homework."

I turned to look at Jack as if seeing him for the first time. Somehow I'd managed to back myself up against him. It felt so right, I hadn't even noticed. He'd also rested his hand on my shoulder, another thing that hadn't felt out of place.

"You people are all crazy!" I screamed before fleeing the house.

I knew it was futile to think I could run away from a vampire, a Kurr prince, and a Mannador-Kurr prince, but I gave it my all. Of course Jack was the first to reach me.

"I can't take any more. Get me out of here Jack," I begged while choking on my tears. "Please!"

He swept me into his arms and we disappeared into the trees at vampire speed.

CHAPTER TWENTY-TWO

He traveled longer and farther than he'd ever traveled while carrying me in his arms. Instead of stopping abruptly as he had in the past, he gradually slowed, giving my body the opportunity to adjust. As a result, when he finally landed us on top of a majestic Canadian mountain I was able to enjoy stable legs that allowed me to walk about immediately. I stood still, waiting for the purging of my stomach to begin. To my surprise and delight, I felt a little nauseous, but nothing came forth.

He took me by the hand and pulled me along behind him. I noticed his breathing was a bit labored. Another fallacy uncovered. Vampires eventually get tired.

When we reached a large flat surfaced boulder positioned securely against the mountainside, he pressed on it lightly and it swung open. With my hand in his, he led me down a long underpass until we reached the other side. My breath caught in my throat at the vision of beauty before me.

It was an immaculate mountain village filled with perfectly designed, perfectly proportioned, and perfectly positioned homes. Flowers of all varieties lined the streets and sidewalks and coated the surrounding fields. Butterflies fluttered their greeting while birds sang their praises. It was like a piece of heaven.

"Where are we?" I asked with awe.

"My home," he replied.

"You live here?" I was stunned.

"Many live here. It is the capital of my kingdom," he said passionately.

"It's beautiful," I whispered.

"My house is this way," he volunteered.

There was pride in his voice.

I followed him down a narrow path and then back up the side

of the mountain. The village grew smaller and I thought what a pity his house wasn't nestled amongst those beautiful structures. I was just beginning to wonder if he might have made his home inside the mountain like he had on Kurr when the ground leveled off and before me was an enormous fairy tale type castle; complete with moat, turrets, and drawbridge.

"This?" I chuckled.

"Too much?" I asked nervously.

"Let's just say I didn't expect it," I replied.

"You're the first to see it," he said softly.

"Aunt Jenny claimed to know where you lived," I said jealously.

"Knowing and visiting are not the same," he replied. "Come," he said before lifting me into his arms and jutting into the sky.

We were flying! Every other time I'd been traveling in Jack's arms or on his back, we ran and jumped at vampire speed. This time we were actually flying and it was slow enough to allow me a panoramic view of his kingdom.

It was magical and I told him so.

When he set us down in his courtyard, we were greeted by the castle staff and residents as if they'd expected him. What struck me the most was the genuine look of pleasure in everyone's eyes as they bowed and welcomed him home. It was in stark contrast to the oppressive ambiance and fearful mood of King Orvis's court.

"You left without breakfast," Jack said softly as he clapped his hands.

"Do you have real food here?" I asked as a young man scurried up and waited on bended knee for Jack's instruction.

He ignored my question and ordered the table set for two in his private rooms. The lad bowed and scurried off to do his bidding. I could have sworn he was skipping with pleasure.

This seemed such a surreal land. For the first time, I questioned whether I was really asleep and if this entire drama was a dream. After all, I'd wanted nothing more than for Jack to swoop me away from it all and take me where we could live happily ever after.

"Am I dreaming?" I asked timidly.

I wasn't sure I wanted to know the answer because I knew that if I was dreaming I never wanted to wake up.

"I love you," he said before kissing me with that familiar passion I'd missed so miserably.

I was sure then I was dreaming and I also knew I never wanted to wake up. Some way, somehow, I'd find a way to keep in dream zone and in Jack's arms.

"Never stop," I said between kisses. "Love me always and in all ways. I beg you."

I knew I was being a bit corny and wimpy, but, since it was my dream and I was the director, I thought why not? If a dream was the only way I could experience Jack's love again, then so be it.

He waltzed me through the great hall. His lips never left mine. His hands roamed my body as if to burn every inch of it in his memory. I did the same. He was wearing a button down linen shirt and jeans instead of the Kurr dress of tunic and leather pants. I couldn't decide which ensemble made him look sexier. As I ripped his shirt open to gain access to his strong, muscular chest, I decided the linen shirt got my vote. He looked like he belonged on the cover of a sexy romance novel.

Instead you're the star of my dream, I thought with a giggle.

We walked, twirled, and kissed up three flights of broad marble stairs to his private rooms, leaving articles of clothing along the way. Had it been real and not a dream I might have worried about what the help would think. Instead, I eagerly disrobed and helped him disrobe without worrying about where we were or who might see us.

He'd barely opened the door to his room before we were rolling around on the bed, sharing, discovering, and enjoying each other in a way that only people in love can do. It was the most erotic, orgasmic, sensual, yet peaceful experience I'd ever had; real or created. I hoped that, when I was forced to awaken, I'd never lose the memory of the love we shared in this most beautiful figment of my imagination.

"Why do you think this is a dream?" Jack asked as he lay next to me and pulled me close.

His heart was beating its usual double time. It was a wonderful beat.

"I love listening to your heart. It's musical," I sighed.

He gave a light chuckle and rolled back on top of me. That's the wonderful part about dreams. It didn't matter whether vampires had incredible stamina for love making or not. In my dream, whatever I desired was what happened. At that moment, I desired a repeat of our love making. I couldn't imagine ever growing tired of it.

I'll admit that by the time Jack was satiated, my body was just a little sore. I found it odd for me to add that to the dream. Perhaps it was my guilt surfacing. After all, I was promised in marriage to two others. One was a kind and loving man who I was promised to since birth and the other was my lifelong friend. Yet, here I was fantasizing a torrid rendezvous with a vampire and I'd turned Mark into a villain in order to justify it.

The food arrived, but we simply lay naked in bed with only a sheet to provide some semblance of modesty. Although they were aware of our presence, the servers didn't seem to mind or bother with us. They laid out a purely vegetarian spread containing fruits and garden vegetables, a wedge of cheese and a round loaf of brown bread. I smiled when they uncorked a bottle of Dom Perignon. Of course! What else would I place in my romantic dream lunch?

When we were alone again, Jack leapt off the bed and headed into the washroom. I heard the shower running and giggled. The marble floor felt cool underfoot as I rushed to join him. We laughed, splashed, made love just one more time, and washed each other until we glowed. Jack presented me with a thick, soft robe to wrap in, donned one himself, and pulled me to the table.

The food was sweet, fresh, and absolutely delicious. It was so satisfying, I never noticed the absence of meat. I wondered why I hadn't fantasized Jack eating meat instead of me being a vegetarian.

He sat opposite me and cocked his head.

"I just can't figure why you keep thinking this is all a dream," he mused.

"Stay out of my head," I ordered playfully.

"Stop broadcasting so loud," he replied with a grin.

"I can't believe my eyes!" screeched a woman from the doorway. "Have you lost your mind, Jack?"

I sat upright and shook my head to clear it. There, before me, stood the woman I vaguely remembered as my mother. I may have been only a toddler when she left, but hers was a face I'd never forget. She glowered at me with a look that I could only describe as hate. What was happening?

My dream was crumbling around me.

"How could you bring Helen of Troy to our sanctuary? Soon they'll follow," she hissed. "Is nothing sacred?"

"You don't understand," Jack actually stumbled over his words, "I... l love her."

"She's not yours to love, you fool!" she shouted as she bared her fangs.

I closed my eyes and told myself repeatedly that it was only a dream.

"Give it a rest, will you?" Sara hissed. "I can assure you this is no dream. It's very, very real."

"Mother?" I whispered.

"Not anymore. I forfeited that abhorrent chore to Jenny," she spat. "She was far more suited for the drudgery of bringing up a kid."

"You're dead," I said timidly.

I was still trying to determine if what was happening was truly happening.

"Send her back, Jack," she demanded.

"The last I knew, I was the king and you were the king's sister, not his superior," Jack said with authority. "You may leave, Sara."

"You're making a mistake," she said vehemently. "Not only will they come looking for her, but the blacks will come calling just as soon as they discover you've brought a human here. Either way, you'll lose her. Send her back."

"Jack?" I whimpered.

I was beginning to think I wasn't dreaming after all. My fairy tale was rapidly turning into a terrifying nightmare.

"It's alright, my love. Sara was just leaving," he said softly.

When he moved to my side, picked me up in his arms, and informed his sister that no one was to even think about touching me, I felt confidence return. I shuddered briefly when she gave one last fangy -and very terrifying- snarl before leaving. I gave thanks that I was in his arms when it happened.

"This isn't a dream," I mused.

"I can see why you'd question my love. I've been a bit of a shit," he said with sincerity.

"I won't argue that," I replied half-heartedly.

He kissed me long and hard before setting me back down in the chair.

"It was a serious move bringing you here," Jack said. "Sara's right about that."

"You're going to send me away?" I cried. "No! Not again. This can't be happening."

He knelt down beside me and cupped my chin with his strong, slender fingers.

"When I conceded to Drake and his marriage arrangement, it felt like someone took an axe to my chest. Every inch of it pained me. When I saw you two talking, I wanted to rip his throat out. When I saw him kiss you.... well... let's just say I can't go through that again. A vampire rarely finds someone who makes him react like that, but when he does, it's a powerful thing. I've always known you were meant for me. So did you. Do you know that when you were just a toddler you sat on my lap and told me you and I would wed? I will never concede to anyone's claim on you again. Friend or no friend... honor be damned. Be assured, my love, that as long as you live I will never send you away."

"I'm going to die before you!" I gasped.

It was a realization that slapped me in the face like a bucket of ice water.

"It's inevitable, as long as you stay as you are," he sighed.

I fell against him and held him as tight as my arms would allow. I wanted to secure him to me while making the world disappear. What started out a romance was rapidly becoming a tragedy.

"Why does Sara hate me?" I whispered.

"She's just afraid of what's to come," he replied softly as he stroked my long, silky air.

"Will Drake come for me?" I asked, even though I didn't want an answer.

"Drake may be a prince, but he is also a soldier; a very confused soldier right now," he said. "Discovering you have been consorting with his half-brother was a shock. My carrying you away probably added to it. I'm not sure how he'll react."

"Do you know him well?" I asked hesitantly.

"No one knows Drake well. He's a prince in disguise as an active soldier for the coalition. Secrecy is a vital part of his make-up," he said and then added, "I suppose I know him better than most."

"He called you his best friend," I said softly.

"As he is mine," Jack almost whispered.

"Will they fight over me?" I gasped.

The realization of why Sara was so upset finally struck.

"They may fight to get you back and then maybe each other," he said. "It's difficult to tell."

"What did she mean when she said the blacks will come for me?" I asked.

"You worry for nothing," he said as he gently set me from him.

I need to tend to a few things. Feel free to stay as you are or dress and explore." A mischievous gleam appeared in his emerald green eyes. "I'd say explore as you are, but I'm afraid my staff wouldn't get any work done."

"Your staff!" I wailed. "They saw us!"

He gave a smile, a wink, and a mischievous nod before kissing me lightly on the forehead and hurrying off to get dressed.

CHAPTER TWENTY-THREE

It was my intention to never leave Jack's rooms again. The thought of facing his staff after the show we'd provided them was mortifying. I did, however, put my clothes on. I didn't want his staff coming in to clear things up and see me lounging around in Jack's robe like some hired prostitute. Perhaps if they saw me dressed and well-coiffed they'd forget about my wanton display.

From the size and number of rooms in his suite, I guessed he occupied the majority of the third floor; if not all of it. Jack had a wonderful array of books in the small library that was part of his rooms. I helped myself to a Jane Austin novel and headed to a light and airy sitting room I'd noticed while exploring. I selected a large floral tapestry overstuffed chair that was positioned next to the floor to ceiling window and settled in for a good read.

I was about to start the third chapter of Pride and Prejudice when Sara burst into the room. I looked around nervously. This vampire may have been my adopted mother when I was young, but it was clear I meant nothing to her now. I wondered if she was a vegetarian like Jack or if I needed to worry about my safety. Without even realizing it, my hand flew protectively to my throat.

"You're still here?" she moaned.

"Why do you hate me so?" I demanded as I stood up to display my full height.

I was actually an inch taller than she was, which was saying a lot since I was only five foot three. I hoped the fact that I had size to my advantage might help balance the situation.

"Do you actually think you can intimidate me?" she chuckled. "You do know I'm an eight-hundred-year old vampire. I could crush you with my pinky."

"You were my mother once. I don't understand," I said wistfully.

"I loved my Berger. I loved him more than I loved life itself," she glowered. "Because of you, he's gone. He died defending you. Did you know that?"

I shook my head.

"That's why I tossed your care off to Jenny. I can't stand the sight of you. If I'd had my way, I'd have left you buried alongside my husband!"

I gasped at her remark. Without warning my claustrophobia affliction kicked in. I started gasping for air as if I was suffocating.

"So you remember?" she preened.

"You...did. You buried me!" I screeched.

"And that stupid brother of mine unburied you. Although, I'll never understand why," she spat. "He should have left you there to rot. You're nothing but trouble."

"I... I'm sorry... I...." I gasped.

"Spare me," she spat.

"You buried me alive?" I said aloud, as if it would help me comprehend her heinous act.

"It was nothing less than you deserved. You were a trouble-some little whiney brat that demanded attention and brought trouble wherever you went," she said coldly.

"You buried me alive?" I repeated.

"Sara's not as evil as she sounds," Jack said as he causally entered the room. Sometimes her emotions get the better of her. When a vampire loves, there is no comparison. She blames you for the death of her one true love before she was able to convince him to turn vampire. Her grief got the better of her."

"He refused to turn vampire because of you!" she spat. "If he'd allowed me to turn him, they wouldn't have gotten the jump on him and he'd be alive today."

"Who is 'they'?" I asked.

"The Mannador, who else?" she replied.

"I don't understand why the Mannador tried to kill me and then try to marry me. Either they want me dead or they want me shackled in marriage, but they can't have both," I complained.

"When you were a child and King Orvis just seized the thrown, there was chaos everywhere. People were murdering just for the sake of murdering. Many Mannadors feared your supporters might find you and reclaim the throne before King Orvis had secured it fully," Jack explained. "Now that he is secure, he seeks appeasing those who still oppose him by marrying you. With you on the throne as his bride, there can be no opposition."

"What about Mark?" I asked. I was now convinced I hadn't dreamt his admission to being King Orvis' bastard and Drake's half-brother.

"King Orvis will kill him to eliminate the competition," Sara interjected.

"His own son?" I gasped.

"She's very soft, isn't she?" Sara chuckled.

"She's perfect," Jack said as he looked at me lovingly.

"Little miss perfect is one walking time bomb and you know it," Sara argued. "Are you prepared for battle?"

"As a matter of fact, we are," Jack said smugly.

"The blacks?" Sara gasped.

"The fiancés," Jack replied.

"Funny," Sara spat as she twirled on her heels and left in a huff.

"She buried me alive," I said as I watched her leave.

"It was an emotional reaction that I know she didn't mean," Jack explained. "Once this is all over and you get to know her, you'll see the wonderful side that I know so well and that Captain Berger fell in love with. Vampires are powerful beings and so are our emotions."

"Would you bury me alive?" I asked.

"I might do it to someone who tried to harm you, but never you," Jack cooed as he stepped forward and pulled me into his arms. "Drake was spotted coming up the mountain. He's an excellent tracker."

"Will you hurt him?" I asked with concern.

"You worry for him?" Jack raised an eyebrow. "Should I be jealous?"

I slapped his chest lightly and kissed his cheek.

"Don't be silly. He's your friend and he's been my guard as well all these years," I said.

"He loves you," Jack murmured.

"Will you hurt him?" I repeated.

"He's my friend. If we can talk it out as friends, then that's what we'll do," Jack said firmly.

"If you can't?" I asked hesitantly.

"I won't let you go," he replied.

I looked at him long and hard before saying, "I hope not." After a long, sensual and very satisfying kiss, I looked Jack in the eye. "Promise me you'll do everything you can to keep the peace with Drake. I love you Jack. You know this, but I am bonded to him in a variety of ways and I like him very much. He's a good, kind man."

"He's also a killer," Jack said firmly.

"He's a soldier, of course, but that doesn't change the fact that he's shown me nothing but goodness and kindness. He loves me. I can't help that," I said with a sigh, "but I don't want to see him killed because of that love."

"If I weren't around, would you love him back?" Jack asked hesitantly.

"You are around," I replied firmly.

"If I wasn't?" he persisted.

"No one has ever made me feel the way you make me feel. Until I met you, I didn't know what love was. I'd never felt the wild abandonment of true passion. I'd never known joy," I said as I took his face in my hands and pulled it close to mine, "If you had never come into my life I would have continued functioning as a half-dead puppet. You brought me to life. I could never love anyone but you, but I can like someone very much."

"Sometimes that's enough," he whispered.

"Maybe once, but not anymore," I replied.

CHAPTER TWENTY-FOUR

It took several hours before the horns sounded the arrival of a visitor. Drake was led into the great room of the castle with all the fanfare royalty deserved. Jack and I stood at the end of the massive hall. My heart broke as I watched his tortured face rotate emotions as he took in the scene of us standing together as king and queen... host and hostess. It was clear to all with eyes that Jack and I were a bonded couple that would be impossible to separate.

When Drake finally stood before us, he looked at me with tortured eyes, but said nothing. He didn't need to. It was clear I'd made my decision and it was equally clear I'd broken his heart. My guilt over hurting him forced me to look away.

"You always were an excellent tracker," Jack said with a smile as he extended his arms in greeting.

"It's easy to track a sloppy vampire," Drake teased as he embraced his friend.

As I watched the warm embrace between friends, every muscle in my body relaxed to the point I almost collapsed.

"It's good you came," Jack continued.

"I needed to be sure she was okay," Drake replied. He looked at me, smiled, and took a deep breath. "It's clear she's where she wants to be. Her happiness it what's important."

"Drake..." I started, but he raised his hand to stop me.

"I knew it was him. I knew it would always be him, but for the sake of honor and the feelings that I developed for you, I had to try," he said as he stood back and looked at us both. "I give you both my blessing and if the baby's a boy I hope you name it after me."

"Vampires can't have babies," I giggled. "Well, they can, but Jack's pretty old and hasn't produced one yet. It's rare for them."

"Vampires and vampires, true, but you're not a vampire,"

Drake replied with a wink.

"Oh," I gasped.

My mind raced back to our love making. Not once did it ever occur to me that precautions against pregnancy needed to be taken. Jack had said vampires rarely had children and, since he was so old and childless, I assumed it meant he couldn't. It never dawned on me to clarify that he meant vampires rarely had children with vampires. My hand moved to my abdomen. Had I conceived?

Jack clapped his hands and ordered a feast to be prepared in honor of his guest, Prince Mandrake. Drake and I laughed when he wrinkled his nose and ordered venison be placed on the menu. The reaction of his staff wasn't much better. Drake finally took pity on them and declared his curiosity over vegetarianism and announced he'd prefer to eat a native meal with the natives. I couldn't help feel a bit of love in my heart for this man. He was a rare find.

Jack slapped him on the back appreciatively and redirected the order for the feast's menu. He then asked me to excuse them as he showed Drake around his castle grounds. I knew he wanted to be alone with Drake to discuss me and the fact that Mark was probably not far behind, so I made no protest. Instead, I went about chatting with whoever felt comfortable enough to stop their task for a minute or two and I dug for information on the blacks.

I discovered that there were two sects of vampires. The ones who broke away in rebellion and made Jack their lord and king were called the whites and the originals who were evil and sinister were the blacks. I found this bit of information confusing, since I'd been told on Kurr that Jack was the king of all the vampires on earth and I didn't remember Drake's story of how Jack let the king he rose up against live and that king was in charge of a small band they called the blacks. They clarified and elaborated on Drake's story. Jack was king of the white vampires and the white vampires made up the majority of the vampire world. Recently, in an effort to enlarge his tiny kingdom, the black king recruited a small force from amongst Jack's subjects and they were now in rebellion. They hated humans and if they discovered that Drake and I were in residence, they would surely come for us. Although no one wished to speak badly of their king, they speculated on how it might have turned out had Jack killed the black king instead of showing mercy.

The cook went so far as to ask me when I planned on becoming vampire. To quote her words, "The sooner the better."

Me become vampire? The thought never even crossed my mind. I thought about Sara lamenting over the fact that Captain Berger was killed before she'd been able to convince him to become vampire. Would Jack expect that of me? From what I'd heard so far, I guessed yes.

I spent the next few hours wandering the castle while alternating my pondering on whether I should become a vampire and whether I was pregnant. When I finally found myself in the company of Jack and Drake once more, I was being seated at an enormous dinner table in an equally enormous dining room. There were no less than fifty chairs around the table and each of them was occupied. I sat on Jack's left and Sara sat on his right. Drake was seated on my left.

Although it was clear the two men had worked things out between them, the energy coming from Drake showed me that he was still trying to gain control over how he felt about me. I understood. I went through the same thing when Jack conceded to Drake. The difference being that my hurt and frustration turned to anger and rage, where Drake transferred his into love and kindness.

I had a lot to learn.

"You didn't dress for dinner?" Sara barked as she stared at my attire.

"Should I have come in Jack's robe?" I replied with the sassiest tone I could muster.

My gumption earned me a few chuckles and approving mumbles from the other dinner guests.

"Sit still and be quite," Jack snapped as he covered my hand with his. "Jessica will be outfitted by Dresser soon enough. In the meantime, you will mind your manners."

I looked around the room. Sara was right. The others at the table were all suited in gorgeous dresses that bordered on being categorized as evening gowns and the men were spit shine clean and in jacket and tie. Even Jack looked like a fashion model. Although Drake wasn't quite as elegantly attired as the other men, he'd somehow managed to secure a dinner jacket for the occasion. I felt like a complete underdressed idiot.

I wanted to be anywhere but sitting at that table.

"My apologies to my lovely companion," Jack bellowed for the vampires at the end of the table to hear, "I was so occupied with our very special guest, Prince Mandrake of Kurr, that I neglected to see to her wardrobe. Please join me in making her welcome at this table, for she is perfect just as she is. As for tomorrow, it is my sincerest hope that one of you lovely ladies will see your way to introducing my princess and love to our Dresser."

Shouts of welcome that were warm and genuine traveled up the table. Drake placed his hand on my knee just long enough to give it a little squeeze to relay his pleasure, while Jack openly smiled at the genuine acceptance his people were giving me. It was enough to bring me at ease so that I could enjoy the good food, great conversation, and fabulous company; Sara being the exception.

As the dinner wound down, the men moved into a different room for a smoke and conversation. It was a little odd to be dining in accordance to Victorian tradition, but I somehow managed without making too big a fool of myself. Drake, on the other hand fit in as if he was born to it. Once again I thought what a wonderful catch he'd make for the right person.

"May I sit next to the woman who managed to steal the elusive heart of our great leader?" a female asked.

I turned to look into the deep brown eyes of a very pretty vampire who appeared to be about my age. Her long dress was tailored to accentuate her slender frame and small perky breasts. Even being a woman myself, I couldn't deny that the only description suitable for her full, well-shaped mouth would be to call it 'kissable'.

"I'm Victoria, but you can call me Vicki," she said with a smile.

"I'm Jessica... Jess for short," I replied with a broad smile that belied how hungry I was for female companionship."

"It's nice to meet you, Jess," she said with a smile. She leaned forward and whispered, "Are you really a princess? Were you really engaged to Prince Mandrake? Did Lord Devon truly steal you away from him? It's so romantic!"

She gave me little chance to respond as she babbled on about the romanticism her king displayed where I was concerned. She confided that the entire kingdom was in shock about it. Most of his subjects were thrilled to see him come alive and find his one true love, while a few were angry because I was human and stolen from a very prominent prince. They worried about the black vampires coming to investigate and trouble brewing as a result. I listened with a heavy heart because I didn't know what to do to stop it, short of leaving. The more I listened to how Jack changed from a gloomy, sad, and lonely leader to an animated, lively, and openly happy one since my arrival, the more I realized that my leaving was something Jack would never stand for.

The conversation eventually turned to other topics. I'd never really had a female friend to talk to about all the things girls talked about. I was enjoying it immensely. I liked Vicki's vibrant personality. It was nice to make a friend. Thoughts of L'oana floated through my head and I pushed them back. Vicki was clearly a vampire and a part of Jack's court. There was no comparison to be made between her and L'oana.

"You two look as thick as thieves," Sara said in a sickly sweet tone of voice before walking past with her head high and her nose even higher.

"Beware of that one," Vicki whispered nervously. "She walks the line between light and dark. I have no idea why Lord Devon allows her to stay."

"She's is sister," I said flatly.

"And your one-time step mother, I'm told," Vicki said and then whistled low and slow. "What a tangled web this is."

"She buried me alive when I was a child," I said.

I was still trying to process that horrific act.

"You don't say? How did you survive?" Vicki asked with genuine curiosity.

"Jack saved me," I said with pride.

"You've known him that long?" she said with amazement.

"Sort of," I replied.

I have no idea why I trusted Vicki like I did. Perhaps it was simply women's intuition. I found myself telling my entire story to her. She gasped in horror at the part where I was trussed up in the food line for the Dragos and laughed with delight when I admitted to giving Jack the middle finger in the woods. When I'd caught her up to date with what was happening, she dove into her own story.

I learned that my newly acquired friend was made a vampire in the year eighteen-ninety-one. She was nineteen and visiting her extended family at their lake house in Montreal when they were attacked by a group of black vampires. She and her brother were turned, but the rest of her family died. I waited for her heart felt emotions to calm down enough for her to continue. It touched me deeply that after more than a century she could still feel this much emotion and pain over the loss of her loved ones. Once again I thought of the stories of vampires and realized just how far off the mark they were.

Her brother refused to eat and eventually perished, leaving her to her own devices. She was unskilled at vampirism, but did the best she could to survive. Jack discovered her prowling around the forest living on rodents and bugs. He cleaned her up, taught her how to hunt and take just enough to sustain her, but not enough to kill the animal. He showed her what fruits, vegetables, and beverages her body could tolerate in its new state. Then, he invited her to stay at his home. It saddened her that she met him too late to save her brother. Had he been shown the correct way of vampirism, she was certain he would have accepted it.

Vicki had no idea he was the actual king when he rescued her. She just thought him a handsome, kindly vampire who took pity on her. I laughed with delight when she described her reaction when she saw the castle and learned of Jack's true identity.

My new vampire friend admitted to having a severe crush on Jack for the better part of the century, but he showed only fatherly interest in return. She said she hardly saw him over the last few decades. Rumor had it that he'd fallen in love and was moonstruck and following her wherever she went.

I giggled at that one, since I was the cause of his absence.

I was surprised to see how much time had gone by when the men finally returned to join us. Jack made the excuse that it was a long day for me and scooted me off to his rooms with him hot on my heels.

If I'd thought of getting any rest, that thought was short lived. Jack had other plans. His passion was unleashed almost as soon as he closed the door to his room.

CHAPTER TWENTY-FIVE

I could barely move the following morning. Every inch of my body was sore and stiff. I moaned involuntarily as I tried to make it to the bathroom without waking Jack. As much as I loved him, I knew I couldn't endure any more love making for a while. This was the one thing that truly spoke the differences between his vampirism and my mortality.

To add to my misery, my head throbbed and my stomach felt like I'd pulled it out in the middle of the night, twisted it into an enormous knot, and then shoved it back in sideways.

Jack was lying next to me, but he wasn't sleeping. Vampires required far less sleep than humans under normal circumstances. The fact that I was exhausted and slept even longer than normal gave him even more time to observe me without my being self-conscious about it.

I struggled through my morning constitution and practically crawled back to bed. When he discovered the reason for my stiffness and lack of agility he was genuinely apologetic and concerned. He promised to give my body a rest and to be more careful in the future. He ordered breakfast be sent up to me and told me he'd be gone for a little while. He needed to hunt for some fresh blood. He reminded me that vampires can't live on fruits and vegetables alone. Ideally, they should have fresh blood daily.

Finally, a vampire myth was proven right.

When I asked him why he didn't just raise farm animals for their blood nourishment, he looked at me in an odd way, smiled, wondered aloud why no one had thought of it before, and congratulated me for a marvelous idea. His praise made me feel all giddy inside, like a young school girl.

Breakfast for one consisted of the most delicious boiled wild yam drizzled with honey, a coarsely mashed applesauce, brown bread and a small wedge of sharp cheese. Tea from the orient was steeping in a pot waiting to help me wash it all down. I made a mental note to complement cook when I saw her.

Sometime between my going to sleep and my waking up a pair of jeans and an Irish cable-knit sweater found their way to the chair by the bed. I tried them on. They were a perfect fit. A knock at the door caught my attention in time to see a note slipped under it. It was from Dresser. My presence was requested in the fitting parlor at my earliest convenience. I had no idea where the fitting parlor was, but since I already felt like I belonged to the castle, I had no problem stopping the staff to ask directions.

The walk to the fitting parlor was more like a trek. The farther I went, the farther I had to go. It turned out Dresser was at the far north end of the castle on the lower level. Jacks rooms were on the far southern end of the castle on the third floor. I didn't time myself, but I'm sure it took at least twenty minutes to get there; possibly longer.

I was treated like royalty by Dresser and her assistants. She outfitted me in couture everything; even bra and panties. She was a native Irish country woman, which explained the source of my gorgeous hand knit sweater and jeans.

By the time Dresser was satisfied that I was outfitted in a way befitting for the mistress of their realm, she thanked me for coming and went about ordering the clothing be taken to the king's room, where they were to be put away in a neat and orderly fashion. She then introduced me to Lizzy, my new hand maid. It took me a moment to realize what a hand maid was. When I did, I had all I could do not to burst out laughing. It seemed Jack's kingdom held on to certain traditions from the past. It would be rude of me to laugh at them.

As I made my way back to the main part of the castle, I couldn't help smiling with satisfaction over the fact that I'd be dressed in style at the dinner table that evening. I couldn't wait to see Sara's face.

I was near the great hall when I stopped and flattened my body against the wall. Beads of sweat formed on my forehead and neck. I had no idea who that tall formidable figure standing in the middle of the hall surrounded by a dozen or so not as tall formidable figures was, but I knew he wasn't good. It wasn't because he was dressed in black, as were his companions. It was the energy he emitted. It was pure evil. He must have sensed me there because he turned and peered with beady red-orange eyes into the dimly lit corridor. Fortunately, not only had I accomplished flattening myself into a small alcove, but Jack entered and distracted him.

I was certain I'd just laid eyes on a classic horror film vampire. Could he be the black king?

I watched Jack standing all alone while talking to the group's leader and was filled with fear. Even though he was the same height, if not a little taller than the evil leader of this pack, Jack seemed no match for these characters, should they decide to attack. He was too kind, too gentle. Where was everyone? Why would they throw their king to the wolves like that? Surely the staff was aware of this evil group's arrival. I was at a loss at what to do. If Jack was no match for this group, then what was I?

Absolutely worthless.

I couldn't tell what was being said, but I knew it wasn't a friendly pow wow; especially when voices started to get louder. As if on cue the hall filled with Jack's people. I hadn't realized I was holding my breath until I felt it pouring forth as relief flooded me. Unfortunately, the sound of the air passing through my relaxed lips was just enough to attract the acute hearing of the evil vampire.

Before I knew what was happening I was back in the alcove flattened against the wall with Jack's weight pressing against me so hard I was motionless. Breathing was an effort. I knew better than to struggle, so I did my best to get enough air into my lungs to sustain me with shallow breathing.

"Get out of the way Devon," hissed the tall figure in black. "You know the rules about bringing humans into the den."

"Your rules don't apply here," Jack hissed. "It's time for you and your friends to leave."

"She's just a human," Jack's opponent spat. "You would risk dying for a human?"

"This is my wife and she's carrying my child. You won't touch her," Jack roared so loud I was sure they heard it on Kurr.

I didn't know which remark shocked me more.

I was Jack's wife? I didn't recall a wedding. Did having sex with a vampire make you his bride?

Then the second thing he said hit home.

I was pregnant!

I wasn't ready for either.

"Now Ralph, do you really plan on battling my brother over a puny human?" cooed Sara as she sundered up behind the evil vampire and kissed him on the cheek. He smiled and put his arm around her waist, pulling her close. "You're early my love. I wasn't expecting you for another week."

"I thought to surprise you, but it seems I'm the one surprised," Ralph chuckled.

He and Jack had a short stare down before he finally bowed his head and turned to leave.

"You're playing with fire, Devon," he tossed over his shoulder as he led Sara out of the great hall to the open atrium. Jack moved forward and I sucked in air with a desperation that surprised him. I leaned my head against his back as I watched the black vampires shoot straight up into the sky and disappear.

I could hear Drake's strides echo down the great hall as he hurried to my side.

"I was fencing when I heard about our ... err... guests. It was the oddest thing. I couldn't find my way here to be near you. I'm so sorry. The castle turned into a maze of twists and turns. I was about to give up when I suddenly found myself here," Drake explained. "Are you alright?" He took my chin in his hand, heedless of the fact that I was leaning on Jack, "Did they touch you?"

"My wife is fine your highness," Jack said softly. "Thank you for your concern."

It was then that Drake realized how inappropriate his well-meaning concern appeared. I could see his face coloring as he mumbled his apologies to Jack and me and started to leave us.

I couldn't bear to see him so embarrassed. I squeezed Jack's shoulder.

"Jack," I whispered. "Do something. Say something. Don't let him leave embarrassed like that."

"Prince Mandrake," Jack called out, careful to use his full title for the benefit of his people, "Will you join us in the parlor for tea?"

Drake turned and smiled, "Did I hear brandy?"

I giggled and said, "Brandy would be appropriate, don't you think?"

Jack tossed his head back. All of the tension that wound his body like a coil funneled into deep bellied laughter. He patted Drake on the back and the two of them headed off to the parlor, leaving me to find my own way.

Men!

I would have found it humorous if I hadn't been so freaked out from the visit by those evil vampires. I really would have preferred being nestled between my two champions. For the first time since I'd met Jack, I was truly happy he was able to get into my head when he turned around and headed back for me.

I slid one of my arms through Jack's and the other through Drake's when we caught up with him. These were the two most important men in my life and nothing made me happier than to see they'd settled the issue of "me" and were back on track with their relationship. Something told me that although Jack was surrounded by his people and Drake was in charge of his coalition sector, neither of them had many real friends. I would have never forgiven myself if I'd come between them.

Brandy was indeed the drink that did the trick. Since vampires can only consume food and drink in moderation, Jack was careful not to partake in too much, but even he seemed to revel in the soothing relief the fiery liquid provided.

"I never could get used to the taste of tea," Drake mused.

"You're missing out," I teased. "You can travel the world while sitting in this parlor just by sampling all of Jack's teas."

"Is that so?" he said with a smile.

"I happen to enjoy a good cup of tea," Jack explained.

"Are you seriously sitting here discussing teas?" asked Vicki from the doorway. She looked in Jack's direction and bowed her head in respect, "May I enter?"

Jack nodded and she bounced in to plant herself on the settee next to me. I glanced in Drake's direction just in time to catch a look of true admiration for my new friend's beauty before he hid it behind a mask of politeness. It seemed my ex-fiancé wasn't all that heart-broken over me after all. I couldn't have been happier.

"More humans have been spotted coming up the mountain," she said softly. "Were you expecting any more visitors, my lord?"

"This certainly does seem to be a popular place," Jack mused.

Since I guessed the newcomers included Mark, I assumed Jack was thinking the same thing.

"Do me a favor, Vicki, and tell cook to prepare for ... how many are coming?" Jack said casually.

"Now, that's where I'm confused," she replied. "Some reports say only three, yet others say at least two dozen. Isn't that odd?"

Jack smiled lamely, "Well then we'll prepare for the two dozen just in case. Run along and tell cook."

Vicki gave my hand a quick squeeze and scooted out to do Jack's bidding. I caught a look of approval about my new friendship in Jack's eyes before they clouded over to focus on the matters at hand.

"Could Mark have rounded backup?" Jack asked Drake.

"Someone's kept him up to snuff with who he is and who she is," Drake said while looking at me. "Who's his mother?"

"Sadly, I never paid the woman much mind," Jack apologized. "I'm afraid I fell short as guardian and protector."

Drake waived his hand at Jack as if to say, "Nonsense".

"I had very little exposure to her over the years. She called Aunt Jenny on the telephone, but I really only spent time in her company once or twice. They'd spend hours talking on the phone.

If they visited, Aunt Jenny went there or they'd meet at a coffee shop or go shopping. I never really thought much of it," I mused.

"Mark was at your place?" Jack asked.

"Every day," I replied.

"Are you sure Jenny knew nothing?" Drake asked Jack.

"If she did know something, she has fantastic mind control," Jack said flatly.

"Do you think he plans on walking into a vampire kingdom and starting a war?" I gasped. "That's insane."

"He's desperate," Drake mused. "There's no telling what he has in mind."

CHAPTER TWENTY-SIX

It took Mark and his troop a few more hours to reach us. The soothing effects of the brandy wore off just before he marched into the courtyard. My body was so tense I could barely move to greet him. Grateful for their presence, I positioned myself between Jack and Drake for support and comfort.

Without any pretense of civility, Mark immediately cut to the quick.

"You have something of mine. I've come to get it back," he said in a demanding and arrogant tone.

"It is a human being, brother," Drake hissed.

"Don't call me brother. You're nothing more than an embarrassment to me," Mark spat.

"I should think it would be the other way around," I bellowed. I was suddenly angry on Drake's behalf. "Most bastards would be grateful to be acknowledged by their legitimate sibling."

Drake placed his hand over mine and squeezed. I wasn't sure if he was warning me to stop or praising me for my support. If he was asking me to stop, it was a lost cause. My anger was out of control and so were my hormones. I felt like a raging bull. The fact that Mark lied to me and looked upon me as nothing more than a pawn in his scheme to rise to glory infuriated me more than anything I could recall. I felt a strong tug in my abdomen. My hand flew to my stomach and I bent over in surprise.

"Take it easy, my love," Jack whispered. "You have a baby in there who wants to defend his mama from the womb. It could get very uncomfortable for you if you don't calm down."

"How can that be?" I whispered back.

"Vampire genes," Jack replied softly, "The gestation for vampire babies is far shorter than humans. We'll discuss it later though, okay?"

He was right. Now was not the time to discuss the fact that I was pregnant with his vampire child. There was no denying it was a huge issue, but we had an even bigger one staring us in the face. Mark was standing in his courtyard demanding what he considered his property back in front of all the residents of the castle and it wasn't going over well. All I saw as a sea of vampire fangs. It was incredibly disarming. Even Drake hedged back just a bit.

"Your words are cutting, my love," Mark said mockingly while he held his hand over his heart. "I'm crushed."

"Your love? Is that what you called me, Mannador?" I hissed. "I was under the distinct impression you considered me your thing."

It was clear to both Jack and Drake that what had started out as a threatening encounter between Mark's troop and my protectors was rapidly becoming an argument between two old friends.

"I can't believe I devoted all those years to us," I spat. "I thought I loved you. I thought you loved me. Oh sure, I knew the sparks weren't there, but the friendship was. We grew up together, side by side. We shared laughter and tears. I thought we had a solid friendship as the base of our relationship. Everyone knows that's important." I took a moment to breathe some composure into my body. No one said a word and the fangs disappeared. It was as though they were mesmerized by the situation. "You lied to me! How long have you known your true identity? How long have you known you were the bastard of the man that killed my parents?"

An enormous gasp echoed through the room as the spectators took in the true intensity of the situation. Even members of Mark's group shuffled uncomfortably.

"This isn't the time or the place to..." Mark started.

It was clear he was beginning to buckle under my onslaught of accusations.

"This is precisely the time!" I bellowed. "What makes you think you have the right to march into the home of the man who has forfeited years of his life to guard and protect me and demand he hands me over like I was a dinner roll? How arrogant you are to think that you can waltz in here and lay claim to me as if you had the right. This isn't the middle ages! As a resident of this planet in a time where women have equal rights... I have the right to say 'no'... and as the princess of Kurr and true heir to the throne, I have even more power and privileges. If I was to honor any pledge of marriage it would be the one my parents made to the legitimate prince of Kurr, not to some snot nosed bastard of their killer!"

The room was abuzz with my last statement.

I stopped only briefly to fill my lungs with air before continuing, "Fortunately for me your half-brother is a wonderful, kind, and understanding man. He realized the love Lord Devon and I have for each other and he politely gave us his blessing. He no longer recognizes the agreement between my parents and him, so there's no harm done. Yet you... You arrogant, poor excuse for a... I don't know what you are... you think you can enforce a childish agreement between two kids? Had you paid attention to history, you'd recall that in the olden days when honor and agreements of this nature played a role of such ridiculous importance, the desires of the parents superseded those of the young lovers. In short... were we living in a time where you might remotely be able to treat me like an object...whatever promises passed between us wouldn't mean shit!"

Jack's low chuckle pulled me from my rage and back to reality. I'd given quite a show to a very large audience. Suddenly embarrassed, I stepped into his embrace.

The hall was so quiet you could have heard a pin drop. I shuffled back and forth on my feet. I was not only suddenly at a loss for words, but I felt 'odd'. I had a strong need to lie down.

I whispered this fact in Jack's ear. He nodded and immediately called for four of his guards to escort me to his rooms. When Mark started to protest, Jack's remaining guards surrounded his troop in readiness for battle.

I smiled to myself when I recognized the brief flash of fear in Mark's eyes before he puffed out his chest and conceded for the moment. I heard my politically correct lover suggest Mark's troop join his men in their quarters for some rest and refreshment while he, Drake, and Mark retired to his den for drink and conversation. It was his sincerest hope that they could have an amiable outcome.

I'd moved too far down the corridor to hear Mark's response, but, from the sound of their footsteps, I assumed he agreed.

We'd reached the second floor before pain gripped my abdomen and I doubled over, unable to continue. Without a word, a large, burly vampire swept me into his arms and continued up the stairs. When we entered Jack's quarters he laid me gently on the bed and ordered the castle doctor be sent for. Vampires moved so fast that she was by my side in no time. It was as if she'd been waiting in the corner of the room.

The guards assured me they'd be right outside the door as they cleared the room to allow the doctor, who introduced herself as Marigold, and me some privacy.

"Now, you lay back miss and we'll get you fixed right up," cooed Marigold.

I couldn't get over the fact that she looked surprisingly like an old crone out of one of Shakespeare's plays. The difference being that she had both eyes intact and very strong and perfect looking teeth. I looked at her wrinkled face and gnarled hands and assumed she must have been made vampire very late in life.

"Have you dealt with many humans carrying a vampire child?" I asked.

"None that were sired by a vampire king," she cackled. "This is a very important first."

"Have you known Lord Devon long?" I asked timidly.

"Since he was made vampire," she replied. "Never in all those years have I seen him go goo goo over a female like he has over you."

"Is that good?" I asked hesitantly.

"You'll have to turn vampire," she said flatly.

I sat up with a start.

"Jack hasn't said anything about...," I began.

Marigold waived her hand in the air to stop me and continued to speak while she poked and prodded at my abdomen.

"He'd never force you," she said. "I doubt he'd even make the suggestion." She looked me in the eye with clear, dark orbs that reflected her years of living. "If you want to be around to see this baby grow up and maybe have children of his own, then you'll need to become vampire. The gestation period is short and sweet, but they mature very slowly. Jack was a young man when he was turned eight-hundred years ago, yet he looks not a day over thirty."

I had to agree.

"You'll die long before your son becomes a man if you don't become vampire," she said briskly.

"It's a boy?" I giggled.

"I believe we have a male vampire in that womb, but, male or female, the fact remains the same. If you want to see your child grow up, you must become vampire."

"But, I'm not a true earthling. I'm Kurr," I explained.

"Yes, yes. You could live a whopping two-hundred years if you're lucky. What is that compared to two or three thousand years?" She said as she stroked my cheek with her crooked thumb. It was surprisingly soft and smooth. "Why would you want to inflict such heartache on someone who loves you as much as Lord Devon does? If you don't become vampire, you will eventually die. One-hundred years, two-hundred years... it doesn't matter. The outcome will be the same."

"Vampires don't die?" I said with surprise.

"We eventually die," Marigold explained, "but it takes thousands and thousands of years. There are a few things that will kill us, but I shan't say what for secrecy's sake. Yes... we eventually will die of old age, but only after centuries of life."

"How old are you?" I asked hesitantly.

Since she said she'd known Jack since he was a young man newly made, it was clear she was at least eight-hundred years old.

"I am five-thousand years old," she boasted.

"Five-thou..." I gaped.

She threw her head back and cackled.

"You thought I looked this old and gnarly when I was made, didn't you?" she said.

I nodded.

"I'm the oldest known vampire to the kingdom. I was born vampire from a humanoid mother like you. These wrinkles are from thousands of years of living," she explained softly. "Like I said, vampires live a long time."

I sank back into the pillow and looked up at the ceiling. The old nurse had given me something to think about.

"I'll have to become vampire," I mused, more to myself than to her.

"Don't let it happen while you're still carrying the child. Vampire women can't hold the seed of a vampire man. They require the seed of a human. Human and vampire only... vampire and vampire usually ends in disaster."

"But, I'm already pregnant," I replied.

"You'll abort," she said as she completed the exam. She patted my cheek to reassure me. "You'll be fine. I suggest bed rest for the remainder of the day. Your little man in there got himself pretty worked up. He can sense your emotions. I believe we have a born leader incubating in that womb."

"It seems so fast for him to be moving," I said with disbelief.

"How long since you first coupled with the king?" she asked thoughtfully.

"On Kurr it was several months, but time is different on earth," I replied.

"You conceived while on Kurr and the baby had time to grow while in Kurr's vibrational atmosphere. I'm surprised you aren't showing more than you are. That must be a Kurr female trait. The gestation process takes about one third the time for a vampire baby as it does for a baby. Throw your visit to Kurr into the mix and I believe you'll be delivering soon."

I felt warm and cozy as she smiled and tucked me securely

beneath the covers of Jack's comfortable bed. The old vampire gave me a sedative to help both the baby and me sleep and it worked like a charm.

It was well into the wee hours of the morning before I felt Jack climb into the bed next to me. He did his best not to disturb me, but I was wide awake and refreshed from sleeping over fifteen hours.

"Hey handsome," I whispered as I laid my hand on his bare back.

He rolled over to face me and kissed me long and slow. I could feel my body reacting to his touch. I positioned myself to receive him.

"Is that wise?" he asked as he placed his broad hand on my abdomen.

"She didn't tell me not to. She just said we were having a boy, to remain calm, and not to become a vampire while I was carrying him. She said nothing about abstaining from making love," I pouted.

My sex drive was suddenly at optimum and if he denied me I was sure I'd explode with need.

"The old witch doctor mentioned you becoming a vampire?" Jack said with surprise.

"If you don't make wild and crazy love to me right this minute I swear I'll go insane!" I complained.

His low, throaty chuckle and wandering hand told me I'd won the tug of war and would soon have my needs satiated.

CHAPTER TWENTY-SEVEN

We lay in each other's arms for several hours while Jack grabbed some much needed sleep. I was wide awake, but had no desire to leave his bed. His slow rhythmic breathing stabilized and comforted my nerves. I felt safe, secure, and at peace.

"Marigold's a witch doctor?" I asked with concern when he finally showed signs of rousing.

"Is that a problem?" he asked sleepily.

"I thought she was a regular doctor," I explained.

"Trust me. You want a witch doctor in a situation like this," he assured me. "I've heard vampire pregnancies require magic as well as regular care."

"Why?" I asked suspiciously.

He shrugged his shoulders with genuine innocence, "It's a girl thing, I'm sure."

A soft knock on the door roused my lover. He pulled on his robe and sauntered to the door. He looked so sexy with his hair mussed and his eyes still clouded over with sleep, I was hard pressed to keep my desires in check. I was a little embarrassed by the fact that my libido was out of control. I wondered if it was because of the pregnancy or just simply because I was a wanton woman who'd been unleashed.

Jack only partially opened the door, which prevented me from seeing who he was speaking to in a low tone. I'm sure it was for my benefit, since the only thing covering me was a thin sheet that clung to my body and left nothing to the imagination. Whoever it was, the news wasn't good. He returned wearing a deep scowl.

"You'll need to get dressed," he said flatly.

"Have I done something wrong?" I asked hesitantly.

He stopped pulling on his jeans and looked at me in surprise. "Why would you say such a thing?"

"The scowl and your face and the gruff way you ordered me to get dressed for starters," I replied.

He finished pulling on his pants, then sat on the edge of the bed and pulled me close.

"Forgive me. I've been alone for too long. The scowl was for the news I just received. So was the tone of voice. I'm sorry I imposed them in my request," he said as he took a deep breath and smiled. "Please dress and join me downstairs for breakfast."

Not wanting to encourage his dark mood returning, I opted to forego asking what was going on and simply smiled and assured him I'd be right behind him.

I felt pretty good that morning. In fact, I felt the best I'd felt in a long time. I made a mental note to ask Marigold what was in that tea as I bounded down the stairs to join Jack -and I assumed Drake- for breakfast. When I reached the great dining room, it was empty. I looked around in surprise until I spotted a guard walking down the corridor.

"Excuse me," I called to him, "Do you know where I might find Lord Devon?"

He looked at me with confusion and bowed slightly, "I was under the impression he was with you, my queen."

Normally I would have swelled with pride from being addressed in such a manner, but, instead, I gave him a slight smile, bowed my head a bit, and did my best to hide my disappointment while I thanked him. I didn't want him to know that Jack pulled a disappearing act on me. It dawned on me that, since there was just a small party for breakfast, perhaps we were to meet in the parlor a few doors down. After all, I hadn't left my room for morning fare prior to this, so I didn't really know where the everyday eatery was.

I found Drake in the parlor having breakfast alone.

"Where's Jack?" I asked as I sat down opposite him at the small round table and poured myself some coffee.

"I haven't seen him princess," Drake replied after first making sure he'd swallowed the biscuit he'd just popped in his mouth. "Or is it your majesty. When did you marry?"

"We didn't," I chuckled. "I'm not sure what's going on with that."

After a moment of silence, I said, "He asked me to join him for breakfast. He left the room before me."

"Then he'll be along," Drake shrugged. "Someone probably waylaid him with a kingly duty."

I smiled and relaxed.

"You're probably right," I said as I looked at the food on his plate. "How are the biscuits? I'm starving."

He pointed to the sideboard, "There's coddled eggs and bacon too."

"Bacon?" I said with delight.

My broad smile was met with an even bigger one.

"Oh yeah," he said enthusiastically.

"Yum!" I squealed as I hopped up to fill a plate with the delicious smelling food. "Is there any orange juice?" I asked as I looked the sideboard over.

"Vampires can't eat oranges, so I doubt it," Drake replied.

"They don't eat bacon either, but it's being served," I pointed out.

"Very true, princess," he chuckled.

After satisfying myself that there would be no orange juice, I sat back down at the table and shamelessly dove into my breakfast. He smiled as he watched me devour my food like a ravenous street urchin.

"Feeling better?" he asked as I washed the last of my food down with piping hot coffee.

"I've never felt better," I informed him. "I had a visit from a five-thousand-year-old vampire witch doctor last night and she fed me some tea. I was told it was to help me sleep, but I have a feeling there was more to that tea than meets the eye. Whatever's in it, it worked wonders. I can't remember when I felt this good."

"I've been making inquiries about your pregnancy," Drake said softly. "It won't last long. Vampire babies don't have the same gestation time."

"Jack told me, but he never said how long. The witch doctor said that since I conceived on Kurr it would probably be soon, but we haven't had time to speak about it yet," I replied. "Did Mark leave?"

"Not that I'm aware of," he replied. "He's probably enjoying the luxury of this place. It's a mighty fine home. Far greater than what we have back on Kurr."

"Are you homesick?" I asked with concern.

He shrugged, but said nothing.

"You don't have to stay here. I'm going to be fine," I said softly.

"I can't leave you," he said in a voice that sounded choked, "until the baby's born and I know you're okay."

"Why wouldn't I be okay?" I asked with concerned.

"Jack didn't tell you?" He looked surprised.

I looked at him quizzically.

"There's a lot we haven't had time to discuss. What do I need to know?" I said firmly.

Drake took a long drink of coffee and then sat back in his chair with both hands on the table. It was as if he was fortifying and bracing himself for what he was about to say.

"From what I'm told," he said quietly, "there's a high mortality rate for human women who give birth to vampire babies."

I gasped and grabbed my abdomen.

"Why would Jack do that to me?" I wailed.

"I wondered the same thing, so I had a conversation with Jack in private when we discovered you were pregnant," Drake said. "It turns out that although vampires can impregnate a human it's an extremely rare event. So rare, in fact, that he's never seen it. He's had sex with plenty of human women over the last eight hundred years and none of them conceived. Your pregnancy came as a complete surprise to him."

I rested my elbows on the table and buried my face in my hands.

"I also don't think he knows you could die. He seemed a bit ignorant on the subject," Drake added.

"The witch doctor said it was something she'd dealt with a lot," I whined.

"The witch doctor is five-thousand years old. Jack is eight-hundred years old," Drake pointed out. "Also, what constitutes a lot to this woman… five, ten, one-hundred, one-thousand? If you ask around like I have, you'll discover that the vampires here are calling this a miracle baby. None of them have seen this before. None of them realized it was possible."

"Who told you I could die if none of them even knew it was possible for Jack to father a baby with me?" I asked.

"I met up with this old crone named Marigold early this morning. She tried to get some gaud awful tea she'd just brewed down me," he chuckled. "I asked her if she was familiar with vampires being born from humans. It seemed okay to ask her since she's obviously lived a long time. She said she was concerned about you and that she needed to do whatever it took to keep you alive," Drake explained. "She mentioned turning you into a vampire immediately after the baby's birth. I figured she was some senile old women. After all, vampires have human DNA so I imagine they can go off their rocker when they get of a certain age, right?"

"She's the witch doctor," I said softly.

"Shit!" Drake hissed.

"Why hasn't she told Jack?" I asked accusingly.

"She asked me to keep it a secret for now. She's a pretty superstitious old woman. She claims that if the black vampires hear that you'll most likely die during childbirth they'll make it a point to attend the birthing just to be the ones to turn you. You'll be too vulnerable to stop them. If they are able to succeed, then you and your baby would be black and obligated to follow them. Since this child was sired by the white king, that would be a very big boon for them."

"She told this to Jack?" I asked.

"I'm not sure, but I think so. I heard her tell one of Jack's personal guards that she needed to speak with him this morning and to fetch him right away," Drake said. His eyes lit up, "That's probably where he is now."

"Well, I hope he hurries up. My questions about this pregnancy are piling up," I said. Then it hit me and I voiced my fear aloud, "I hope he isn't marrying me just because I'm pregnant!"

Drake chuckled and grabbed a biscuit before saying, "That's the most ridiculous thing I've ever heard."

"It happens," I pouted.

"Have you met Jack Devon?" he replied sarcastically.

CHAPTER TWENTY-EIGHT

When afternoon came around and there was still no sign of Jack, the entire castle was in an uproar. Since I was the last to see him, the sergeant at arms interviewed me extensively. Unfortunately, I was of little help.

As the day wore on, I heard whispers from a few disgruntled residents blaming me for Jack's disappearance. They pointed out that I'd only been there a few days and already they'd had more upheaval than they'd had in the last century. I felt horrible.

Drake heard the whispering as well and decided to stick to me like he was stuck with glue. Short of going to the toilet, I was not allowed to be alone. He sat in a chair while I napped and offered me his arm when I went downstairs to dinner. I could have stayed in my room to eat my meal. I think a few of my dinner companions would have preferred it, but I wanted to be there to hear any news of Jack, should it come in.

Light conversation was buzzing around the table, but nothing that would really concern me or even allow me to join in. It was like I didn't exist. Drake didn't suffer quite as badly. In fact, many of the men approached him for insight on possible solutions to locating Jack. I was grateful for the friendship shown me by Vicki as I sat next to Jack's empty chair and awaited my meal. Seeing my pain, she pulled a chair up between mine and Jack's empty one and began a light dinner table conversation with me about absolutely nothing. It was exactly what I needed.

It wasn't until the meal was almost over that the conversation between the men and Drake grew animated. Apparently some new bit of information or strategy surfaced as a result of their joining of the minds and it had them quite excited. Vicki and I stopped our conversation in hopes of catching a bit of theirs.

We didn't need to worry about eavesdropping. The conversation was about me and, as soon as they realized they had my attention, they directed Drake to fill me in. He didn't seem happy about it, but he did as they asked.

"Those weeks that you were recovering in Jack's cave on Kurr... you were fed the same meal every day," Drake began.

I smiled and said, "Jack said it was all he knew how to make that was palatable."

Drake smiled back.

"I wouldn't doubt that to be true," he agreed. "That stew served a dual purpose. It was filled with healing herbs to aid you with your recovery and nourishment, but it also had another ingredient placed in it."

I waited patiently for him to continue. It was clear he was hesitant, but, I knew if I waited and didn't push, he'd eventually get it out.

"For crying out loud man, tell her or I will," shouted a male from the end of the table.

Drake scowled at him and then turned back to me to continue.

"We were concerned about the possibility of you being kidnapped again," he said hesitantly. "So, at my suggestion, Jack put his blood in your stew."

"What?" I gasped with disbelief. "Do you mean Jack fed me his blood for two months!"

I was thunder struck. I had no idea what to think of this bit of news. Why would he do such a thing?

Drake didn't keep me in suspense.

"You see, with his blood in you, Jack is able to connect with your mind no matter where you are," Drake said.

"You mean read it?" I asked.

"Yes," he replied. "This way, if you were captured he'd be able to find you by tracking you through your mind."

"That explains a lot," I said. "Is this temporary or permanent?"

"It will only last a while longer. Eventually your body will have processed and eliminated all traces of his blood. Until that happens, there's still a connection," shouted someone from the other end of the table.

I stood up and looked down the dinner table at the sea of worried vampires. It was clear what they were alluding to. I agreed.

"If Jack can track me through my mind, then I should be able to track him, shouldn't I?" I bellowed so all could hear.

The room went abuzz with affirmative answers.

When I sat back down Drake leaned forward and whispered, "It's dangerous, and not as easy as it sounds. It could drive a human crazy. With you being pregnant, I just don't know."

I thought about Drake's concerns for a moment and stood up again. Silence permeated the room as my dinner companions waited for me to speak.

"I've just been informed by Prince Mandrake that this type of connection could be dangerous for me. Is this true?" I asked boldly.

The room remained silent until finally a small voice to my left said, "Yes, your majesty."

I looked to see a lovely fair haired female who looked to be no older than sixteen. I smiled my thanks for her consideration and bravery and continued, "For me, I am not concerned. Let's remember that I'm Kurr, not human. Who's to say I would have the same danger? Unfortunately, I do not just have to consider myself. I carry life within my womb. I carry your king's child. If it is dangerous to me, there is also danger for the child. I will tell you now that I love Jack Devon more than my life and if it were just me I wouldn't hesitate at all. To risk the life of my innocent child and a child that may very well be the only child your king sires... well... it is a decision I can't make. I need your help." The room was abuzz with whispers about what I'd just said. I raised my hand to silence them and continued, "I place the decision with you. I will do as you decide. If you desire I risk the life of this child to save your king, you need only say "yes" once and I will do it."

The room went wild as the vampires argued amongst themselves as to what I should do. It was clear they didn't all agree with risking the life of the baby. Drake stood up and raised his hand for the room to quiet down. It took a few moments, but they eventually obeyed.

"This is not an easy decision, I know," he said. "My suggestion is that you vote on it and let majority rule."

They did just that. Within minutes, I was whisked into a room with a few of the older vampires to learn how to track someone through their mind.

Drake was right. It wasn't an easy thing to do. My head hurt as I struggled to connect with Jack. My body temperature rose. At one point, Drake demanded they stop and allow me a little rest, pointing out the obvious... I wasn't vampire and I was pregnant. The older of my instructors, Jeremiah, apologized profusely for their lack of consideration. He was one of the vampires who voted "no" out of fear for the child. He called for Marigold and ordered her to prepare a tea to assist me in recovering. She gladly obliged.

Fifteen minutes later I was feeling on top of the world and ready to try again. I closed my eyes and thought of Jack. The face that flew in front of me made me jump. It wasn't Jack's face, it was Marks! I told them of my vision. Drake swore under his breath and Jeremiah called for the sergeant at arms and relayed my vision to him. The sergeant bowed his expressionless face in acknowledgement of the information and left us. I could only assume Mark would soon be in their custody.

"Just because his face flashed in my head doesn't mean he's done something to Jack," I said with despair.

"You worry about him?" Jeremiah asked with surprise.

"No... yes... I mean no. It's not him per se; it's the fact that I don't trust myself yet. What if I just conjured his face? What if he's guilty of nothing but stupidly thinking he's still my fiancé? I don't want that on my conscience," I replied.

"If he's innocent we can tell. Do not worry," Jeremiah assured me. "Now, what else can you see?"

I closed my eyes.

"I see... no, I smell dampness. It's dark and damp. My head hurts. No! His head hurts. There's something wrapped around his head and its paining him," I wailed as I held my temples with the flat of my hand and writhed with pain. "Make it stop!"

Drake stepped up and stopped us one more time. Jeremiah gave him no argument. I stood up and walked to the window. I needed air. It felt like I was still attached to Jack. I hadn't broken the connection, but at least the pain was tolerable.

"He needs air. It smells like rotten flesh... road kill. It smells like road kill. It reminds me of the stench of the Dragos." My eyes flew open, "You don't think the Dragos have him do you?"

"No, but I'm beginning to think I know who does," Jeremiah hissed. "Are you able to continue just a little more?" he asked gently.

Drake growled deep in his throat, but did nothing else as I closed my eyes and focused on what I was receiving.

"He's weak," I said. "He's lost blood. Someone has been taking blood from him. His wrist and ankles have something wrapped around them. It burns. It's the same thing that's around his head. Its... metal...some type of metal. It burns and pains him so much he wants to die to make it stop." I started pacing the room, "He's thinking of me. He's connecting. He knows I'm connecting!" I said excitedly. "He's telling me something. I... I can't make it out."

I slammed my fist into my palm to help release some of the frustrated tension and pain that was building up in me.

"Take it easy Princess," Drake cooed, "Don't force it. Let it come naturally."

He walked up to me, wrapped his arm around my shoulder and led me back to the chair I'd been occupying. He then knelt down in front of me, picked up one of my feet and rested it on his knee. He removed my moccasin and started massaging my foot. I paid no mind to the curious looks of the vampires in the room as they watch this scene that hinted of intimacy. What he was doing felt wonderful and I quickly fell into a relaxed state.

The information poured through me.

"He says to tell Drake to assemble his army and prepare for war. You have the wrong man. He received a message to meet with Mark, but while enroute to their rendezvous he was waylaid by Sara on the pretense of an emergency with Ralph, but it was no emergency. It was a trap. He's being held in Ralph's dungeon and drained of his blood, little by little, until he agrees to relinquish my baby to Ralph!"

"That son-of-a-bitch!" Drake roared.

"He said they injected him with something that paralyzed him for the journey and is only now wearing off. They have him chained in silver." I gasped, "Silver really does burn and incapacitate vampires?"

"It most certainly does," Jeremiah winced. "Our poor king."

CHAPTER TWENTY-NINE

I managed to get the location of the black vampires, some-thing they'd been able to keep secret since the black king's return. Drake and Jeremiah were meticulous about recording everything I told them. When I'd said all I could and was so exhausted I couldn't hold the connection with Jack anymore, they made ready for their rescue mission.

Not long after that I was nestled in Jack's bed with Marigold administering some of her wonderful tea to help me rest. I didn't think I needed it. I was exhausted and wanted to sleep until Drake returned with Jack, but I took the tea anyway, since she claimed it also had healing properties to keep the baby well and happy.

Vicki volunteered to sit with me and a guard was posted out-side. We chatted about fashion and giggled about men and sex until the tea took hold and I drifted off to sleep. It seemed as if I'd just settled into a deep state of relaxation when I heard a commo-tion in the distance. Vicki was shouting at someone. Furniture was being overturned and I was being bound and lifted off the bed. Since it resembled the state I'd seen Jack in, I assumed I was having a nightmare and forced myself to shake it off and go deeper into sleep.

When I awoke, I was no longer in Jack's room. I wasn't sure exactly where I was, but from the décor I suspected I was still in Jack's castle. Vicki was bound to a chair with silver chains. She had a silver chain gagging her as well. Blood trickled down her chin where the odious metal burned into her flesh.

I shook my head and squeezed my eyes shut in hopes I was still dreaming. When I tried to sit up I found that I was bound to the bed with jute rope around my wrists and ankles. The more I struggled, the more it burned into my flesh. If the burning pain I was experiencing from the jute rope came anywhere close to what Vicki and Jack were experiencing from the silver chains, my heart went out to them. What a horrible thing to do to someone.

I looked around the room until my eyes settled on Mark looking thoughtfully out the window. I hadn't been gagged so I used my cutting tongue to let him know exactly what I thought about his antics and demanded he set us free.

"Spare me the theatrics princess," he drawled. "The father of that bastard vampire you carry will be dead soon and your Kurr protector will follow. You have no one to rescue you."

"Let us go and I won't let anything happen to you," I said with a confidence I definitely didn't feel.

"Is this a joke?" he chuckled. "Take a good look at the situation, Jess. I'm the one with the leverage, not you." He closed his eyes, took a deep breath, and said with authority. "You'll remain quiet until that damn baby is born. Then it becomes a thank-you gift to the black king for his help in retrieving you and we're off to Kurr as husband and wife to seize the throne from dear old dad."

"You're mad," I hissed. "You can't keep me locked up in Jack's castle without someone finding us."

"Who said we were in Jack's castle?" he chuckled.

I twisted my head around to better view my surroundings. I'd never been in this room before, but the castle had over one thousand rooms and I'd only been there a few days. The décor looked similar to the rooms I'd visited, so I simply assumed that's where we were.

When Sara popped her head in the door and made a sarcastic remark about Sleeping Beauty finally waking up, I knew I was in trouble. I watched in horror as she ordered one of Mark's men to tighten the chain gagging Vicki, reminding them that if she managed to get free they'd be dead in seconds. I could smell her searing flesh as the guard tightened the chain to the point it imbedded in her flesh. She allowed herself one crisp cry before regaining control. It ripped through my heart.

"How could you partner with someone like her?" I spat at Mark when Sara finally left.

"I didn't partner with her. I'm working with King Ralph. She's just a pawn he tolerates... a means to an end," Mark boasted.

"Why do this?" I wailed.

"It seems that brat in your belly has value to the black king. You have value to me. We happened to bump into each other outside the castle walls and plotted a way to separate you from those annoying males who fancy themselves your protector. Jack lies in the dungeon four stories below us and is close to being drained of his blood. Ralph is one sick mother. He's draining Jack slowly to prolong his agony. From what I understand, the white king is experiencing torture in its purest form." I thought for a minute by the look on Mark's face that he was experiencing a bit of compassion and remorse for the role he played in Jack's capture until he spoke again. "But then, he is in the torture chamber, right?" he chuckled.

"I don't know you at all," I said sadly.

"Drake will soon follow," he spat. "He and those fools are about to walk into an ambush. You see, the true king... King Ralph... well he has ways of reading minds... and so do some of Jack's subjects. We were banking on them connecting to Jack through one of those fools and getting the information on where to find him. When King Ralph's seer felt one of Jack's subjects connecting with him, he literally stepped into the line of communication and fed a phony location for Drake to take his army... Clever, huh?" He took a deep breath and puffed his chest, "It'll take them a few days to reach it. When they do, they'll be tired from their journey and Ralph's army will be waiting for them. It's like out of an old western, isn't it?" he chuckled.

My eyes flew open wide and my heart pounded erratically when I realized I was the one they tricked into giving the phony information to Drake and Jeremiah. I'd literally played a role in sending my love and my very dear friend to their death!

"My baby won't be born in a few days," I said.

"I understand the gestation time is shorter than with humans," he said as he walked over to me and sat on the edge of the bed. The weight of his body as he lowered it onto the mattress caused friction against my wrists and I winced. "I'm only going to keep you bound until Jack and Drake are gone. Then you'll be free to enjoy King Ralph's hospitality as my wife. He's even going to provide a lovely wedding ceremony for us."

"Are you for real?" I screeched. "Is any of this real?"

I closed my eyes and fought against the tears that were threatening to consume me. It was hard enough to look at Vicki and feel her pain and realize that Jack was in far worse condition. It was even harder to think that he was just floors below me.

'I'm here Jack. I'm in a room above you. They have me bound, Vicki too.' I communicated and prayed Jack was able to hear me.

'Don't... communicate. They'll find out we have a connection,' Jack replied weakly.

I wanted to ask him what would happen if they discovered Jack and I could communicate telepathically, but the intensity of his message made me fearful of even one more thought sent his way.

My wrists were burning and my arms were aching from being pulled over my head. To add to my misery, I had to go to the bathroom.

"I'm hungry, I'm thirsty, and I have to pee," I said forcefully.

"Quiet, I'm thinking," Mark ordered.

"Or do you intend on starving me and my baby to death and allow me to lie here in my own urine?" I went on to say. "I can see where it'd be necessary to bind a pregnant female to a bed to keep you and your...err how many?" I audibly counted the men in the room, "One, two, three, four. It's your duty to keep your four men from being harmed by one pregnant woman. I get it." I sighed heavily, "I only encountered King Ralph briefly. He seems a formidable king to anger, but if you think he'll be fine with the fact that my baby was damaged, or possibly even killed, by your inattentive care, then I'll just piss my pants and drink my spit."

How she managed while in such pain was a mystery to me, but I'm sure I heard Vicki's weak giggle.

My baby went wild within my womb as Mark untied the ropes and gave me my freedom.

"I suppose you're harmless enough," he said thoughtfully.

"Where's the commode," I asked.

I really did have to relieve myself. I'd never been such a slave to my bladder as I had over the last few weeks. I assumed it was the pregnancy. I recollected I conceived the first time Jack and I made love.

He directed me to the bathroom down a short corridor and I did my business as slowly as possible. Not only did I want time to think, but my baby was going absolutely wild and causing such surges of energy in me that I thought I'd burst. I needed to release it somehow. I got my chance when Mark sent one of his men to see what was taking me so long.

Mark's comment about how the ambush on Drake and his men was like an old western played over and over again in my mind. As crazy as it sounds, I began to play out movie scenes in my head that I'd seen where the spy gets the jump on her captors. When one of Mark's guards popped his head through the door to check on me, my actions were fluid and automatic; just like the visions in my head.

A surge of energy and strength poured forth that surprised me as I reached up and grabbed Mark's man by his head and broke his neck almost as easily as I would snap a chicken wishbone in half. Without a moment's hesitation I stepped over him and slipped quietly into the short corridor, all the while familiarizing myself with every nook and cranny of the space. Mark called a warning to the dead man that he'd better not be touching me inappropriately.

Still portraying the escaping spy, I smiled at the irony of his fear.

When his man didn't respond, Mark flew into the corridor in a jealous rage. I didn't stop to think that it was my lifelong friend I was dealing with. I didn't stop to give him the benefit of the doubt for being confused and misguided in his actions. I simply waited for him to get within range of the alcove I'd flattened myself into and then with lightning speed that resembled the speed of a vampire I snapped his neck in the same easy manner I'd snapped the guard's. I looked at his limp body with zero emotion, stepped over it and continued toward the bedroom.

There were two men left.

It was insane what happened next. Adrenaline pumped into my thighs to the point I felt I'd explode if I didn't run it off. I raced with surprising power and speed into the bedroom, took the two remaining men by surprise and snapped their necks with the same ease and effort of opening the tab of a coke can.

Unbelievable.

Vicki looked at me in wide eyed shock before smiling as best she could with the silver in her mouth. I went to unbind her and jumped back in surprise from the burning sensation in my hands. I didn't take the time to try to understand why the silver was burning my skin. I sensed that the death of these men would be felt by the resident vampires soon. Time was of the essence.

I grabbed a cloth napkin off the table Mark's men had been eating their lunch on and once again began the ardent task of freeing Vicki. It was a slow and tedious job because I had to be careful not to cause her any undue harm. I'd just finished pulling the last chain from her when one of the guards gave a weak groan and moved his foot.

"I thought I'd killed them all," I said in a voice that didn't sound like mine at all.

As I started to move toward the man Vicki stopped me.

I watched her struggle to stand and then waddle over to the semi-conscious man. She knelt down beside him, extended her fangs and sunk them deep into his neck. The sucking noise as she replenished her stamina with the power of life giving fresh blood echoed in my ears. I found myself wanting to kneel next to her and partake in it myself. I shook my head and pushed that ridiculous idea right out of it. It was clear my baby was taking control of the situation and for that I was grateful, but enough was enough.

CHAPTER THIRTY

When Vicki returned to a more normal looking vampire, she shoved a gag in the man's mouth and bound his wrists and ankle in a way that made it impossible for him to even fidget, let alone move. She tossed his big bulk over her petite shoulder with surprising ease, held her finger to her lips to let me know I needed to keep quiet, and tip toed out of the door Sara passed through not long ago.

I was amazingly light footed as I hurried behind Vicki. We made our way to the dungeon below. We slipped into alcoves and behind doors to avoid meeting up with an occasional vampire. Fortunately, the majority of the black king's subjects eagerly left to join in on the ambush, leaving us with only a skeleton group to deal with.

At one point, Vicki stopped to take more nourishment from the bundle over her shoulder. I watched the robust color I knew to be her natural state finally return. That last feeding brought a resurgence of power to her just in time as we stumbled onto a guard without warning. She had the element of surprise and pure rage on her side. The black vampire may have been twice her size, but she had twice the rage. The fact that she'd fortified herself with human blood brought her level of vitality and strength equal to his. It was over within seconds. She pulled the dead vampire into one of the many maid closets throughout the castle and closed the door tight. Retrieving her food source from where he lay after she'd tossed him unceremoniously away in preparation for battle, she motioned me to continue.

My heart was so filled with gratitude and love for this petite little vampire whose bravery was astounding that I completely neglected the fact that she had a bound human slung over her shoulder and was feeding off him to the point he just might die.

Although I was sorry for the suffering she'd endured, I was grateful to have her with me. I questioned how I'd have managed saving Jack without her.

It was like Vicki had a homing device set for Jack. She made her way to the dungeon like a bee to its beehive. There was absolutely no hesitation and no confusion. The two guards at the door proved a little more challenging for her. Although she was holding her own, they were making a lot of noise and I feared others would come to investigate. Once again my little babe in the womb stepped forth and gave me the wherewithal to step in and assist. Since it was something the black vampires never would have expected, we had the element of surprise.

I grimaced as my fist drove deep into my opponent's chest and I pulled out his beating heart. It was a necessary act, but it was also a gross act. My body shook with emotion, disgust, and adrenaline as I followed Vicki down the steep steps into the dungeon.

After some serious searching, we finally located Jack sitting in the recesses of a cell all trussed up in silver. I moaned with compassion as I rushed to him. Remembering the burning I'd experienced while freeing Vicki, I pulled off my shirt and used it as a barrier against the myriad of metal that bound my love. The air reeked of scorched flesh and my stomach lurched several times before the task was completed and he was free.

He fell to the floor in weak, exhausted relief. Vicki shoved her bundle before him and urged him to drink and regain his strength. She apologized for taking more of her victim's blood than intended, but she'd needed it to fortify and regain strength for the battles that ensued. I thought he wasn't really paying attention to her babble as he drained every ounce of blood from Mark's man, but I was wrong. As I watched the life come back to him, he smiled at Vicki and thanked her for all she'd done and assured her she'd left him enough to bring him back to life.

When he stood up and stumbled, I realized that, although he'd been brought back to life, it would take more blood than what he'd been able to get from the carcass at my feet to make him strong enough to fight.

"How much more blood does he need to be back to normal?" I whispered to Vicki.

"I drank too much. I feel so bad. It's just that those guards were so big..." Vicki bemoaned.

"Tell me how much more blood he needs," I insisted.

"A few pints, I would think," she replied wistfully.

I rushed forward and extended my wrist to Jack, "You need more blood. Take it."

He pushed my arm away and leaned against the wall.

"I can't do this without you, Jack. Take the blood!" I insisted.

"You need that blood for the baby," Vicki cried softly.

"Jack needs this blood to get out of here. Right now, that takes precedence," I said firmly. "Besides, I've developed a pretty strong bond with the little hero in my womb and something tells me it'll take a lot to get the better of him."

"It'll weaken you," Jack said meekly.

"Seriously?" I scolded, "Are you seriously saying that my strength is more important that yours in this situation?"

He looked me in the eye and smiled slowly. I could feel his love radiating from him even in his weakened condition.

"Drink the blood, my love. We don't have much time. The black king is planning an ambush on Drake and your men. We need to warn them," I said with urgency.

Although I'd offered my blood freely, it still took me by surprise when he pulled me close and sank his fangs deep into my neck. The sucking sound as he fed on me filled my ears and my head went dizzy. I could feel the life force draining from my body and wondered if he'd be able to stop before he killed me. Although filled with fear, I relaxed my body and let him drink until he felt he'd had enough. When he pulled away, I was certain I saw concern in his eyes. Or maybe it was guilt. Whatever it was, we had no time for it and I told him so.

He was his old self as we made our way out of the dungeon. I silently spoke to the babe in my womb and apologized for depleting my body's life source and jeopardizing him in the interim.

Warmth spread through my body and I knew it was him telling me that everything would be alright. Even so, I found it difficult to keep up with Jack and Vicki as they bounded out of the dungeon and made their way toward freedom.

Once we were at the castle walls, Jack motioned us to remain in the shadows while he observed our surroundings. Beads of sweat coated my forehead and neck. I wiped at it with my sleeve, not wanting to show my weakened condition to my companions. When I pulled my sleeve away I saw traces of blood from the puncture wounds made by Jack. I gasped. Vampires had an uncanny ability to smell blood from literally miles away. I was a walking billboard of our presence.

I tapped Jack on the shoulder and silently showed him my sleeve before pointing to my neck. He understood immediately and ripped his own bloody shirt to bind my throat. With the scent of my blood disguised by vampire blood, we made our way to the castle wall. I was grateful Jack had stopped long enough to survey the area. It provided me with much needed rest.

We climbed the guard's steps to the top of the wall with no mishap. It seemed the castle was barely occupied, so eager were they to slaughter Jack's people.

He pulled me in his arms and held me close and whispered, "I took too much blood from you. You should have stopped me."

"Better I'm feeble at a time like this than you," I smiled.

"What about the baby?" he asked with concern.

"He may not be showing like normal babies do at his stage of development, but he's as strong as an ox. I wouldn't worry. Just let's get to Drake and then go home, shall we?" I said with as much bravado as I could muster.

I could see in Vicki's eyes that she knew I was more worried than I was letting on. She reached over and stroked my cheek with affection, but said nothing. What was there to say? We had a mission to accomplish. I suppose I could have asked Jack to take me home first and then continue on, but I was the one with the knowledge of how to get there and I also didn't want to waste the time it would have taken away from our reaching them in time.

Jack placed me on his back and asked me to whisper the directions in his ear as we went along. He noticed my weakened grip and scowled. Setting me back down again he went into the tower room and returned with rope. Although the thought of being trussed to anything ever again repulsed me, I knew he was right. I ran the risk of falling off his back while traveling at vampire speed at heights even birds didn't reach while in flight. The fall would surely kill me and our baby. I closed my eyes and nodded for him to go ahead and do what he must.

Being strapped to the back of my strong handsome lover had an entirely different connotation to it than being trussed to a bed. I actually enjoyed it. I teased him softly that it was something we might want to try in the bedroom someday. He smiled, emitted a low sensual growl from deep in his throat, squeezed my buttocks affectionately, and leapt into the air.

I found myself able to see my surroundings better than I had during past journeys of this nature. Even so, I closed my eyes and funneled the information to Jack's mind that I'd received and given to Drake and Jeremiah. Vicki stayed a respectable distance behind her king, but was close enough to be of use if needed.

We soared through the air, leapt from tree to tree, and occasionally ran on the ground. The place of ambush was far enough away from the black king's castle that if something did go amiss and they needed to retreat there'd be no tracing them back to it.

Mark told me it was a two-day journey from Jack's castle to the ambush point. They were at least three-quarters of a day ahead of us. Our only hope was that as a small party we'd be able to travel faster than them.

I could feel myself growing weaker and weaker as my remaining life force was absorbed by the babe in my womb. He was gearing up for battle, I could feel it. My heart swelled with a mother's pride over his bravery even while my body sank deeper and deeper into the danger zone.

I did my best to disguise my worsening condition to Jack. When he stopped to rest and set me down on the forest ground, I stumbled and blamed it on the mode of travel. Having seen me do similar things from this type of travel in the past, Jack accepted my explanation with no reservations. Vicki, on the other hand, assessed me carefully. It was clear she didn't believe a word I said.

"I need to use the privy," she said to Jack. "Jess looks like she could use a little attention as well. I spotted a lake just over the ridge. What say Jess and I go freshen up a bit?"

Even in my weakened state I mused at the concept that vampires went to the bathroom. I'd never noticed Jack doing it, but apparently it was something they did. Another myth debunked.

Vicki grabbed me by the waist and before I realized what was happening she'd lifted me off the ground and was carrying me a good distance away from Jack. I suddenly felt very vulnerable.

When we stopped, I saw no lake and looked at her curiously.

Without a word, she bit into her wrist and forced it against my mouth. I tried to protest, but when I parted my lips to speak she shoved her blood filled wounds against my lips so powerfully it forced blood into my mouth. As the blood built up, I had no choice but to swallow it.

"I'm sorry to force this upon you, but you're going to die if you don't drink this. Jack may accept your lame excuse for the way you look, but I know better," she said gently.

There was no other way to define the blood's taste except to say it was metallically delicious. Once again my baby took control and I drank greedily.

I heard more than saw Jack's arrival. The world had shrunk since giving my blood away to a small view within a tunnel of darkness. My peripheral vision was long gone.

"Vicki, no!" he roared as he ripped her wrist from my mouth.

I wined in protest, but was unable to do more. I felt odd. I wasn't tired, but I wasn't energetic either. I just...was.

"She's dying, Jack, can't you see that?" Vicki hissed, mindless of the fact that she was addressing her king by his first name.

I got the distinct impression that this wasn't the first time she'd done this. Jack seemed not to notice as he continued to berate her for her actions.

"You took too much from her," Vicki said defensively. "I can't believe you couldn't see that. She was dying before your very eyes! She still might," she shrugged, "You stopped me too soon."

Jack took my face in his strong hand and moved it left, right, up, and down. He pulled my lower eyelids down and looked carefully. Finally, he put his ear to my chest and listened.

"You're right," he said softly. "I'm sorry."

"Well, fix it," Vicki demanded.

"I can't," he said as his shoulders sunk low.

"Of course you can!" Vicki shrieked. "Just give her blood and it'll all be alright."

"It'll kill the baby," he whispered.

"What? How? It's a vampire child. That doesn't make sense," she said angrily.

"Marigold told me that if Jess was turned before the baby was born, it would kill the child," he explained.

"Then kill the child!" Vicki ordered.

"Wait a minute!" I interrupted weakly, "No one is killing my baby."

"It's between you and the kid right now and my vote is for you," Vicki said in a choked up tone. "What say you Lord Devon?"

He looked at me with sorrowful eyes, "I have to agree with Vicki. I couldn't bear to lose you."

"You would have lost me eventually. You said so yourself," I spat defensively as I backed away from them.

"I thought I had time to get you used to the idea of becoming vampire," he explained as he advanced toward me. "I wanted to discuss it with you when we had time to do it at length and I could answer all your questions fully. We've just never had that time."

"You would kill our baby?" I said incredulously.

"I don't want to, but I see no other way," he said sincerely.

"Does Marigold know firsthand the baby will die?" Vicki broke in. "Has she seen it with her own eyes?"

"I don't believe so. I think it is just wisdom handed down through the ages," Jack replied.

"Another vampire myth," I said softly.

"What did you say?" Vicki's attention was turned on me full force.

"Jessica was filled with misconceptions about vampires when we met. One by one their being dispelled," Jack explained as he looked at me lovingly.

"Maybe this is another myth," Vicki said excitedly.

"Yes! Yes! Maybe it is..." I agreed, "I mean... you guys even pee!"

The absurdity of my last comment struck us all at once and we burst into a peel of laughter. It was enough to lighten the mood and give us hope.

It took a little more convincing to get Jack to allow me to drink a little more of Vicki's blood and not his. Both Vicki and I were concerned that even a drop of blood lost from him would shift the odds of battle, should we find ourselves in one. In fact, she encouraged him to hunt for a deer or a bear to nourish him while she nourished me. After we'd vowed to be careful and have me take only enough blood to balance me out, but not so much that it would weaken Vicki or turn me vampire, Jack disappeared into the forest.

CHAPTER THIRTY-ONE

""I'm sorry it's come to this Jess. I know you were given no choice but it's the only thing I know to save you. I knew the minute I set eyes on you that we would be lifelong friends. I can't bear the thought of losing you either," Vicki explained while I sucked greedily on her arm.

I could feel the power of her blood flow through my veins. My baby responded immediately. Once again I felt the surge of adrenaline and energy fill my body. Although she said nothing, I could see that I was very close to taking more blood than was safe for Vicki. I forced myself to stop. It had to be one of the hardest things I'd ever done.

Vicki stepped away and stumbled a little. I reached out to steady her.

"Now look who's caring for whom," she said weekly.

"I took too much," I said with concern. "Why didn't you stop me?"

"You're living is far more important than my dying," she explained. "I make the sacrifice willingly, my queen."

"Are you going to die?" I wailed in dismay.

"No one's going to die," Jack barked as he approached us with an enormous black bear trussed over his shoulder. "Drink and replenish, Vicki, so we can be on our way."

His matter of fact order was just what we needed to keep our emotions in check.

I watched Vicki partake in the bear's blood and licked my lips. I craved its taste.

"You'll crave it for a while until you fully turn," Jack explained.

"I'm vampire now?" I asked.

"No, but if you die you'll become one," he explained.

"I feel like I could be one now," I said uneasily. "I feel very... odd."

"You drank a lot of her blood," he replied.

"I didn't mean to. I had to force myself to stop," I explained.

"She didn't stop you?" he roared.

"N... no," I said meekly.

I watched Jack process the emotions that were raging through him. He was angry with Vicki for jeopardizing her own life, but also grateful that the baby and I were well and safe. When he finally gained control enough to speak, he prompted Vicki to complete her feeding so we could be on our way.

She surprised me with the tenderness and consideration she showed the bear as she positioned it in a way that it would be comfortable for the length of time it took it to recover and thanked it for providing its much needed life source. The bear blinked at her as if he understood and was saying 'you're welcome.' It was an amazing thing to witness.

"Do you always do that?" I asked anyone in general.

"Always," Jack replied as he positioned me on his back.

Even with the surprising increased bulk of my stomach that occurred after I'd fed on Vicki to deal with, this time there was no need for securing me with ropes.

We traveled the last stretch of our journey with speed and efficiency. Jack's power was returned to him full force and Vicki seemed none the worse for wear. I secretly questioned if I might have died from the blood loss caused by my baby and Jack's needs prior to Vicki giving me her blood. There was a brief moment when Jack stopped her that I was looking through a dark tunnel at the world and all sounds were muffled and barely audible. I questioned if the only thing that kept me from completely expiring was the little bit of blood I'd ingested before Jack stepped in. I would always be grateful for my friend's keen astuteness, loyalty, and chutzpa for standing up to Jack.

I ran my tongue over my teeth. I really felt I'd turned already, but if that was true I'd have fangs. I felt nothing. I admit I was a little disappointed. The anticipation of dying and coming back to life left me a little unsettled. I would have much rather had it have already happened and be behind me, but it was probably for the best, since there was speculation that the baby could die if I became vampire while carrying it.

Even so... there was something distinctly different about me overall. I couldn't put my finger on it but something was different that went beyond the fact that my stomach experienced a growth spurt. Since I'd been fed Jack's blood for almost two months and not felt this way, I knew it was more than just the fact that I had vampire blood in me. If it hadn't been for the lack of fangs, I would have sworn I'd morphed into vampire.

"I'm a humanoid, but not an earthling," I shouted in Jack's ear as we continued our journey. "Have you ever turned a Kurr?"

He shook his head with concern. It hadn't dawned on him that he was dealing with an alien species and not a human from earth. Even though we resembled each other greatly, there were some slight differences. What if those differences were enough to make a significant impact on my becoming vampire?

"I think I'm a vampire already," I said firmly.

"Do you have fangs?" he asked over his shoulder as he bounded from one tree to another.

"Let me see," Vicki said as she clung to a nearby branch.

I opened my mouth as she kept steady with Jack's movements and looked into my mouth.

"I don't see any," she shouted as she bounded to another tree.

"I still think I am," I replied.

"Is the baby okay?" Vicki asked with concern.

"It feels like he's stronger than ever," I replied. "I can feel him growing inside me."

"Let's focus on saving Drake and my men and then we'll look into it, okay?" Jack reasoned.

I nodded and remained quiet for the rest of the journey.

By nightfall, we'd reached the point of rendezvous. Vicki spotted the black king and his army off in the distance and signaled Jack. We dropped into the forest and found refuge in a small but serviceable cave. It was clear we'd reached the point before Drake and Jack's men. He wanted to warn them and get them turned around immediately, but was insistent on seeing to my safety first. After making sure I was snug and secure and well hidden in a small cave on the mountainside he and Vicki took off to locate Drake.

As I sat in the cool darkness, I assessed my body. It had changed. It morphed with incredible speed that was similar to how it morphed after losing my virginity on Kurr. I was convinced something was happening that was out of the norm. I just didn't know what.

I felt my stomach and gasped. In the short time since Jack and Vicki had hidden me, my stomach had grown in size. Could that be why I felt so strange? Was my baby having a Kurr style growth spurt? If so, that was quite some spurt. I thought back on when I could have possibly gotten pregnant. My suspicions of it happening on Kurr my first time with Jack had to be correct. That would explain things. Even though a vampire's gestation was less than a human's, a few days was still awfully short. A few months, on the other hand, made more sense. All the times I was vomiting and blaming it on other things, it was probably due to the pregnancy.

I smiled as I massaged my belly while whispering sweet nothings to my baby. I was happy and content and looking forward to the future. I no longer thought I was a vampire. The odd feeling must have been the baby getting ready have its growth spurt. I could only reason the intake of vampire blood brought it on.

As time wore on, what started out as an exciting experience became something that was extremely uncomfortable and frightening. Not only was my stomach growing larger, but it was paining me.

Something was terribly wrong.

I sat in pitch black coolness of the cave with perspiration pouring off me as if I was sitting in a sauna. Not only was my stomach cramping to the point it took my breath away, but the baby was moving around like a scuba diver fleeing a shark! I had no clue what to do to ease the pain, nor did I understand what was happening.

I was frightened.

I wanted Jack.

I listened in the night for signs of Jack and Vicki's return, but could hear nothing over my panting. My breathing was getting so labored I decided to try controlled breathing like I'd seen in a movie. Of course I had no clue what I was doing, but the steady rhythm of air going in and out seemed to help a bit.

I'd lowered the waist of my pants to accommodate my stomach, but even then they were too constricting. I needed to find comfort some way, somehow. I inched my way up the wall until I was standing. I don't know what possessed me to be all brave and assure Jack and Vicki that I'd be fine in the dark like this. It wasn't that I was afraid of the dark because I wasn't. It was the intense sensation of claustrophobia that overtook me when I was unable to see and realize an exit. Now that I was aware of Sara's attempt to bury me alive I at least understood it.

Bracing myself against the wall, I removed my pants from my cumbersome body. They felt wet and sticky. Could I be bleeding? I held them near my nose. It smelled like vaginal bleeding to me, maybe a little worse.

It suddenly struck me that I might be giving birth.

I couldn't believe my situation. I was alone and giving birth to a vampire baby in complete blackness of a cold dirty cave without a clue on what to do.

I closed my eyes and tried to connect with Jack. It wasn't working. I didn't know why it wasn't working. He drank my blood. We should have been connected. The baby's head moved down and pushed on my cervix and I clenched my teeth. I didn't dare scream the scream that was trying to force its way out. Sounds echoed through the mountains and I couldn't risk the black vampires hearing me.

I tried to connect to Jack again.

Nothing.

Why wasn't it working?

I went over the explanation both Jeremiah and Drake had given me about why Jack fed me his blood and how because I had his blood in my system he could connect with me and vice versa. It just wasn't making sense.

Then it dawned on me. Jack drank most of my blood. It felt like he'd practically drained me of it. That left little trace of his blood in me. It was Vicki's blood in me now, not Jack's. Did this blood connection thing work with all vampires? I hoped so.

I focused on Vicki.

Her face flew up in front of me and I told her I was in labor. She assured me she was on her way and disappeared. I lowered myself back down to the cold earthen floor of the cave and sat in a pool of bloody mess while I waited for my friend to come to the rescue.

By the time Vicki arrived the baby's head was crowning. I looked for Jack, but saw only Vicki. I was in too much pain and panic to even bother asking why she came alone.

Sadly, Vicki knew even less about birthing babies than I did. We relied on instinct and scenes from television shows and movies to get us through. Vicki bemoaned Marigold's absence so many times I lost count.

The sun was just peeking over the horizon when my little ball of vampire flesh took his first breath. We were both so emotionally and physically exhausted from the ordeal that we didn't even bother with the fact that his cries might attract the enemy.

We had no water to clean him with so we cleaned him the way we'd seen animals clean their newborns. I thought it would be a disgusting process, but it was actually a soothing act for both us and the baby. I removed my shirt and wrapped him in it. When he was clean, warm and quiet I focused on Jack.

"I was surprised Jack didn't return with you," I said hesitantly. If the black king had gotten him, I wasn't sure I was up to knowing.

"I didn't tell him," she said quietly. "We arrived just minutes before the ambush. We barely had time to warn Prince Mandrake and the soldiers. We were in the middle of battle when I got your message. I had no idea where Jack was and, quite frankly, I felt he was needed there more than he was here." She smiled enthusiastically, "From where I stood when I was leaving, it looked like we were winning!"

"How long do these battles usually take?" I asked.

"Sometimes days, but I doubt that long for this one. Ralph's people looked disconcerted that we were on the ready for their attack. They were starting to retreat when I left."

Vicki gathered some soft foliage to create a bed for the baby and then helped me to the cave opening so I could breathe in fresh air and admire the sunrise. It was beautiful.

With the sun providing light for me to actually see the state I was in, I gasped in horror. Not only was I wearing nothing but a bra, I was bloody and bruised from the birthing. It was a far cry from the beautiful new mothers you'd find in the hospital maternity wards. I was still bleeding and there was a sac coming out of me that neither Vicki nor I knew what to do with. It was a frightening sight.

Just then Jack and Drake landed nearby. Drake jumped from Jack's back and made way for us, mindless of the pleas we made for him to keep his distance for modesty's sake. Jack stood looking in shocked horror at the state of me.

"She's lost the baby," he shouted as he rushed to my side. "I can't believe I left you alone to go through this."

"What am I, invisible? I came to be with her," Vicki said indignantly.

"How did you know to come?" Drake asked.

Vicki looked at him hesitantly, so I said what she and Jack couldn't.

"I drank her blood so we were connected," I said boldly.

"Not Jack's?" he mused, clearly confused.

"I'd like to clean up and put clothes on," I said softly to Jack.

He swept me up into his arms and then planted me back down again when he saw the sack between my legs.

"What's that?" he asked with panic in his voice.

"It's her placenta. Where's the baby?" Drake said with urgency.

"Do you know about these things?" Vicki asked excitedly.

"I've delivered a few babies in my day," Drake replied.

"Oh thank the saints," I said. For the first time since they left me alone I was not overwhelmed with fear. "The baby's inside. He's fine, but neither of us have any idea what we did or what to do about... what did you call it?"

"Afterbirth," Jack said as he rested his head against mine.

"Go see your son," I whispered as I gave him a little nudge.

"I'll get him!" Vicki shouted as she rushed into the cave and emerged only seconds later with my red faced newborn.

While Jack hedged and hawed about the prospect of possibly breaking his son if he attempted to hold him, Drake dove right into the clearing and cleaning up the mess Vicki and I made of my body. I was self-conscious about being so naked and vulnerable in front of him for a few minutes, but soon forgot my embarrassment as he worked his magic and my body returned to normal.

As he'd done several times before, he removed his tunic and offered it to me. I accepted it gratefully.

"She needs to be checked by a physician," Drake said sternly. "The sooner, the better."

He walked over to where Jack was standing. He'd finally accepted the baby from Vicki, but was not in the least bit comfortable holding him. Drake stroked my son's little cheek and said it would be wise to have him looked at as well.

Neither Vicki nor I took offense by these suggestions. We just prayed our bumbling didn't damage the baby or me too badly.

Jack had me hold the baby tight to my chest and swept me into his arms. We didn't travel home at vampire speed out of respect for our son and me, but we still made rapid time. Drake was able to keep up with us at a fast jog. His stamina amazed me. I noticed he took extra care to make sure Vicki was keeping up and doing alright. I wanted to remind him that she was a vampire, but thought better of it. It was obvious he was doing the macho thing for her benefit and from the looks of things she was eating it up. She was certainly enjoying the view of his strong broad and very defined back muscles as he moved with the grace of a wild beast through the jungle. If I hadn't known better, I would have thought giving me his tunic was part of some male strategy to get the woman; a Tarzan thing. It may have been on a subconscious level.

CHAPTER THIRTY-TWO

Marigold had the staff hustling and bustling about as they made Jack's room more suitable for mother and baby. She fussed about the fact that the castle had over one-thousand rooms, yet I was being cramped into his quarters with him. We heard all about how it was done in the old days with mild amusement. Marigold's outrageous ranting were just the ticket to take our minds off what we'd just been through. For Vicki and me, it was the trauma of giving blood and losing blood and then birthing a vampire child and, for Jack, it was being drained of blood and then almost killing me by drinking my blood and then joining Drake in a difficult battle followed by discovering my situation and what followed.

All this within a twenty-four-hour period!

Drake stuck to me like glue, refusing to leave even with all of Marigold's scolding and carrying on. She finally settled for him sitting at the far side of the room with his back to us so that I could have some semblance of privacy while she examined me. It seemed a little silly since he'd seen all I had to offer just hours earlier, but he went along with it.

Vicki sat in a chair next to Drake and carried on a soft, animated conversation with him. I smiled to myself and secretly wondered if his refusal to leave was really about concern for me or possibly to spend more time with Vicki. I hoped the two would hit it off. They had to be the two most wonderful people in my life. Nothing would please me more than to see them together as a couple. I began to scheme ways to make that happen.

When Marigold was satisfied that both baby and mother were healthy and doing fine, she called in a wet nurse to tend to the child. I resisted the notion of some other woman nursing my baby at first, but when Marigold whispered in my ear that for the moment my milk was not the healthiest for a vampire child,

I conceded.

Jack was foolish enough to allow himself hustled out of the room when Marigold arrived and finally gained permission to re-enter. He scowled with open jealousy when he saw Drake sitting smugly in the chair by the window before turning his attention to me.

"We could use some alone time," he growled at Drake as he lowered himself on the bed next to me, "Or do you need to protect her from me as well?"

"I believe you've already done your worst," Drake smirked as he bowed low and guided Vicki from the room.

"Was it really wise to speak to him like that?" I heard Vicki ask Drake.

"He can take it," Drake laughed.

"Can you take it?" I asked as I snuggled into the crook of his arm.

"I can take just about anything," Jack sighed and raised himself on one elbow, "but I have to admit I need to process the fact that the man you were once engaged to has had full access to your most private area and now knows you as well as I do."

"Rather than be jealous, you should be grateful," I cooed as I stroked his hair. "Marigold said I could have contracted a very dangerous fever if he hadn't cared for me like he had. It's called childbirth fever and it's what most women die of."

"I don't like the fact that you had the baby and we're not married," Jack continued.

"You are old fashioned in so many ways," I laughed.

"I am what I am," he declared as he pounded his chest like Tarzan.

That lightened the mood and he soon forgot about the fact that Drake had tended to my naked body and focused on naming his son and the heir to his empire. He asked me if I had any preference in names, but I shook my head. Maybe I still had a small connection to his thoughts or maybe it was just women's intuition, but something told me he had a name he'd always wanted to name a child, should he ever be blessed with one. Of course he'd given up on that ever happening. I gave him carte blanche to name our son whatever he chose as long as I could pronounce it.

That afternoon, on his first day of life, the castle bells rang out in joyous declaration that Joshua Angus Devon, prince of the white vampires, had arrived.

I was confined to my bed and Jack seized the opportunity to stay with me behind closed doors and discuss all that needed to be discussed, knowing there'd be no interruptions out of respect for the mother of their miracle prince. He told me how he'd been lured into thinking he was meeting Mark for a discussion about me and instead was jumped by black vampires and taken to their torture chamber. I relayed my story of being the one to unwittingly lead Drake and his men into the ambush Jack was able to foil and then how I'd been abducted by Mark. When I told him how the baby had taken control of my body and killed Mark and his men he was one proud daddy.

I was concerned about the public announcement of Joshua's birth for fear the black vampires would attempt to steal him. Jack was aware of the boon it would be for Ralph to raise the baby as his own. Vampires that were born were far more powerful and valuable to a den than vampires that were made. The fact that Joshua had the blood of the White Vampire King in his veins would make him extra special if he was raised to be black. It would be a feather in King Ralph's cap.

Jack sent word for his sergeant at arms to come to his suite. They conferred at the far end of the room near the window at such a low tone that I was hard pressed to hear what was being said. I managed to grasp enough of the conversation to realize that, although Jack was acting casual with me about the threat of the black vampires, he wasn't taking any chances and had ordered the guards to be on the alert and ready. I smiled as I sank back into my pillow. All would be well. My baby and I were in safe hands.

"When do you want to wed," Jack asked as he climbed back onto the bed.

"Is that what you two men were gabbing about so mysteriously?" I giggled.

He pulled me so that my back lay against his chest and rested his chin on the crown of my head, "I want to do it tomorrow. Will you be up to it?"

"What's the rush?" I gasped. I'd just given birth to a baby. My body felt like it'd been ripped in half and was incredibly stretched and distorted and he wanted me to act the blushing bride for all to see. Had he lost his marbles?

"We should have married before the birth of our son," he mused.

"What's the big deal?" I asked impatiently.

Jack pulled me around so that he could look into my eyes.

"You have to understand," he said with serious directness, "my kingdom is made up of vampires older than me. They have held onto many of their traditions. As their leader, I must honor and respect that. If Joshua is not recognized as born legitimate, he will not gain easy access to the throne. Even if we marry say... next month, he'd be labeled a bastard for all eternity. I don't want to make life hard for him. Do you?"

Joshua's happiness was an absolute must for me. The fact that I'd walked into an antiquated society struck home. If I wanted to fit in and be a part of it, I needed to embrace their beliefs and traditions.

"He's already regaled as the prince," I said, confused.

"I lied and said we married in secret," he confessed.

I searched his eyes and saw nothing but love. True, he was marrying me for the sake of our child, but I believed he would have married me anyway.

"He might be the only child you'll ever have," I said softly.

Jack looked at me, but said nothing. It struck me that not only would Joshua be labeled a bastard for life, but he could very well be Jack's only opportunity of producing and heir to the kingdom he fought so hard to protect. If he was born on the same day we were married, then no one could claim him a bastard. I looked at the clock. We had four more hours until midnight.

"Can we do it now?" I whispered.

CHAPTER THIRTY-THREE

Vicki managed to rustle up a gown that was suitable for a blushing bride to wear on her wedding day. I was barely able to squeeze into it, but it was the best we could do without Dresser's help, so I shrugged and told her not to worry. Since the ceremony was to be kept hush, hush, only the castle chaplain and our two witnesses were in attendance; the witnesses being Vicki and Drake of course.

If I said I'd never fantasized about a big white wedding while growing up, I'd be lying. Even so, the ceremony was so lovely, so touching, and so meaningful that I felt I'd forfeited very little for the sake of my son. Since it was late and we'd all had an incredibly unbelievable few days, we were in unified agreement that the celebration could wait.

Vicki and Drake gave their heartfelt congratulations and said their good nights. Jack had a snifter of brandy to help ease him into a restful sleep while I partook in the tea Marigold ordered I drink prior to retiring for the night. I didn't mind toasting our marriage with a cup of tea since I inherently knew that it was the tea in my system that helped get me through my birthing ordeal and it was definitely doing its magic for rapid healing. I drank miracle tea and gave birth to a miracle baby.

Sleep came easily to us both. Before we knew it, Anna - the personal maid who was assigned to me by Dresser- was tapping lightly on the door with a tray of tea and biscuits. She seemed unaffected by Jack's sleeping body lying next to me as she bustled around the room to get me ready for the day. Marigold assured her that I would be up to some small activity, but I was to remain within my rooms. I smiled when I heard her refer to Jack's rooms as mine.

Jack mumbled something about lack of privacy before rolling

onto his stomach and emitting an incredible snore.

"We seem to be disturbing my husband," I said softly, fully aware that Jack could hear. "Perhaps I should move to rooms of my own."

"The hell you will," he slurred sleepily into his pillow before flopping on his side and resuming his snore fest.

Anna and I stifled our giggles as I allowed her to help me out of the bed and over to the chair at the small table she'd set up for me. The biscuits were piping hot and delicious. Cook sent up some extra butter and honey, which I slathered on liberally. I was ravenous. If my husband wanted a biscuit he'd better get it soon or there'd be none left.

Had my crotch not felt like it'd been attacked by a chain saw, I would have scooted over with a biscuit dripping in honey and waived it under his nose, but fantasizing about the tease was about all I could manage.

The tea tasted different than it had the day before, yet it was what Marigold prescribed. She'd mentioned giving me something to dry up my milk so that I wouldn't be so uncomfortable. Since it was agreed that a wet-nurse was the better option for Joshua, I agreed for her to do it. I forced the unappealing beverage down as a good patient would and then hobbled back to bed.

Drake bounded into the room unannounced just as the warning bells filled the air. Jack was up in a flash and looking out the window.

He turned to Drake, "They're here."

"I was coming to tell you," Drake replied.

Jack rushed to dress.

"Stay in this room and lock the door," he ordered. "Have the baby brought in here with you. Do it now!"

I rang the bell for the wet nurse and asked her to set herself and Joshua up in my room, explaining we were under attack and it was the safest place for them. She scurried to do my bidding. The frenzied jousting and juggling of my son by his terrified caretaker brought on an onslaught of tears. I did my best to calm him down and eventually managed to get him to sleep. She started to take him from my arms, but I shook my head. I knew who "they" were without Jack telling me. The black vampires had come for my baby. There was no way I was going to let go of him until my husband walked into the room and told me all was well.

There was a loud bang outside and the walls. The battle was on.

Vampires battled much differently than humans did. They themselves were a force to be reckoned with. They rarely had need for a weapon of any kind. Because King Ralph's pride was injured by Jack and my escape and the foiled ambush, he brought some assurance of winning the battle with him. He'd brought cannons.

Another loud boom rang through the castle. Two guards entered the room, pulled the iron shutters closed, and then locked them. They then activated an electrical current through the bars. If a vampire tried to enter through the windows he would be immobilized by the high voltage passing through the bars.

I was just starting to feel confident about our safety when Sara bounded into the room. It was clear by her disarrayed appearance that she'd been in the thick of the battle at some point.

"So, you gave birth to the brat," she hissed as she approached the bed.

"Stay back, bitch," I warned.

I no longer had my son in my womb to give me the strength should a battle ensue, but I had the rage of a mother protecting her child on my side. That had to count for something.

The wet nurse whimpered from the far side of the room. Sara's eyes glowed reddish orange like the black vampires she ran with as she peered to see the source of the noise.

"So we have company," she cooed as she made her way toward her victim.

"Leave her alone. She's terrified as it is," I barked.

"Quite the little protector, aren't you?" Sara chuckled. "Funny, since you couldn't come to her aid if you tried. Right before I tore her head off, your little maid Anna told me you can hardly walk from one side of the room to the other."

"She's not a part of this fight, Sara," I insisted as I stretched my arm toward the wet nurse and wiggled my fingers, indicated I wanted her near me.

"Will you look at that?" Sara teased. "Touching, but not necessary. Ralph wants the brat so she'll live to feed and care for him. You, on the other hand, are worthless and will die." She looked at her watch and then walked over to the overstuffed chair and fell into it. "It shouldn't be much longer for that poison I slipped into your tea to take effect. You'll be nothing but a lifeless corpse in a matter of minutes. Any last words?"

As if on cue, my throat constricted and my breath grew labored. My body was saturated with perspiration as I did my best to maintain consciousness. I looked down at Joshua and burned his sweet little newborn face into my memory. I didn't know what really happened when one died. Did the world just cease or was there more in another dimension? I hoped there was more and if there was I wanted to remember him; every inch of him.

Without warning the sweating and struggling for breath stopped and I was filled with peace. Darkness surrounded me, but it didn't seem to matter because I somehow knew it was temporary. I felt euphoric; free of worries, fear and pain. My body felt light. In fact, I felt free of my body. In the distance I heard a baby crying. It sounded familiar, but my mind wouldn't wrap around who was crying or why. I simply listened as I floated in the darkness without a care in the world.

More sounds invaded my euphoria. Men were shouting, but I couldn't make out what it was about. It didn't matter. I tried to shut out the commotion. I was actually annoyed that my bliss was being tainted by shouting and loud banging. It sounded like they were fighting. As I focused on remembering why men would be fighting, the image of Joshua floated before me. I smiled. He was the product of Jack's and my love. He was perfect and he was mine.

Coldness invaded my perfect space. It was a cold darkness that didn't belong there. I could feel it creeping around me and Joshua. It left me, but I just knew it was still enveloping Joshua.

I was no longer content to float around the darkness in blissful peace. I needed to get into the light so that I could see what was going on. This was not a time to focus on my joys and pleasures. It was time to care for my son. Something was happening. He needed my help. I had to get to him.

I tried to move, but my body wouldn't cooperate. I got the sense that I was too far out of my body to be able to command it. I focused on re-entering. When I did, the sounds around me grew louder and clearer. Jack was in the room. I could clearly hear him ordering Ralph to stay away from his son. His voice was choked with emotion.

Sara was there. Something about her sounded worried. She was trying to convince Ralph not to kill Jack! She asked him to just take my son and leave Jack bound in silver, claiming she had plans of her own for him. What plans could she possibly have for my husband? Why was he bound?

Drake. I remembered Drake. What happened to him? He was always nearby in a crisis and this was definitely a crisis. And Vicki, where was Vicki?

The cries of my son crew fainter until they were no more. The room felt still. Suddenly I heard a noise. Someone was pacing the room.

"I had to do it, Jack. You can't see it now, but in time you will," Sara said. "That baby was trouble, just like that girl was trouble. You should have left her in the ground. You should have never dug her up."

"She's my wife, you bitch, and he's my son!" Jack roared. "The only trouble in this room is you and when I get free of these chains I'll rectify that right away."

There was a pounding at the door.

"Is everyone alright?" asked a familiar voice.

It was Drake!

"Hello, Jack? ... Princess? The door is bolted like Fort Knox. What's going on in there?" he bellowed.

"It's that meddlesome prince," Sara hissed. "He's part of the reason my Berger is dead. Him and that corpse over there."

"You shouldn't have killed her," Jack said slowly. "You've made a huge mistake."

"How is that?" she asked arrogantly.

"There are some things that are better experienced than explained," he said with mild amusement.

"Oh, so you're going to tell me you gave her your blood and she's going to return as a vampire?" Sara spat.

"I didn't give her my blood," Jack said softly.

"I should say not. I poisoned that bitch almost an hour ago. If she was going to shift she'd have done it by now," Sara said confidently. "It's wishful thinking on your part Jack. You need to just get over it and move on. She was only a human... and a troublesome one at that."

"You forget, Sara. She was raised by humans, but she's not human. She's Kurr," Jack continued.

"Whatever. I see no difference. She's lifeless on the bed and that soldier of hers is powerless to get past a few locks and bolts. It's pathetic the way he's pounding on that door. They seem human to me," she hissed.

Just then Drake burst through the door, followed by Vicki and Jeremiah.

"Sisterly love at its finest I see," Jeremiah spat.

I was just starting to be able to see through the slits of my eyes. The light hurt them and my body was still not able to function, but at least I could see fuzzy shapes and my eyeballs were able to keep up with the action at the far end of the room. Surprisingly, my hearing had come back even better than before. I could hear a mouse scurry across the floor. Amazing!

I wanted to shout for Drake to follow Ralph and get my son back. I wanted to scream they were wasting time. It was clear Sara had no intention of harming Jack. She simply wanted to keep him subdued so that Ralph could escape with our son and then wait for Jack to accept his losses and calm down enough for it to be safe for her to release him. Knowing Jack, it could take centuries.

My suspicions were confirmed when Sara responded to Jeremiah's taunt.

"He's bound for his own good," she said. "That child is the spawn of the devil and he belongs with the devil. Jack is good and pure. That Kurr witch put a spell on him or something. Now that she's dead and the baby's out of the way, things can go back to normal. I'm just restricting him until he calms down enough to see that I am right in this. I would never hurt him. He's my only family."

"She married Jack," Vicki hissed. It was clear she disliked Sara. "That makes her family too."

"Bah!" Sara spat.

"Release him now," Drake ordered.

My sight was clearing enough to see the mixed emotions on Sara's face. She appeared to be assessing the situation. Drake proved to be a strong warrior and formidable opponent and he was accompanied by two vampires that would give their life for their king. She doubted she'd get out of a battle alive.

I could feel Vicki's anger. It surged through my veins. With so much of her blood just recently taken into my body, the connection was strong. She looked at me with a start, but said nothing.

'You'll be rising soon,' she said in my head. 'Don't move until you have all your faculties functioning. You'll know when that is. You'll feel a power surge. If you move before that happens, you're still vulnerable and she might see and truly kill you.'

So, I'd really died this time and was now coming back as vampire. The thing I'd dreaded had happened. The experience wasn't bad at all. Unfortunately, the situation was.

I listened as Drake, Jeremiah, and Vicki struggled to talk some sense into Sara. They clearly didn't want to hurt her since she was Jack's sister. I, on the other hand, wanted to wring her neck. Because of her, my son was in the clutches of the dark vampires. If we didn't get him back before they reached their hideout, it could take centuries to find him. The black vampires worked with magic to keep themselves hidden from the white vampires. If they were seen and encountered, it was by their choice.

I sent a message to Vicki to go after the baby and leave me

with Jack and Sara. She nodded slightly to indicate she'd received it and whispered in Drake's ear.

"You are right," Drake said to her.

"Jeremiah, we have a situation here that needs to be addressed," Drake said boldly. "Your king is bound," he looked at me with eyes that expressed his deep loss, "Your queen is dead, and your miracle prince is in the clutches of the dark vampires. We could stand here and try to reason with this insane vampire and allow King Ralph to steal your future leader or we could leave now and rescue him before he's lost to you forever. The choice is yours."

"Go," Jack ordered. "She won't hurt me," he hissed while glowering at Sara, "but I can't claim I won't kill her when I'm free."

"See what I mean? He needs time to calm down," Sara chuckled nervously. "It's too late for that bastard half-breed. Ralph's probably gone underground by now."

Without realizing it, Sara had given them a clue as to where to search for Ralph and his band of dark vampires. He may be using a cloaking spell to hide them, but there were only two entrances to the underworld in the area. If he'd gone underground already then he had to have gone to the nearest one, just a few miles north of their village.

Drake, Vicki, and Jeremiah thanked Sara for giving them direction and were off before she could spit her frustration about their trickery. She walked over to look at me more closely. I let my eyes go out of focus so they wouldn't give away my true condition.

It was so difficult for me to lay motionless while this vile woman who'd tried so hard to kill me twice inspected me. I wasn't mobile enough to be breathing yet, which was good. My limp, lifeless body had her completely convinced I was dead. Had she realized Vicki's blood was morphing me into a very angry vampire that would awaken any minute she might not have looked so smug.

CHAPTER THIRTY-THREE

Vicki managed to rustle up a gown that was suitable for a blushing bride to wear on her wedding day. I was barely able to squeeze into it, but it was the best we could do without Dresser's help, so I shrugged and told her not to worry. Since the ceremony was to be kept hush, hush, only the castle chaplain and our two witnesses were in attendance; the witnesses being Vicki and Drake of course.

If I said I'd never fantasized about a big white wedding while growing up, I'd be lying. Even so, the ceremony was so lovely, so touching, and so meaningful that I felt I'd forfeited very little for the sake of my son. Since it was late and we'd all had an incredibly unbelievable few days, we were in unified agreement that the celebration could wait.

Vicki and Drake gave their heartfelt congratulations and said their good nights. Jack had a snifter of brandy to help ease him into a restful sleep while I partook in the tea Marigold ordered I drink prior to retiring for the night. I didn't mind toasting our marriage with a cup of tea since I inherently knew that it was the tea in my system that helped get me through my birthing ordeal and it was definitely doing its magic for rapid healing. I drank miracle tea and gave birth to a miracle baby.

Sleep came easily to us both. Before we knew it, Anna - the personal maid who was assigned to me by Dresser- was tapping lightly on the door with a tray of tea and biscuits. She seemed unaffected by Jack's sleeping body lying next to me as she bustled around the room to get me ready for the day. Marigold assured her that I would be up to some small activity, but I was to remain within my rooms. I smiled when I heard her refer to Jack's rooms as mine.

Jack mumbled something about lack of privacy before rolling

onto his stomach and emitting an incredible snore.

"We seem to be disturbing my husband," I said softly, fully aware that Jack could hear. "Perhaps I should move to rooms of my own."

"The hell you will," he slurred sleepily into his pillow before flopping on his side and resuming his snore fest.

Anna and I stifled our giggles as I allowed her to help me out of the bed and over to the chair at the small table she'd set up for me. The biscuits were piping hot and delicious. Cook sent up some extra butter and honey, which I slathered on liberally. I was ravenous. If my husband wanted a biscuit he'd better get it soon or there'd be none left.

Had my crotch not felt like it'd been attacked by a chain saw, I would have scooted over with a biscuit dripping in honey and waived it under his nose, but fantasizing about the tease was about all I could manage.

The tea tasted different than it had the day before, yet it was what Marigold prescribed. She'd mentioned giving me something to dry up my milk so that I wouldn't be so uncomfortable. Since it was agreed that a wet-nurse was the better option for Joshua, I agreed for her to do it. I forced the unappealing beverage down as a good patient would and then hobbled back to bed.

Drake bounded into the room unannounced just as the warning bells filled the air. Jack was up in a flash and looking out the window.

He turned to Drake, "They're here."

"I was coming to tell you," Drake replied.

Jack rushed to dress.

"Stay in this room and lock the door," he ordered. "Have the baby brought in here with you. Do it now!"

I rang the bell for the wet nurse and asked her to set herself and Joshua up in my room, explaining we were under attack and it was the safest place for them. She scurried to do my bidding. The frenzied jousting and juggling of my son by his terrified caretaker brought on an onslaught of tears. I did my best to calm him down and eventually managed to get him to sleep. She started to take him from my arms, but I shook my head. I knew who "they" were without Jack telling me. The black vampires had come for my baby. There was no way I was going to let go of him until my husband walked into the room and told me all was well.

There was a loud bang outside and the walls. The battle was on.

Vampires battled much differently than humans did. They themselves were a force to be reckoned with. They rarely had need for a weapon of any kind. Because King Ralph's pride was injured by Jack and my escape and the foiled ambush, he brought some assurance of winning the battle with him. He'd brought cannons.

Another loud boom rang through the castle. Two guards entered the room, pulled the iron shutters closed, and then locked them. They then activated an electrical current through the bars. If a vampire tried to enter through the windows he would be immobilized by the high voltage passing through the bars.

I was just starting to feel confident about our safety when Sara bounded into the room. It was clear by her disarrayed appearance that she'd been in the thick of the battle at some point.

"So, you gave birth to the brat," she hissed as she approached the bed.

"Stay back, bitch," I warned.

I no longer had my son in my womb to give me the strength should a battle ensue, but I had the rage of a mother protecting her child on my side. That had to count for something.

The wet nurse whimpered from the far side of the room. Sara's eyes glowed reddish orange like the black vampires she ran with as she peered to see the source of the noise.

"So we have company," she cooed as she made her way toward her victim.

"Leave her alone. She's terrified as it is," I barked.

"Quite the little protector, aren't you?" Sara chuckled. "Funny, since you couldn't come to her aid if you tried. Right before I tore her head off, your little maid Anna told me you can hardly walk from one side of the room to the other."

"She's not a part of this fight, Sara," I insisted as I stretched my arm toward the wet nurse and wiggled my fingers, indicated I wanted her near me.

"Will you look at that?" Sara teased. "Touching, but not necessary. Ralph wants the brat so she'll live to feed and care for him. You, on the other hand, are worthless and will die." She looked at her watch and then walked over to the overstuffed chair and fell into it. "It shouldn't be much longer for that poison I slipped into your tea to take effect. You'll be nothing but a lifeless corpse in a matter of minutes. Any last words?"

As if on cue, my throat constricted and my breath grew labored. My body was saturated with perspiration as I did my best to maintain consciousness. I looked down at Joshua and burned his sweet little newborn face into my memory. I didn't know what really happened when one died. Did the world just cease or was there more in another dimension? I hoped there was more and if there was I wanted to remember him; every inch of him.

Without warning the sweating and struggling for breath stopped and I was filled with peace. Darkness surrounded me, but it didn't seem to matter because I somehow knew it was temporary. I felt euphoric; free of worries, fear and pain. My body felt light. In fact, I felt free of my body. In the distance I heard a baby crying. It sounded familiar, but my mind wouldn't wrap around who was crying or why. I simply listened as I floated in the darkness without a care in the world.

More sounds invaded my euphoria. Men were shouting, but I couldn't make out what it was about. It didn't matter. I tried to shut out the commotion. I was actually annoyed that my bliss was being tainted by shouting and loud banging. It sounded like they were fighting. As I focused on remembering why men would be fighting, the image of Joshua floated before me. I smiled. He was the product of Jack's and my love. He was perfect and he was mine.

Coldness invaded my perfect space. It was a cold darkness that didn't belong there. I could feel it creeping around me and Joshua. It left me, but I just knew it was still enveloping Joshua.

I was no longer content to float around the darkness in blissful peace. I needed to get into the light so that I could see what was going on. This was not a time to focus on my joys and pleasures. It was time to care for my son. Something was happening. He needed my help. I had to get to him.

I tried to move, but my body wouldn't cooperate. I got the sense that I was too far out of my body to be able to command it. I focused on re-entering. When I did, the sounds around me grew louder and clearer. Jack was in the room. I could clearly hear him ordering Ralph to stay away from his son. His voice was choked with emotion.

Sara was there. Something about her sounded worried. She was trying to convince Ralph not to kill Jack! She asked him to just take my son and leave Jack bound in silver, claiming she had plans of her own for him. What plans could she possibly have for my husband? Why was he bound?

Drake. I remembered Drake. What happened to him? He was always nearby in a crisis and this was definitely a crisis. And Vicki, where was Vicki?

The cries of my son crew fainter until they were no more. The room felt still. Suddenly I heard a noise. Someone was pacing the room.

"I had to do it, Jack. You can't see it now, but in time you will," Sara said. "That baby was trouble, just like that girl was trouble. You should have left her in the ground. You should have never dug her up."

"She's my wife, you bitch, and he's my son!" Jack roared. "The only trouble in this room is you and when I get free of these chains I'll rectify that right away."

There was a pounding at the door.

"Is everyone alright?" asked a familiar voice.

It was Drake!

"Hello, Jack? ... Princess? The door is bolted like Fort Knox. What's going on in there?" he bellowed.

"It's that meddlesome prince," Sara hissed. "He's part of the reason my Berger is dead. Him and that corpse over there."

"You shouldn't have killed her," Jack said slowly. "You've made a huge mistake."

"How is that?" she asked arrogantly.

"There are some things that are better experienced than explained," he said with mild amusement.

"Oh, so you're going to tell me you gave her your blood and she's going to return as a vampire?" Sara spat.

"I didn't give her my blood," Jack said softly.

"I should say not. I poisoned that bitch almost an hour ago. If she was going to shift she'd have done it by now," Sara said confidently. "It's wishful thinking on your part Jack. You need to just get over it and move on. She was only a human... and a troublesome one at that."

"You forget, Sara. She was raised by humans, but she's not human. She's Kurr," Jack continued.

"Whatever. I see no difference. She's lifeless on the bed and that soldier of hers is powerless to get past a few locks and bolts. It's pathetic the way he's pounding on that door. They seem human to me," she hissed.

Just then Drake burst through the door, followed by Vicki and Jeremiah.

"Sisterly love at its finest I see," Jeremiah spat.

I was just starting to be able to see through the slits of my eyes. The light hurt them and my body was still not able to function, but at least I could see fuzzy shapes and my eyeballs were able to keep up with the action at the far end of the room. Surprisingly, my hearing had come back even better than before. I could hear a mouse scurry across the floor. Amazing!

I wanted to shout for Drake to follow Ralph and get my son back. I wanted to scream they were wasting time. It was clear Sara had no intention of harming Jack. She simply wanted to keep him subdued so that Ralph could escape with our son and then wait for Jack to accept his losses and calm down enough for it to be safe for her to release him. Knowing Jack, it could take centuries.

My suspicions were confirmed when Sara responded to Jeremiah's taunt.

"He's bound for his own good," she said. "That child is the spawn of the devil and he belongs with the devil. Jack is good and pure. That Kurr witch put a spell on him or something. Now that she's dead and the baby's out of the way, things can go back to normal. I'm just restricting him until he calms down enough to see that I am right in this. I would never hurt him. He's my only family."

"She married Jack," Vicki hissed. It was clear she disliked Sara. "That makes her family too."

"Bah!" Sara spat.

"Release him now," Drake ordered.

My sight was clearing enough to see the mixed emotions on Sara's face. She appeared to be assessing the situation. Drake proved to be a strong warrior and formidable opponent and he was accompanied by two vampires that would give their life for their king. She doubted she'd get out of a battle alive.

I could feel Vicki's anger. It surged through my veins. With so much of her blood just recently taken into my body, the connection was strong. She looked at me with a start, but said nothing.

'You'll be rising soon,' she said in my head. *'Don't move until you have all your faculties functioning. You'll know when that is. You'll feel a power surge. If you move before that happens, you're still vulnerable and she might see and truly kill you.'*

So, I'd really died this time and was now coming back as vampire. The thing I'd dreaded had happened. The experience wasn't bad at all. Unfortunately, the situation was.

I listened as Drake, Jeremiah, and Vicki struggled to talk some sense into Sara. They clearly didn't want to hurt her since she was Jack's sister. I, on the other hand, wanted to wring her neck. Because of her, my son was in the clutches of the dark vampires. If we didn't get him back before they reached their hideout, it could take centuries to find him. The black vampires worked with magic to keep themselves hidden from the white vampires. If they were seen and encountered, it was by their choice.

I sent a message to Vicki to go after the baby and leave me

with Jack and Sara. She nodded slightly to indicate she'd received it and whispered in Drake's ear.

"You are right," Drake said to her.

"Jeremiah, we have a situation here that needs to be addressed," Drake said boldly. "Your king is bound," he looked at me with eyes that expressed his deep loss, "Your queen is dead, and your miracle prince is in the clutches of the dark vampires. We could stand here and try to reason with this insane vampire and allow King Ralph to steal your future leader or we could leave now and rescue him before he's lost to you forever. The choice is yours."

"Go," Jack ordered. "She won't hurt me," he hissed while glowering at Sara, "but I can't claim I won't kill her when I'm free."

"See what I mean? He needs time to calm down," Sara chuckled nervously. "It's too late for that bastard half-breed. Ralph's probably gone underground by now."

Without realizing it, Sara had given them a clue as to where to search for Ralph and his band of dark vampires. He may be using a cloaking spell to hide them, but there were only two entrances to the underworld in the area. If he'd gone underground already then he had to have gone to the nearest one, just a few miles north of their village.

Drake, Vicki, and Jeremiah thanked Sara for giving them direction and were off before she could spit her frustration about their trickery. She walked over to look at me more closely. I let my eyes go out of focus so they wouldn't give away my true condition.

It was so difficult for me to lay motionless while this vile woman who'd tried so hard to kill me twice inspected me. I wasn't mobile enough to be breathing yet, which was good. My limp, lifeless body had her completely convinced I was dead. Had she realized Vicki's blood was morphing me into a very angry vampire that would awaken any minute she might not have looked so smug.

CHAPTER THIRTY-FOUR

The more I listened to Sara's attempts to convince Jack that she'd done the right thing, the angrier I got. I kept myself connected to Vicki so that I could know their progress in finding Joshua. They found the entrance to the underworld and were heading in there. She warned me that it would be more difficult to keep connection since the surface world dealt with the third dimension and the inner world was ruled more by the second dimension. Crossing dimensions when you're a novice can be tricky.

I explained to Vicki that I was building up a type of rage toward Sara with every passing moment and wanted to snap her neck like I'd done with Mark and his men, even though Joshua was no longer inside me. She said that was the vampire blood taking over. When a new vampire is made, all emotions and senses are heightened to maximum and the energy level is intense. She assured me it would level off as time passed, but warned me not to kill Sara when I was finally able to move. She explained that although Sara exasperated Jack, she was still his sister and he took family ties very seriously.

Although I found it difficult to tolerate that fact that Jack would want to protect the bitch that repeatedly tried to kill me and stole our son, I took Vicki's warning to heart. The last thing I wanted was for Sara to come between us.

Sara moved back to Jack and sat next to him. He was so angry his face was almost scarlet red. It didn't look safe for him to have such a buildup of pressure and I was concerned. Sara devised a way to secure him where the only time the silver that bound him came in touch with his flesh was when he tried to move. He was angry and frustrated and, although she was his sister, I questioned her safety. She may have stepped over the line this time. The way I felt at that moment, I actually hoped she had stepped over the line. If ever in my life I hated someone, this was the time. I don't believe it was all vampire hormones. She'd done enough harm to me to make me hate her no matter what I was.

'I'm ready to move,' I said telepathically to Vicki. *'I need to free Jack. If I can't kill the bitch, what do I do to get near him?'*

'Take her by surprise and push her through the window. The bars will shock her enough to immobilize her, but they shouldn't kill her. She's an old vampire. It takes a lot to kill old vampires,' Vicki replied.

'Have you got my son?' I asked.

'We're above ground again. The underground route was just *a rouse. We don't have him yet, but we're on their tail,'* Vicki assured me. *'Get Jack out of that contraption and come help us. The rage between the two of you is enough to kill Ralph's army while we just sit back and watch!'*

I smiled in my mind at her wit and the truth behind it. Jack was angry enough to kill them all himself and I wasn't far behind him. I played out the scenario of shoving Sara through the window in my head like I'd played out the spy escape scenes with Mark and his guards. I wanted to make sure I didn't fail at planting her in those bars. She was an old vampire who truly wanted me dead. If she got to me again, it would be the true death. I needed to be careful and precise with my movements.

I needed to get her out of the chair so that I could have decent leverage when I pushed her. She'd lost interest in me and was completely focused on Jack. After playing it out several times in my mind, I took a deep breath and hoped it worked just as well in reality.

The deep breath caught her attention. She was up in a flash and standing over me. As she bent down to examine me, I made my move. I grabbed her by the shoulders while leaping off the bed with speed I never dreamed I could achieve. She stumbled back in surprise. I took advantage of her loss of balance and plowed her through the window. Her scream told me of the excruciating pain she was in, but it did nothing to move me to help her.

I rushed to Jack's aid and soon he and I were both leaping

over tree tops with me in the lead and getting my direction from Vicki telepathically. If I hadn't been so focused on saving my son, I might have enjoyed the rush that flowed through my body when I called upon my muscles to move me at vampire speed. It felt far more natural now that I was a vampire.

We caught up with Drake and Jack's guards within the hour. I was shocked to discover I wasn't even tired. If anything, my adrenaline was pumping stronger than ever. I stood in front of Drake hesitantly. I wasn't sure if he'd accept the fact that I'd become a vampire, even if it was through no fault of my own. In truth, I would have asked Jack to turn me anyway. I was in love with and married to a vampire and the mother of a vampire baby. Of course I'd want to become one with them. Even so, I was hesitant to reveal it to Drake.

To my surprise, Drake looked at me long and hard, nodded his head and said, "Good. Welcome. Are you ready for battle?"

Boy was I!

Relieved, I nodded my head vigorously and squared my shoulders. I was beginning to wonder if Vicki's joke didn't have some truth behind it. From the way Jack was pacing and coiled for action and the way my body was about ready to explode if I didn't find an outlet for my rage soon, we could very well have been all that was needed to conquer Ralph's army.

I'd just finished lamenting to anyone who would listen about Jack, Vicki, and my sloppiness in not paying closer attention to the route we took to escape the castle when the scout returned with the information we needed. He started to address Drake with his news, but when he noticed us he stopped short and bowed to his king. Jack bid him stand and finish giving his report. The scout had not only located King Ralph enroute to his castle, but the magical veil had been lowered so that Ralph could find his way home. Because of this, the guard not only knew its location, but how to enter the castle as well.

It was unanimously decided that, once Joshua was safely back in our hands, Jack's army would perform a raid on the dark vampire's castle. The scout was clever enough to mark the trees near the opening of the magic shield so that when it closed again we could find it. Jack patted him on the back and praised him for his courage and intelligence. The young scout's smile was so broad and genuine I was sure he'd revel with pride over his king's praise for centuries to come.

Jack insisted I stay behind with Drake and the army while he and a party of six vampires set off to steal our son back. He was afraid if we approached them head on and a battle ensued, Joshua may be killed. After all, he was only one day old. I was disappointed, but I could also see the logic in his thinking. I urged him to remember to save the wet nurse as well and kissed him long and hard. I could feel his power through the kiss and knew my son would be back in my arms in no time.

I was right. In less than an hour Jack was standing before me holding our newborn in his arms. The wet nurse was none the worse for wear, but truly frightened. Fearful that her milk would dry up, I did my best to soothe her nerves and assure her all would be well and she was safe. It was unfortunate that I happened to have been full of vampire blood when I gave birth. I didn't understand the reasoning, but Marigold insisted that a vampire baby born of a human mother required only human milk for the first few weeks and then could be weaned from the milk and placed on blood. I prayed she wasn't quoting some superstitious wives tale because that wet nurse was the only one we were able to locate on such short notice. If she was unable to nurse my son because of the trauma she'd experienced, I wouldn't be able to do anything. The tea Marigold fed me dried up my milk almost immediately.

Jack asked Vicki to accompany me, the baby, and the wet nurse home. He and Drake were going on to finish it with Ralph once and for all. Vicki asked to speak with Jack in private and was granted her request. It wasn't until we were just outside the castle when she told me what they'd spoken of.

"I spoke to Lord Devon about the situation here at the castle with Sara. With any luck, she's still passed out from the electric shock, but she'll be coming around soon. I felt uncomfortable with this. After all, she just keeps trying to kill you and one of these times she might be successful. Now, there's our miracle prince to think of as well. Sending you back to a castle that contains that evil vampiress is risky business," she explained.

"What was his suggestion?" I asked.

"He expressed great reluctance, but finally made his decision," Vicki replied. "We're to go to the remote part of the castle and wait there for him. Hopefully when Sara revives she'll head for King Ralph's and not realize we're back."

"What if she sticks around and finds us?" I asked hesitantly.

"We have permission to kill her," she said flatly.

It was odd, but now that I had my baby back safe and sound, I'd lost the rage that consumed me earlier. I had no desire to fight with anyone over anything and I definitely had no desire to kill. I sighed heavily.

"Can we walk like normal humans the rest of the way?" I asked Vicki. "I'd like time to think and I'm sure the wet nurse wouldn't mind solid ground beneath her feet."

It was then that I realized no one had ever told me this poor woman's name. In fact, I knew nothing about her. I rectified that while we walked. Her name was Lynette and she was recruited by Jack's people when her newborn baby died at childbirth. She was considering refusing because we were vampires, but the sum offered to her was astronomical and, since she had family other than the infant that died and could really use the money, she accepted the assignment. Had she realized what would happen, she would have refused because no amount of money was worth dying and leaving her babies without a mother for. I made a mental note to ask Jack to double what they offered her, no matter what the original sum. One advantage of being with an eight-hundred-year-old vampire king is that he'd had time to amass wealth beyond description. Also, no amount of money was too much when it came to Joshua's welfare. I was sure Jack would agree.

We made it to the castle with no mishap and circled around to the entrance that led to the less used rooms. They were opened only when Jack was entertaining a vast amount of guests.

This hadn't happened since he'd assumed the task of guarding me twenty-two years earlier. The rooms were dusty and needed airing. I planned on speaking to housekeeping about that. Even though the rooms weren't being used, they still needed to be cared for to avoid decay.

We managed to get the room we'd selected aired out and habitable without having to call any of the staff for assistance. It was our goal to hide in the castle until Jack returned and the fewer who knew about it, the less risk of it slipping out.

Lynette calmed down considerably and was off in the corner cooing at, and cuddling, my son while he suckled at her breast. I felt a pang of envy over a scene that should have starred me and my baby instead of this stranger, but I pushed it back into the recesses of my mind and reminded myself that it was in Joshua's best interest that things were done this way.

Vicki and I gossiped the time away with stories about my childhood and what I could remember about Sara and Captain Berger. We talked about the Dragos, at first openly and then at a low whisper when we realized we were frightening Lynette. She asked me about Drake and his history. I told her what I knew of his history and then what I knew of him from personal experience. She confided in me that she had fallen for him and wondered if I thought she had a chance. I told her I truly hoped so.

We discussed Kurr and my rights to the throne. I told her that I didn't feel I had any rights. Drake was of equal royal blood and had been fighting with the coalition for over twenty years to overthrow King Orvis and seize the throne back in my name. I admitted that he was engaged to me and probably thought we'd rule together, but, even without me, I felt he was the one who should rightfully rule. He was a born leader with a love for his homeland. I couldn't make that claim.

CHAPTER THIRTY-FIVE

The sun brought in yet another day before Jack, Drake, and a very exhausted army returned to us. They not only managed to infiltrate the castle, but they'd killed the Black King. Those in the Black King's army who weren't killed or didn't escape were given the opportunity to become Jack's subjects once again. Most of them readily agreed. The few that didn't were taken to the castle dungeon. Of course, although they were being locked up out of necessity to assure safety for Jack's kingdom, they were more fortunate than he was when he was their prisoner. Jack didn't believe in torture.

We went to our rooms to see what became of Sara. I had half hoped she'd revived and run away so we wouldn't have to deal with her.

We weren't that lucky.

The power behind my shove was far greater than I'd realized. Sara was still unconscious. Jack seized the opportunity to order her comatose body taken to her rooms where she was to be barricaded in with bars on the windows, locks on the doors, and guards outside her doors at all times until she came to her senses. I had a feeling that would take a very long time.

When I finally found myself alone with Drake, I took the opportunity to broach the topic of Vicki. To my amazement and delight, he was absolutely crazy over her, so I told him about my conversation with her. I thought I was playing matchmaker. I later discovered they'd already started a relationship, but just didn't know how I'd take it; which was why Vicki felt around during our conversation.

Drake confessed that falling for Vicki showed him that the feelings he had for me were more those of a protective brother who loved his sister. His feelings for Vicki were so potent he couldn't even describe them, but I understood. I felt the same for Jack.

We discussed Drake asking Vicki to marry him. He wondered how Jack would take it. I was touched that Jack's and my opinion meant so much to them. I asked him if he planned on taking Vicki back to Kurr and he said 'yes'. It suddenly made sense why she asked me so many questions about the Dragos and my experiences on Kurr. I had no doubt in my mind that Vicki would be able to hold her own on my native planet, but I felt I needed to tell her as much as I knew about the Mannador at my earliest opportunity. If she was going to follow her man into a war zone, she should be warned with as many facts as possible. The image of L'oana floated in my head and I put her on the information list as well.

"You don't need me anymore, Princess," Drake said as we walked the gardens.

"I wish you'd call me Jess, or even sis... anything but princess," I said.

"Sis... I like the sounds of that," he smiled.

I tucked my hand in the crook of his arm and leaned my head against his shoulder.

"I would have liked to have grown up with you...brother," I mused.

"We are, you know," he said softly. "You are my sister and I'll love you always."

"Ditto," I whispered as I wiped the moistness from the corner of my eye.

"No more mush," he chuckled. "What say we find that hot little vampire I've grown so fond of and see if she'll elope with me?"

"Oh, no you don't," I said with indignation. "I was denied a big wedding for myself out of necessity. I won't let you take that away from Vicki when there's no need."

"Argh!" he spat. "I hate big too-doos."

"A prince who hates to be in the lime light?" I chuckled.

"Alright, alright, but can we do it soon?" he asked. "I'm eager to get back to Kurr."

Three days later Vicki looked like she's stepped off the cover of Bridal magazine. Dresser pulled off yet another miracle and created a dress for her that rivaled that of any queen in any century gone by and the most beautiful maid of honor gown for me. It almost made up for the hideous way I looked at my own wedding.

Jack was as handsome as ever when he stood next to Drake as his best man. Jeremiah was flattered and proud to walk Vicki down the aisle. He smiled so broadly at the attendees you would have thought he was her true father.

The ceremony was short, but beautiful. The newlyweds surprised me by saying their own vows. Their words were so touching, so sincere, that it brought tears to almost every eye there.

When the ceremony was over, we gathered for a celebration in the ball room. The staff did such a beautiful job at cleaning up that part of the castle I would have never guessed that just three days earlier it was full of dust and stale air.

Merriment filled the room. We danced and drank and ate wedding cake. In honor of the kingdom's vegetarianism, Drake forgo having meat.

When it came time for speeches, I stood up to make mine. The room was so silent it surprised me. I realized that -other than when I asked my dinner companions what to do about finding Jack- this would be my first time addressing them as their new queen and they were all curious.

With Jack close at my side, I called Drake up to stand next to me and addressed the room firmly with my words.

"For the sake of clarity I wish to inform all of you that this man, Prince Mandrake, is not only Prince of Kurr, but he is my step brother who I look upon as a blood brother." The room went abuzz with whispers and speculation. I waited until they quieted down again to continue. "As you know, I am Princess of Kurr by birthright. I was brought to earth when I was very young to preserve my life after King Orvis killed my parents and seized the throne. Who is King Orvis? Well, just think of the black king and you'll have an idea of who King Orvis is." I took Drake's hand. "For the last twenty-two years my brother has been leading a coalition to remove King Orvis from the throne and return it to me. Along with this arduous task, he assisted my wonderful husband –his best friend- in maintaining my safety. They are, and always will be, my champions." I pulled Jack's hand to my lips and kissed it lightly and then pulled Drake's hand to my lips and kissed it lightly as well before continuing. "I owe so much to this wonderful, beautiful, and considerate man that I have the privilege of knowing and calling family. To add to my joy, he has married a woman I consider to be my lifelong friend. I will miss her dearly when she follows her husband to Kurr, but I completely understand her doing it... and I give thanks for the teleportation launch." The room chuckled softly before quieting down for me to continue. "I have thought long and hard about how I could possibly repay this beautiful couple for the role they played in protecting me and your miracle prince. I want to do something for them that would mean as much as what they've done for me. I can think of only one thing. Therefore, I wish to relinquish my claim to the throne of Kurr and turn it over to my brother, Prince Mandrake."

The room went wild.

"You can't do that!" Drake said in surprise. "It's yours by right."

At the sound of Drake's protest, the room went quiet again. They were all eager to hear my response.

"It may be my right by custom, but it's your right by action," I said. "Let's face it. I don't remember Kurr and what I saw of it recently didn't leave a warm and fuzzy feeling in my heart." I caught my proud husband smirking with the corner of my eye at that comment. "You love Kurr. It's your home, not mine. I belong here on earth, with my husband and my son. Take your bride, return to Kurr and fight for what is yours by right. If you need my help, I'll be there for you just as you've always been there for me." I bowed my head in his direction for emphasis and then added. "I have one request. I ask that you locate the Orvis' slave named Sheshua, free her, and reward her well. Were it not for her, I would be wed to that evil Mannador right now."

"Spoken like a true queen," Drake said softly as he brought my hand to his lips and the tiniest tear of admiration filled the corner of his eye.

Eileen Sheehan lives in her native upstate New York where she enjoys the beauty of the Southern Tier Country side.

When she is not setting her imagination free at her computer, she can be found helping her clients through her holistic business as Lena Sheehan a.k.a. Psychic Lena.

She takes advantage of her experiences and encounters with others while going through life, plus wisdom, and knowledge of the paranormal to help with inspiration of her stories. She occasionally finds ways to insert them into her writings.

An incurable romantic, she has a love affair with at least one character... one book at a time.

Visit her online at: http://www.sheehan-author.info

email: contact@sheehan-author.info

A Sneak Peek at "The Vampire, The Handler, And Me"
by Eileen Sheehan

Chapter One

The clock struck midnight.

Finally.

Time dragged far more tortuously than I could have ever imagined. I have no idea what possessed me to attend a New Year's party stag. Adding to the emptiness of no one to kiss when the television showed the ball dropping in Times Square as the clock struck midnight, was the sting of not knowing a soul in the room. I felt completely out of place. My promise to myself to do something new on New Year's Eve never failed me, until now. This party crowd was a cliquish and unfriendly lot.

I didn't belong here.

I should never have come.

I'm not bad looking. Although, this particular night I felt like an unattractive wallflower, standing alone and unnoticed. I suddenly understood the meaning of being lonely in a crowd.

Well, the clock struck midnight. I'd brought in the New Year doing something new. I was surrounded by the new people I'd been sure I needed in order to bring new experiences into my life for the year to come.

Whoopee! The wallflower could now leave.

With an exaggerated sigh, I carefully tipped the cheap plastic, exceedingly precarious, poor excuse of a wine glass to my lips. I shuddered as the sourness of the equally cheap yellowish liquid forced its way down my throat. I'm sure my host was under the illusion he was successfully passing it off to his array of eclectic guests as champagne. I was on my fifth or sixth glass of the abhorrently vile stuff. One would have thought its pathetic taste would have grown on me a bit by now.

Nope.

My stomach threatened rebellion.

Doing my best to hide the embarrassment of attending a predominantly couples party solo, I inched as far into the wall as possible. I hoped to be even more invisible than I already felt while I watched couple after couple lock lips in celebration of the year to come.

The party's stench assaulted my sensibilities. I eagerly downed the questionable beverage someone shoved in my hand in hopes it would dull my smeller enough to tolerate the blend of overly heated humans mixed with expensive perfume, cheap cologne, cigarette smoke and pot.

My couples envy was short-lived as my attention jerked toward my own physical condition. I could feel the pressure of saliva building up under my tongue. This was a major warning. My stomach would tolerate no more abuse.

Great. Not only was I stag amidst groping couples on New Year's Eve, but I was about to barf.

That would certainly attract attention. I did my best to focus on breathing steadily while I frantically searched past the sea of drunkenness for a bathroom. My brain flashed a fuzzy memory of passing a door with a hand written sign indicating it was the designated party potty. I squeezed my way through the herd of drunken bodies. I didn't know how I would ever make it through the mob with my stomach threatening acute rebellion. I needed to reach that door as soon as possible.

A middle-aged couple bumped against me. They were so lost in performing tonsillectomies on each other with their tongues, I doubt they even noticed. In fact, I doubt they had a clue where they were at this point. I'd never witnessed a kiss of such intense nature in real life before.

Fascinating.

I would have inspected it more in depth if the jolt to my body hadn't been all the opening my stomach needed to coerce purging of the horrendous hors d'oeuvres and swill I'd pummeled it with for the last few hours.

I clamped my hand over my mouth and pushed my way

through the crowd. I ignored the outraged gasps following me as party-goers witnessed sludge oozing its way between my freshly paraffin waxed and manicured fingers.

So much for being the anonymous wallflower.

If people hadn't noticed me before, I'm sure my trek to the bathroom made me the talk of the party, and not in a good way.

I wanted to crawl under the thick Persian carpet that looked like it'd been abused far more than my stomach by the party's fare.

It took tremendous strength and perseverance to push my way past an overly large woman as she crammed her way out of the door the crowd had not left room to fully open. I desperately yearned to disappear. I could hear the woman's utter of disgust while she slapped her hand over her wrinkled nose for emphasis. If I hadn't been on what felt like death's door I would have laughed in disbelief. Surely the stench of my vomit could not have exceeded the stench of the room.

Of course, I'd eaten some pretty dicey looking hors d'oeuvres consisting of an unidentifiable gray stuff spread upon whole wheat and rye cocktail toast, salted peanuts and deviled eggs. Of course, let's not forget the cheap champagne.

Maybe the woman had a point.

Locks of my long strawberry-blond hair scattered around the outside of the toilet bowl as I flung to my knees. I cradled the cool porcelain like it was my new best friend and savior. At this moment, it was. Sweat pebbled on my brow and down my back while I violently purged my stomach of an amazing amount of contents. Had I eaten that much? It looked like it was enough to equal my food intake for the last three days.

Was there corn in the bowl? I don't recall eating corn. Had I eaten corn?

My muddled mind couldn't think strait. I'd always been a nervous and absent minded eater. Tonight was obviously no exception.

I stared, mesmerized by the sight in the toilet bowl—or perhaps I was just more affected by the alcohol than I realized. Whatever the reason, it took some time before I came to my senses enough to coax my body into cooperating enough to flush the toilet and get up off the floor.

I clung to the edge of the yellowed ivory antique pedestal sink and splashed water into my mouth. The water was cool, sweet, and refreshing.

One look into the gilded antique mirror mounted over the sink brought a gasp of horror. All the grueling labor of wresting with my curling iron to produce a beautifully coiffed head of hair was for naught. My naturally curly—and barely tamable—hair was all over the place. I looked like Mufasa from The Lion King! My mascara smeared down my cheeks from the tears caused by heaving up what felt like my entire insides.

I was a sight.

Grateful I thought to tuck a small comb, an eyeliner pencil, and a tube of lipstick in my evening bag; I did my best to rectify my appearance. I was almost satisfied when yet another horror met my eyes. All I could do was stare dumbly at pert and perky nipples that stared right back at me. My cocktail dress was a flimsy teal and cream-colored satin with an incredibly poor excuse of a built in bra. Had I looked like this all night? I should have known it was a bad choice in dresses. My sister, who enjoyed antagonizing me, gave it to me. I'm sure she had a good laugh when I accepted it like some idiot. The tags were still on it when she presented it to me, which showed she had smarts enough to know not to wear it herself.

I should have thought twice about wearing anything gifted to me by her. I should have immediately passed it on to the local charity thrift store. I'm a bit superstitious about making sure I wear new things and do new things when bringing in the New Year. It was the only new dress in my closet. Since the invite to the party was so last minute and I had no time to go shopping, I'd ignored the voice in the recesses of my head shouting, Don't do it!

To add insult to injury, tiny bits of vomit clung to the side of my left breast. There was no way of removing it without wetting down the fabric. I was sure such and act would only accentuate my highly visible nipples even more. Of course it would…

Oh, happy freakin' New Year.

It wasn't off to a very good start.

I sucked air into my lungs—only then realizing I'd forgotten to breathe. Grabbing a paper towel, I wet it and carefully wiped at the vomit. As expected, the flimsy, dry clean only whetted fabric left nothing to the imagination. I might as well have stripped the dress completely off for all the covering it provided.

I was mortified.

With such a large party and only one bathroom to accommodate both genders, it wasn't long before fists pounded, impatiently, on the door. I frantically searched the cupboards in hopes of finding a hair dryer to dry my cursed dress or, at least, warm my nipples enough to stop them from dramatically beaming at the world.

No such luck.

Bang! Bang! Bang!

The door reverberated from the impact of a drunken fist. I wondered if the offender on the other side realized how heavy fisted he was. I was sure it was a male by the sheer impact of the pounding. I knew of few women could pound like that. The door shuddered precariously with each impact of fist to wood. There was nothing to do but accept the fact I had to relinquish the bathroom before the door splintered into pieces.

I ran my fingers through my ridiculous looking hair and smoothed my wild curls as best I could. There was no help for it. At least my face looked half way decent again. I squared my shoulders and then thought better of it since it only served to jut my nipples toward the world even more. Instead, I shrugged my shoulders forward and squeezed my way through the door and out into the crowd.

I was so concerned about my perky nipples and crazy hair I completely forgot about the fact that my vomit putrefied the air in the compact bathroom. The howls of a baritone as he gagged and bellowed for an air freshener quickly reminded me.

I willed my feet to move through the crowd as quickly as

possible and made my way toward the door. To hell with saying good-bye. I'd call in the morning and thank my host for inviting me to this garishly ornate and ancient estate home. The truth of the matter was I didn't even know who was hosting this party. A friend had invited me. It could have been anyone in the room—even the bellowing drunk who'd almost broken down the bathroom door.

My invite was last minute. I knew this but I didn't care. It was an opportunity to go somewhere new for New Year's Eve. Tradition stated it was supposed to bring good luck. I now questioned tradition.

I don't know why, but I didn't want to be in the company of my house mate, Frank, even though we'd both been invited. I actually lied about it. I figured karma was sure to come back and bite me in the ass, but I hadn't expected it to be immediately at the party.

Either Frank hadn't realized my lie or he'd chosen not to acknowledge it. Maybe he'd known more about this horrendous party than I did. He probably knew he'd been invited. Whatever the reason...he sent me off to the party with a hug and a kiss on the cheek and a 'have a good time' before settling down in front of the television set with a sandwich and a beer.

I almost succeeded in elbowing my way through the dense crowd to the exit before I felt a hand in my crotch. It happened so quickly it took me unawares. By the time I regained myself I was unable to catch the identity of the culprit. My head spun from side to side. I couldn't tell if the brazen act had been performed by a man or a woman. Well, I guess I could blame whomever. After all, it seemed the theme of the party.

The fact that I understood the inability of a drunk to resist such a temptation did little to reduce my humiliation. I lowered my head and forged my way through the remainder of the crowd to the safety of the abandoned parking area. My cup runneth over with emotions flying about in all directions. Part of me was outraged and felt violated, while the other part was understanding and forgiving.

I immediately forgot my dilemma when the crisp January night slapped my inebriated butt sober. With the faint sounds of celebration behind me, I shivered my way to my car and crawled in behind the steering wheel.

It was then I remembered I needed gas.

Just great.

I turned the ignition and listened to my engine groan as it shimmied and shook for an easy thirty seconds before settling down to run like a normal engine should. This was a regular occurrence in the bitter cold with my old, almost worn out Mazda. I often joked it belonged in the south where it was warm year round. Under any other circumstance I would have been a little embarrassed about my car's winter start up routine, but there was absolutely no one at this party I cared the least bit about impressing.

I focused my attention on my empty gas tank instead.

There weren't many gas stations in the quaint little New England community where the party was being held. I racked my brain to remember if I'd seen any en route there. I recalled passing a gas station/convenience store while maneuvering my way through a myriad of secondary roads. The pathetic map my friend drew on a thin paper napkin that afternoon served as my guide. I decided to take a chance the station would be open. If not, I was in big trouble. My tank was registering empty. I counted on the reserve in the bottom of the tank being sufficient to get me there. but since I'd already tapped into the reserve, I questioned my wisdom in trying to go further.

What were my options?

I could go back into the party and see if someone amongst the inebriated strangers would be willing to take me home. What if someone said yes? Should I risk it?

Calling Frank was another option. He was normally a heavy sleeper. This was New Year's Eve. He was drinking a beer when I left him. He was probably comatose by now. I doubted he'd hear the phone ringing.

Another option was to risk having enough gas to make it to

the gas station.

I opted to try for the gas station.

I prayed my memory of its location served me right and my gas held out. Now was not the time to be guessing about distances or direction.

A crusty layer of snow coated the gravel of the long, tree lined driveway leading from the estate house—that must have been a beauty in its day—to the secondary county road echoed in the night as it crunched and gave way under the weight of my car. I pulled out onto the snow-free macadam road and shuddered at the desolate January morning. The branches of the baron—yet majestic—trees sported residue of snow that had melted from the day's sunny rays—only to freeze in the bitter darkness that followed. The occasional pine tree wedged amongst the forlorn looking wooded perennials softened the eeriness.

I hovered closer to the steering wheel. I felt the need to camouflage myself from any bogeyman lurking about. You never knew who or what might be waiting for some unsuspecting lone driver foolishly make her way down a desolate county road on a cold winter's night.

I'd never taken the time to wonder about how much of life happened as a result of a person's actions or if fate predestined much of life until New Year's Eve when my luck held true. I was able to see the illumined sign belonging to the little convenience store/gas station. Oh, thank you, thank you, and thank you.

I'm sure my car glided up to the pump on vaporous gas fumes, but it made it and was all that mattered. This part of the state was big on having motorists pump their own gas. I didn't even wait to see if it offered full service. I hitched my collar up around my neck, secured my hat, and adjusted my gloves as far up under my sleeves as they would go before I hopped out of the car. I searched the face of the pump for a place to swipe my credit card. No such luck. I had to schlep inside to pay the attendant when I finished pumping. After emitting a long groan, I reminded myself it could have been worse. I wasn't forced to go into the heat of the store to pay first and then have to stand in the freezing cold to pump.

At least this way I could hop into my car right after I paid and would not have to suffer such an exaggerated temperature drop as I would have, had I been in the heat of the store first. I always kept my car just warm enough to keep the chill away, but never actually hot. I hated the onslaught of cold when I left it. This kept the temperature transition minimal.

New Year's Eve superstitions—to which I was no stranger—must have been running rampant. I found myself standing in a long line at the cash register waiting for those ahead of me to buy scratch-off tickets. There was a cut off time for the lotto—something I never played. The fact that they were allowing customers to buy only scratch-off tickets and not the lottery numbers didn't seem to matter. Apparently, the fact that it was New Year's Eve made it an especially auspicious time to gamble no matter the game.

I stood in line long enough to be infected by the fever that consumed the inhabitants in the checkout line of the immaculate, well stocked little store. When it was my turn to step up to the cash register, I couldn't resist the temptation of purchasing at least one scratch-off ticket.

Maybe I'd have beginner's as well as New Year's Eve luck.

After taking my money—which included the payment for the gas—the heavy set and exceedingly homely girl behind the counter robotically pulled my ticket off a rather large roll and unceremoniously shoved it toward me. She dismissed my presence completely and looked arrogantly over my shoulder to indicate her desire for the next customer in line to step forward. Normally I would have made a point of her rudeness, but my night had been so hellish, a little rudeness was the least of my troubles. In fact, it actually seemed to fit right in to the theme of the evening.

I'd always loved the thrill of gambling. I could easily understand why some people found it addictive, which was why I'd never allowed myself to play the lottery. I had a hard enough time staying away from Atlantic City and its money gulping slot machines. My only saving grace was the fact Atlantic City was a three-hour drive and not just around the corner. I promised myself this would be the first and last time I purchased a lottery ticket of any kind. The last thing I needed was to get addicted to handing dollar bills over to lottery sellers every time I bought gas or groceries.

I stepped to the far end of the counter so I wouldn't be between Miss Congeniality behind the counter and the next poor frozen soul standing in line behind me. Savoring the suspense, I carefully scratched at the silver on the ticket. I knew there was a way to just scratch-off the bottom of the ticket to discover if you were a winner or not, but that deflated the thrill.

I was so engrossed in the moment it took a little time for me to realize someone was standing behind the counter opposite me. It wasn't Miss Congeniality. In fact, it wasn't a girl at all.

It was a man.

A beautiful man.

A beautiful, tall man.

A beautiful, tall man with skin kissed by the sun.

He had to be the epitome of the old cliché 'tall, dark, and handsome.'

My heart leapt from my body when our eyes met. I could feel myself sinking into those deep, dark orbs, lined with thick black lashes. They were the kind of lashes any girl would kill for and mascara companies would pay millions to use them in an advertisement. They drew me in. I felt as if they were speaking to me in a silent language I could not understand, but was somehow familiar. I suddenly had the sensation of being where I belonged—yet where I should not be. It felt comfortable, yet dangerous.

Very weird.

Very unsettling.

Very gorgeous man.

"Do you want to share a ticket?" The words reverberated past his Adam's apple in a smooth, rich, sexy tone as it sent shivers down my spine. If this guy wasn't already doing voice over or radio, he should be.

"Huh?" was my unintelligent, unwitty, and unsexy reply.

His broad smile displayed perfectly straight, perfectly white teeth.

Of course it did!

I found myself embarrassed and self-conscious of my own, slightly crooked, off-white set. I pursed my lips together in the hopes he hadn't noticed them.

"Would you like to split a ticket with me? If we win, we go fifty-fifty. Sound good?"

He was oblivious to my tooth situation.

I'm not the most gorgeous woman to walk the planet, but people consider me attractive. Sure, I'm a little tall and a little fluffy—my friend's polite way of stating someone was slightly overweight—but I managed to maintain a flat stomach and an hourglass figure and could pull off wearing most styles of the day. My hair had tamed down over the years, but it was still a little too frizzy for my taste and required a lot of attention to keep it presentable. Even so, I managed to secure a boyfriend now and then.

At best, these boyfriends came from the "B" crowd. Never, in my twenty-four years of being on this Earth, had a quintessential "A" crowd man paid attention to me...until then. This man was the quintessential hunk. I was sure he belonged at the top of the "A" group list.

I couldn't believe it. He was flirting!

The overwhelming fact that an "A" list hunk had actually noticed me, combined with the fact my body was still half pickled from cheap champagne, left me stuck on stupid. All I could do was nod.

A chill traveled all over my body and I shivered involuntarily as he moved away to procure a few more scratch-off tickets. The faintest scent of his cologne trailed behind him.

Oh yeah, Fahrenheit, my favorite scent.

Questioning my good fortune, I wondered if I should look for hidden cameras or something. It would be just my luck if someone hired this person for a New Year's Eve gag. That would be something my sister, Lisa, would do.

Being in the company of this god-like man emphasized the

memory of what I had waiting for me at my cozy little historic home. Frumpy Frank was definitely from the "C" list, but then—I consoled myself—Frumpy Frank and I weren't boyfriend and girlfriend. We were simply house mates and good friends. Not that we hadn't thought about it. We'd even gone as far as making out. He'd wanted to go all the way—or at least do a tad exploring—but I just couldn't go that route.

First and foremost, I wasn't attracted to Frank. Sure, he was a nice guy and all, but his plain and forgettable looks did nothing for me in a way a man should attract a woman. His mannerisms were nothing to brag about either. Don Juan he wasn't. On a scale of one to ten, my attraction for him was a two…maybe two and a half. My sleeping with him would have been out of sheer desperation and loneliness. Most importantly, I was still a virgin.

I know being a virgin at my age and in today's times isn't the norm. Nevertheless, I was and I had no intention of giving it up to a guy I had only a slight attraction for—which was pretty much every guy I'd dated so far. Frank fit right into that category.

We managed to remain friends in the end. When he needed a place to stay, I was happy to rent him a room in the little historic cottage I'd inherited. I enjoyed the company and the extra money his rent provided. The arrangement worked out great.

Certain my tall, dark, and succulent hunk was a set up. Hell… New Year's Eve gag or not, I intended on enjoying every second of it. After all, it wasn't every day I was paid attention to by a man such as this.

I watched as he sauntered back to me with his beautiful fist loaded with scratch-off tickets.

"I did not know what game you liked to play, so I have one of each. Okay?" he asked smoothly.

It was then I noticed the slight trace of accent and realized he was foreign. My eyes finally looked past my hormones to see him for the first time. He was lightly bronzed, like the rich tan you'd find on someone in Florida who never seemed to leave the sun. He had immaculate and stylishly cut thick, pitch black hair that etched itself over the top of his ears and barely grazed his collar. Although his shoulders were suitably broad, he looked to be medium boned. He had to be at least six foot two. The faint accent when he spoke hinted of island heritage, but I couldn't even begin to fathom what island.

He leaned over the counter so we could both look at the scratch-off tickets he'd spread out. I hadn't a clue what the names of those scratch-offs were. Who cared? With him so close to me, I was lucky to be able to breathe, let alone look at a stupid scratch-off ticket. My entire body quivered in the most delightful sort of way. The sensation was glorious.

It wasn't just that he was gorgeous and smelled great. It was something more. He felt...powerful...different. That's the only way to describe it.

I don't believe it was his accent, height, or build that gave him this sense. He was an imposing figure, true, but it was something more. Something I just couldn't seem to put my finger on.

I closed my eyes and tried to concentrate, but nothing came.

It figures. My stupid ability never works when I want it to.

I was born with a type of psychic ability my friends called a "gift." They were forever grinding at me to get help honing and developing it. I, on the other hand, found it to be a disturbing annoyance. I certainly didn't look at it as a gift and I tried my best to ignore it as much as possible.

Because I hadn't done much to develop my ability, it just happened when it happened. It seemed the only time I got useful information was when an unpleasant occurrence was imminent. Good stuff never stood out.

Heaven forbid if I'd have been able to pick lotto numbers or something wonderful like that!

I was the only one out of three children who was born with the "gift". In fact, to my knowledge, I was the only person in my family lineage with it. Now that I think about it, it's a strange thing since the consensus is you inherit abilities. For some time, I contemplated the idea that my parents adopted me. It felt like it was a strong possibility. After studying my looks against that of my siblings and parents, I looked too much like them, so I abandoned the theory.

Where my psychic ability came from remained a mystery.

He leaned so close to me I could feel the heat of his breath against my cheek. A faint scent of a mixture of cloves, cinnamon, and...what was that, ginger, perhaps...circulated the air. I would have thought the scent of spiced breath mixed with Fahrenheit body would be offensive. It was just the opposite. I found it to be heady.

"My name is Nevi, Nevi Sharpe," he said with a deep, sultry accent. "May I ask with whom I have the pleasure of sharing scratch-off tickets?"

I wanted to answer him but I was still stuck on stupid. I opened my mouth to speak and absolutely nothing came out.

How embarrassing.

How ridiculous.

How mortifying.

He was just a man, after all. What was my issue?

I just couldn't move past the sense of magnificence that permeated the air around him. It was both electrifying and nerve wracking.

"You have a phone call," blurted the bland voice of Miss Congeniality as she approached my newly discovered god-man with a cordless phone.

"Please excuse me," he murmured in my direction as he snapped the phone from the clerk's hand, obviously unhappy to be disturbed.

"Lizzy. Lizzy Ewing," I forced past my lips as he stood up. "My name's Lizzy Ewing."

I could feel flames consume my cheeks when I realized how desperate my voice must have sounded. He studied me with dancing eyes—momentarily forgetting his annoyance about the phone call.

"Nice to meet you, Lizzy Ewing," he said warmly. "Please excuse me."

With that, he lifted the phone unceremoniously to his ear and disappeared through a doorway behind the counter. I assumed it led to his office. At the faint sound of another door shutting behind that door, I felt I assumed right.

The clerk shuffled through the array of lotto tickets spread out on the counter in front of me with a notable smirk on her broad, acne infested face before looking up at me. "That'll be twenty-five dollars," she stated smugly.

I stood there looking at her for a brief moment while it registered with me...I was getting stuck with the entire bill of my not so private scratch-off tryst! Had I just been a victim of some sort of scheme to sell scratch-off tickets? Did someone plant this hot guy to seduce unsuspecting women into falling for the 'let's share a ticket' scenario? Did they have a woman planted for the men as well? I looked around, but saw no one. Surely, Miss Congeniality would never qualify for such a task, even if she could have cleaned up enough for it. Not with her attitude.

Oh yeah, this New Year was starting just great.

I was tempted to tell her about my little arrangement with the man who I assumed was her boss to see her response—or possibly just settle for slapping the smirk off her incredibly homely face—but thought better of both ideas. I unceremoniously reached into my wallet and produced the money her outstretched hand so blatantly demanded.

As I slapped two tens and five ones into her palm, I couldn't help emitting a soft note of indignation when she grabbed them briskly and walked away without so much as a "thank you." After sneaking—or at least I thought I was sneaking—a fleeting look in the direction my god-man had gone, I slipped the scratch-off tickets I'd been forced to purchase into my purse. Securing my coat, gloves, and hat against the bitter cold that awaited, I hurried out to my car.

I'd been inside the convenience store just long enough for the little bit of heat that managed to build up in my car getting there to dissipate. It was freezing! My breath billowed like smoke from a smokestack. I held my breath while I turned the key in the ignition of my pitifully worn out Mazda. Fortunately, the car's engine hadn't cooled down enough to bring it the point where it would spat and sputter like it had when leaving the not so wonderful New Year's Eve party. Of course, at the party there was no one I wanted to impress. Now, it was a different story. I heaved a sigh of gratitude for this little bit of luck when I spotted Nevi looking out his office window in my direction. He was still talking on the phone. Although he did not acknowledge me, I felt pretty certain he saw me. I didn't want to make a more pathetic an impression than the one I'd already managed to make with him.

After an uneventful thirty-minute ride back to my little cottage on the lake, I dropped my keys into the basket on the top of the hall table near my back door. I smiled as I listened to Frank's snores rumble through the dimly lit interior. His snoring was one of the reasons he'd had such a difficult time rooming with people. It drove them crazy. Not me. I actually found the rumblings of a good snore soothing. They acted like a sound machine to sleep by.

I scooted to my bathroom and checked my hair for bits of vomit. It looked relatively clean so I decided it was safe to just brush my teeth, scrub my face, and pull on my slightly worn—yet still cuddly—pink flannel nightgown. I' barely settled beneath my thick down comforter before I was consumed by blissful darkness.

Chapter Two

New Year's Day.

Groan.

The effort of opening my eyes to face the trickle of sunshine peeking through my bedroom window was grueling. After a long cat-like stretch, I swung one leg over the edge of the bed and then forced the rest of me to follow. I've always disliked getting up in the morning. Today was especially hard. Not only was I hung over and worn out from my vomiting party the night before, but I knew I had to prepare myself for New Year's Day dinner at my parent's house. It wasn't my parents I dreaded seeing. I loved them dearly and enjoyed spending time with them. It was my know-it-all sister, Lisa, and her equally know-it-all husband, Brad, who I dreaded spending time with.

Lisa and I were born exactly two years apart to the day. She—being the elder—constantly bemoaned her fate at having to share her birthday with me...the freak. Not only were we born on the same day...we were true to our Irish heritage by being St. Patrick's Day babies.

Oh lucky us.

Lucky me.

The commonality of birthdays and parents was literally all Lisa and I shared. I'm of average height—five foot, four inches. I'm robustly shaped—another of my friend's choices of definition. I have well-endowed breasts and my waist is exactly thirteen and one half inches smaller than my hips. I sport a waist-length mane of full, curly, and incredibly wild strawberry-blonde hair that reflects the paleness of my Irish heritage. Lisa, on the other hand, was lucky if she reached five foot two inches in height. She had straight dark hair that fell in a silky mass down her back and a slender figure that was in stark contrast to mine and her skin tone leaned toward my mother's Mediterranean heritage. So, how would someone know we are sisters?

Our eyes.

I may have taken after my father's side of the family and Lisa after my mother's in overall looks, but we each inherited the rich, blue Ewing eyes that our bloodline favored from generation to generation since as far back as anyone knows. It does not matter the strength of the spouse's genes. Ewing genetics win out every time in the facial area. Ewing children always have rich, cobalt blue, almond shaped eyes set above high cheekbones and below high foreheads.

For years, I envied Lisa's slight build and beautiful straight hair. She knew this, of course, and did her best to find ways to rub it in at our every meeting. I sometimes fantasized she was as jealous of my looks and me as I was of hers. That's all it was...a fantasy. There's no way someone who looked like her could ever have been jealous of someone who looked like me. She was your perfect, all American, turn- "A"-list-guy's-heads-wherever-she-went girl. She was a totally-put-together-and-pretty-enough-to-be-a-model kind of girl. All she lacked was the height. How could she possibly envy me, with my bulky body and barely tamable hair? My mother insisted I turned just as many heads and could land an "A" list guy as a boyfriend if I would just open up and be more self-confident. I didn't agree. No, Lisa was the "A" list magnet of the family. Me? "C" list... "B" on a lucky streak. I'd resigned myself to the fact.

Lisa may not have been jealous of me but she certainly resented me. This I'm convinced to be true. Although for the life of me I couldn't tell you what her reason was. It ran deeper than having to share a birthday with me. Sometimes people just don't need a reason to feel the way they feel. They just feel it.

My brother, Greg, is another story. We simply adore each other. He is the eldest of the siblings. He's a whopping thirty-two and resembles Lisa more than he resembles me. Something my dear sister loved to gloat about. Greg did a few tours of duty in the Marines, which messed him up just a tad. For the most part, he's a good guy. I have him placed on such a high pedestal that I can only imagine his pain should he ever fall off. Unfortunately, he's in California and not here. No Greg to buffer things at the dinner table today.

Bummer.

I looked at the clock. Ten o'clock already? Mom and dad lived in Scarsdale. It wasn't far, as the crow flies, but there was no accounting for the holiday traffic. I've always tried to give myself plenty of time to sit on the highway for a cumulative of twenty minutes—or thereabouts—when planning my trip to my parent's house on an average day. Because of the holiday, I would need to allow a little longer to be safe. That meant I needed to be ready to leave in ninety minutes.

Dashing to the mirror, I inspected my hair more closely. Was it passable without washing? I pulled a handful of locks to my nose and sniffed. I reeked of vomit, cigarettes, and pot. Not to mention a cumulative of colognes that permeated the putrid air of the party.

Nasty!

My cheeks reddened as I recalled how closely my newly discovered "A" list guy, Nevi Sharpe, had leaned toward me the night before. Had he smelled me? He must have.

Oh mortification.

My parents would have probably been polite enough to overlook the condition of my hair, but certainly not Lisa. I had no desire to provide her with any more ammo against me. I had no choice but to wash it.

Washing my hair has never been an easy process. My thick, unruly mane hangs just below my waist. I keep it long in hopes the weight of its length will help tone it down somewhat. Also, people are so enthralled with its length that they tend to forgive its unruliness. Unfortunately, because of this admirable mane, my locks require a special method of lathering and rinsing that is long and tedious. The drying procedure is no simpler.

Doubting I'd make it on time, I decided to do the right thing and call my parents to inform them of my anticipated tardiness. When I picked up the receiver to dial them, I heard the beeping notice of a message waiting. I decided to listen to the message first. I dialed the code and hear my mother's voice message. They were postponing our dinner hour. Apparently, Lisa and Brad had to make a stop at Brad's parent's house in North Salem before they could go to my parent's house. My parents decided to back dinner up by a few hours to accommodate the dears.

I smiled with relief. The fact that no one took into consideration the possibility that changing dinner time would screw up my schedule never bothered me. I dropped the receiver into its cradle and slipped into the bathroom.

A long, long, long shower was in order.

* * * *

Several hours later, I was huddled behind the steering wheel of my Mazda and headed toward the interstate. It was freezing outside! My heater squealed as it attempted to pump the little bit of heat I asked of it into the car's cavity. I buried my nose into the furry scarf I'd wrapped around my lower face and neck. I was sure the heater would generate enough heat to allow me to remove the scarf before I reached my parent's house. I had no desire to give Lisa any fuel for her sarcasm. My car's age was enough of a topic without scrutinizing its working condition.

As I passed the exit to the county road that would take me to the little convenience store I'd met Mister Gorgeous at the night before, I fought the temptation to detour and see if he was there in the light of day and not just a figment of my drunken imagination. If time had allowed, I would have probably done just that. As it was, I would barely make it to my parent's house before they expected us at the dinner table. I could see the table in my mind's eye. It was certain to be set with mom's favorite linen tablecloth and napkin set. Neatly arranged and strategically spaced would be the family's elaborate one-hundred-year-old Royal Albert china, Waterford goblets, and twenty-five-year-old Rogers gold-plated flatware. All in immaculate condition.

Lisa and Brad were just getting out of their car when I pulled up the drive. Great. I'd hoped to slink into the house without the usual criticism that poured forth from Brad's arrogant mouth every time he saw my car. He worked for a large car dealership and was constantly onto me about embarrassing the family with my choice of rides. I didn't have it within me to explain to him that I drove my beat up old Mazda out of financial necessity and not by choice. That type of a confession would only have led to further criticism about the fact that I'd dropped out of culinary school and ended up working in a small town diner where I fluctuated between short order cook and part time waitress. Under the best of conditions, I would not have been up to the confrontation. After coupling with the party commode the night before, I definitely wasn't.

I ignored Brad's smirk as I got out of the car and rushed past him, denying him the opportunity to utter a word. I couldn't help giggling at the shocked look on his face over my swiftness of feet. Nor could I resist a quick peek out the door window to see if he was still standing like a dumb statue without a clue while I removed my coat and hat.

He was.

Pleased with myself, I bounced into the living room to find my father sitting in his favorite chair with the newspaper spread wide open. Dad just loves to read the newspaper—unlike me who barely has a clue about world issues. I don't read the paper and I rarely watch the news. I had drama enough in my own life not to want to dwell on the troubles of the world. I figure if it is something I should know about, someone will inform me of it.

I received a gentle smile and a cozy pat on the back of my hands as I laid them on top of my father's shoulders and kissed the top of his head. He always smelled as if he'd showered with Irish Spring.

Lisa and Brad weren't long to enter. I'm sure their announcement of their arrival was loud enough to alert the neighbors. It brought my father to his feet and my mother rushing from the kitchen. I don't know what it was about Lisa and Brad that made my parent's react in such a way. It's like the queen and king were gracing us with their presence and all the serfs had to rouse to the occasion or risk offending.

I leaned against the archway frame that separated the entry foyer from the living room and watched in amazement—as well as mild amusement—while my mother and father adulated over my sister and her spouse. They assisted their royal highnesses with the removal of their winter coats and hung them on the coat tree near the door.

"Now that the royal couple has arrived, shall we eat?" I asked, admittedly a little more sarcastically than I'd intended.

Raising her eyebrows ever so slightly in a display of disapproval, my mother nodded and motioned us toward the dining room.

Dinner was delicious, but I wouldn't have expected anything less from my mother. A former chef, she gave up her culinary career when she and my father decided to have children. She hadn't given up her love of cooking though, and certainly not lost her talent for it. Mom had a way of turning something as simple as a peanut butter and jelly sandwich into a gourmet work of art.

Invitations to dine with the Ewing family had always been a much sought after and treasured thing. Which was why I was surprised to discover such a small dinner party. The attendees were only my father, mother, sister, brother-in-law, and me. I couldn't remember our table this sparsely seated for a major holiday dinner before. I was about to question mom about it when the doorbell rang.

Dad excused himself from the table and disappeared to answer the door.

"So, tell me Lizzy, how's your career going these days?" Lisa leaned forward and whispered in a taunting voice that was for my ears only.

Oh, why did my mother insist on seating us next to each other? You would think that after all the years of bickering between Lisa and me, my mother would have gotten the hint that her daughters were never going to be friends. The richly polished mahogany table could easily accommodate twenty-five diners when fully extended and twelve without the extension leaves. There were only five of us yet Lisa and I sat elbow to elbow. Couldn't she have placed me across from Lisa where Brad sat? Better yet, at the far end of the table away from them all.

Sometimes I questioned whether my mother harbored a secret sadistic side.

The sound of joyous greetings in the foyer distracted me from my annoyance. Lisa's question went unanswered. It hadn't merited a response anyway. She had, once again, been needling me about my choice of dropping out of culinary school and going to work in a small town diner. I would think if my mother—the culinary expert—was able to move past it, my exceedingly annoying sister could have left it alone as well.

I swung my attention away from her goading and turned it toward the new arrivals that were following my father into the room. My mother leapt to her feet and rushed to greet an older couple and a younger man. I immediately measured them as parents and son. I had never laid eyes on them before. From the heartfelt warmth of the greetings, it was apparent the couple knew my mother and father well.

The older man and woman—the Jenkins—looked to be about the age of my parents. I estimated the younger man, who they introduced as their son, to be around thirty. He was clearly less comfortable in our company than were his parents. It didn't take long for me to discover why. It was his first time meeting everyone.

The Jenkins met my parents several years earlier while on one of the many cruises my parents so enjoyed taking. The foursome formed an immediate friendship and were cruising buddies several times a year. Since I lived away from home, I wasn't surprised that my parents had friends that I'd never met. What I was surprised about was that I'd never met them even though they also lived in Scarsdale.

They seemed your average, happy couple. Mister Jenkins was a retired accountant and Mrs. Jenkins a retired teacher. An average couple leading average lives. They were the mirror of my parents.

The son, Geoffrey...that's right...Geoffrey Jenkins...was of medium height and rock solid build. Although he kept himself reservedly in the background, his demeanor didn't fool me. I sensed a power housed within his muscular body. His muscular upper torso strained against the navy blue Henley he was wearing. I found it amusing to see we had something in common. We both sported a head of hair that clearly had a mind of its own. Albeit mine was waist-length and his barely touched his collar, the texture and color were mighty similar and the unruliness...well, let me just say I could sympathize with the man.

My mother settled the newcomers at the table and asked her newest domestic helper—a Filipino woman named Lela or Lea or some such name—to bring everyone dessert and coffee. Mister and Mrs. Jenkins sat across from me, next to Brad, with Geoffrey on my left between Lisa and me. It was with great joy that I accepted the deviation from the company of my annoying sister.

Much to my dismay, things didn't improve much. Geoffrey proved to be an annoyingly quiet companion. It took significant effort on my end to strike up any type of conversation. I brought up the concept of a new year beginning and got a curt smile and what sounded like a grunt. I discussed the frigid weather—a one-sided conversation at best. Finally, I'd had enough and I broke into audible reverie about the party I'd attended the night before and the yummy man I met at the convenience store afterward. I don't know why I did it. Perhaps it was because I was bored and frustrated with the way things were and I wanted to see if I could get a rise out of him or anyone else at the table, for that matter. Perhaps I wanted to show Lisa she wasn't the only one who could draw the eye of a handsome man. Maybe I just wanted to reminisce about my dreamy "A" list guy who battled for occupancy in my mind since I left the convenience store the night before. Whatever the reason, I never expected the response I got.

Geoffrey's hand clamped my forearm in a vice grip. It felt like if I moved to try to break free it would snap in half. His deep brown eyes grew a smoky black as they burrowed into mine. His lips never moved, but my mind received his message loud and clear. "You stay away from that man if you value your soul." Then he released his hold of both my forearm and my mind.

It all happened so fast that if not for the pain and red imprints of his fingers on my forearm, I would have sworn I'd imagined it all. Clearly shaken, I excused myself from the table and made my way upstairs to my old bedroom. I definitely needed some alone time.

My legs threatened to collapse under my weight while I struggled up the winding oak staircase and down the hall. How many times had I bounded up those very stairs with the ease of a gazelle? That day it seemed like I was climbing the equivalent of Mount Everest and the walk to my room at the end of the hall the longest mile.

An eternity later, I finally made it.

I threw myself onto the familiar old four poster bed I'd slept in throughout my formative years right up until I'd dropped out of college and decided it was time to go out into the world and make it on my own. My parents offered to let me take my bedroom furniture with me, but I wanted to prove to myself I could make it on my own. This meant in all ways, including furnishing the little lake cottage that had been in my family for generations. After many family conversations, I'd conceded it was all right to accept the quaint dwelling as an early inheritance. My siblings gave no argument, since neither had an interest in it. It was neglected for years and most of the furniture needed replacing as a result. I'd managed to refurnish it and make my little historical dwelling quite cozy by way of frequent visits to thrift shops and lawn sales.

I rolled onto my back and closed my eyes. What just happened? Had I actually heard Geoffrey's words in my head? It sounded so real. His lips never moved, I'm certain of it. No one else at the table seemed disturbed by his statement. It wasn't just imaginary thoughts popping up was it? No...I'd actually heard his voice loud and clear in my head. No one could have convinced me differently. His masculine voice was deep and angry. Was he a ventriloquist? That would explain his lips not moving. What about the fact no one else was the least bit disturbed by his weird, angry, and creepy statement? They were also quite oblivious to my taunting conversation about my evening out as well. Perhaps they were simply shutting the two of us out altogether. Since I hadn't a clue what their conversations consisted of, I couldn't know for sure.

"Hello."

I nearly jumped out of my skin by the unexpected sight of Geoffrey standing in the doorway of my room.

"The door wasn't fully closed," he added softly.

"What do you want?" I snapped in the most uninviting tone I could muster.

His broad frame filled the doorway in an appealing sort of way.

"To talk...we need to talk," he replied as he moved further into the room.

"Stop right there!" I barked as I leapt from my bed. Handsome or not, he was overstepping the boundaries of propriety by entering my room uninvited. Call me old fashioned, but it's the way I felt.

"I'm not going to hurt you. I just want to talk to you," he coaxed as he inched forward. His actions reminded me of the animal trainer I'd observed at the zoo over the summer as he inched his way into the confidence of a newly arrived lion cub. "I was a little too harsh downstairs. I'd like to explain if I could."

"You're in my bedroom," was the only thing my outraged and muddled mind could come up with.

He looked around as if seeing his surroundings for the first time, "It's very nice."

"You shouldn't be in here," I said, with as much authority as I could muster.

"Please...Let me talk to you for just a moment and then I'll go. Please," he persisted.

I stood my ground and folded my arms across my chest in hopes I would come off just a little intimidating.

"Talk," I barked, more boldly than I felt.

I used the few moments Geoffrey took to formulate his thoughts into a comprehensible conversation with me to observe him more closely. He was quite attractive. I estimated his height to be around five feet ten or eleven inches. He had a ruddy look about him that reeked of masculinity. His clothes fit like a glove over his well-muscled body. I couldn't tell which I found more appealing; his well-developed upper torso or the perfectly sculpted backside I'd managed to catch a glimpse of when he was seating himself next to me at the dining table. Sculpted was a good term for him in general. He looked as if he could easily model nude for an artist's sculpture of the perfect physique. He had sizable doe-like eyes. They were brown now, but appeared black when he was angered. Soft, thick lashes that were just brown enough to stand out lined his doe-like orbs.

Although Geoffrey was fair and rugged looking and Nevi was dark with a more streamlined and sophisticated look, both emitted a mysterious power that I just couldn't place.

I found this power incredibly sexy.

Wow! Being thrown into the company of two handsome, charismatic, and mysterious men back to back; both with eyes any woman would beg for...What were the odds?

I was just thinking the new year was starting better than I'd thought when I heard him say, "I think you should sit down."

Other Books by Eileen Sheehan

The Vampire, The Handler, and Me
ISBN: 978-0692589311

For Love of a Vampire
ISBN: 978-0692588796

Vampire Witch
ISBN: 978-0692594599
Vampire Queen
[A Continuation of Vampire Witch]

Vampire Iniquity
[Book One of the Tugurlan Chronicles]
ISBN: 978-0692619070
The Cure
(Book Two of the Tugurlan Chronicles)
ISBN: 978-0692624692
Vampires and Werewolves
(Book Three of the Tugurlan Chronicles)
ISBN: 978-0692629642

Dark Escape
ISBN: 978-0692629918
The Search for the Crystal Key
[A Continuation of Dark Escape
ISBN: 978-0692630037

****

Books by Ailene Frances
[A.K.A. Eileen Sheehan]

Love Misunderstood
ISBN: 978-0692590003

Books By E. F. Sheehan
Toast With Jelly
ISBN-13: 978-0982056219